C000004197

CRC
YOUR
HEART

ALSO BY KIERNEY SCOTT

Forget Me Not

Detective Jess Bishop Series Book 2

CROSS YOUR HEART

KIERNEY SCOTT

Bookouture

Published by Bookouture in 2018

An imprint of StoryFire Ltd.

Carmelite House
50 Victoria Embankment
London EC4Y 0DZ

www.bookouture.com

Copyright © Kierney Scott, 2018

Kierney Scott has asserted her right to be identified
as the author of this work.

All rights reserved. No part of this publication may be reproduced,
stored in any retrieval system, or transmitted, in any form or by
any means, electronic, mechanical, photocopying, recording or
otherwise, without the prior written permission of the publishers.

ISBN: 978-1-78681-335-0
eBook ISBN: 978-1-78681-334-3

This book is a work of fiction. Names, characters, businesses,
organizations, places and events other than those clearly in the
public domain, are either the product of the author's imagination
or are used fictitiously. Any resemblance to actual persons, living or
dead, events or locales is entirely coincidental.

For Claire Ayres, slayer of dragons.
And for Alistair, the most thoroughly decent human I've ever met.

PROLOGUE

Special Agent Jessica Bishop's body hurt everywhere. Pain pulsed through her with every beat of her heart, and her mouth tasted like someone had cut out her tongue and shoved a moldy dishcloth in its place.

Her knees were folded hard against her chest and her arms stretched behind her. Her cheek was pressed to the ground, slick from sweat or drool.

The room was completely black. She blinked a few times to clear her vision but it didn't work, so she tried to rub her eyes, but metal bit into her wrists when she tried to move her hands.

"What the hell?" she croaked. Even speaking hurt.

She pulled again but her arms wouldn't move more than an inch. She was handcuffed. Her wrists burned as she pulled against the restraints, cutting into her. Panic shot through her; it squeezed her lungs in a vise grip and made her heart hammer painfully against her chest. She pulled fruitlessly against the handcuffs. She winced at the sharp pain but kept pulling until she screamed out in agony.

"Stop," she commanded. Her instinct was to fight against the restraints but that would only injure her and waste energy. She needed to calm down and think, remember where she was and how she got there, and figure out how to get out.

She closed her eyes and took in a deep breath, pushing oxygen down even after her lungs burned, and then slowly exhaled. She had to stay calm. Fear would not serve her now. The first thing she needed to do was get her hands in front of her.

She tried to sit up but her head hit something hard. She tried to shuffle to the side so she could try again but a wall confined her. She moved in the other direction but another wall kept her firmly in place.

"Fuck!" she screamed until her throat was on fire. She was in a box. She was folded over, huddled in a fetal position because that was the only way she would fit.

CHAPTER ONE

9 Days Earlier

"Thank you for agreeing to see me, Dr. Rogers," Special Agent Jessica Bishop said, arm outstretched to shake the medical examiner's hand. The woman had a snowflake tattoo on her wrist just above her blue surgical gloves. Jess's eyes narrowed to look at her, wondering if they had met before but she would have remembered the jet-black hair and nose piercing. She was definitely new to the coroner's office. Jess wondered how long she would last.

"Please call me Elle. I'm glad you called when you did. The body has been released for burial. We're just waiting on a family member to claim her. I hope it happens soon because I need the room." When she spoke, the light glistened off the stud in her tongue.

"Does she have any known kin?" Jess asked. The details the paper had published were general and vague: a girl's body found on a path beside a DC fire station. She needed to see for herself if this case was related to the other two murders Jess was looking into.

Dr. Rogers shook her head. "She may as well not have family. Her mom was too strung out to answer my questions coherently and her stepdad only wanted to talk about how he refused to pay for a burial because it wasn't his kid so it wasn't his problem."

Jess frowned. She had heard of other families refusing to claim a body because they didn't want to pay for a funeral; it was the reason she had already paid for her own cremation. Not that her family would refuse, just that in all likelihood her parents would be dead and there wasn't anyone else in her life she would want to burden with that, so she took out a policy at a firm that would handle everything. "Can I see the body?"

"Of course. I didn't know the FBI was investigating this until you emailed me."

Jess's skin warmed. She wasn't here in an official capacity but it was better if Dr. Rogers didn't know that. Jess was still a federal agent, even if she had not been reinstated, so this wasn't illegal. Even if she were just a concerned citizen trying to get justice, she wasn't committing a crime.

Dr. Rogers pulled on the lever of the stainless-steel door of the body locker and pulled out the body. The wheels of the gurney squeaked as metal rubbed against the polished floor. "Here she is. This is Jade Peters."

Jess stared down at her. Thick dark brown hair, almost the same color as her own, fell just below her shoulders, like a cape, shielding her, offering some armor against her nakedness. Her tiny body had been cut open, examined, and then sewn crudely back together. "She's so young. I knew she was only ten but I had forgotten how young that is. She's just a baby."

Dr. Rogers nodded. "Sadly not my youngest homicide victim."

Jess wasn't surprised at all. When it came to the evils of humanity, nothing surprised her. "Are you sure it's homicide?" She needed a definitive answer to link the cases together.

"She died of an opioid overdose." She shrugged. "I can't say if it was intentional or accidental. But given the circumstances of her disappearance and the staging of her body, my gut says it was murder."

Jess glanced up, her curiosity piqued. "How was the scene staged?" The paper had not mentioned any staging. That was a new development.

Dr. Rogers squinted. "Have you not seen the crime scene photos? This is your investigation, right?"

Jess blinked, momentarily back-footed. "I'm trying to determine if this is related to two other homicides." That much wasn't a lie, but she left out the part that she had no jurisdiction here and that the FBI had not sanctioned an official investigation. She had started an investigation off her own back after reading through crime reports while she waited for her hand to heal so she could go back to work. Two months had given her a long time to examine every unexplained death on the Eastern Seaboard in the last five years.

There was a serial killer in DC targeting little girls. She knew it, she had seen the evidence, she just needed to get back to work so she could prove it.

"I have all the crime photos in my report; I can send you a copy. Is the email you sent your inquiry from good?"

Jess's heart picked up speed. That was exactly what she wanted. She paused for a second so she wouldn't sound so eager. "Um… yeah," she tried to sound nonchalant, "please, that would be great." She pressed, "How was the body staged?"

"Well, she had been dressed in a satin party dress and her nails were painted. She even had a bow in her hair. This guy went to a lot of effort with the body."

That sort of elaborate staging sounded like a fetish kill. Seeing his victims laid out was a turn on for him. He got off on it. "What are all these scabs and scars? It looks like a rash of some description. What is that?" Jess asked. Clusters of small, crusted lesions covered her torso and upper thighs.

"Those are cigarette burns," Dr. Rogers said.

Jess looked up. "The killer burned her?" That was not consistent with the other victims.

She shook her head. "No, the injuries are historic. Look at this one." She pointed to a raised white bump just under the clavicle. "That keloid scar is at least a year old. She was physically abused over a sustained period of time. Notice how all of the burns are focused on her torso. That's so no one would see them. Whoever did this knew what they were doing." Dr. Rogers walked around the table and flipped a switch. The light on the X-ray film reader flickered on. The negatives of a child's forearm and hand lit up. "You can see here a healed spiral fracture. She has a matching one in the other arm."

"Is that sort of break consistent with abuse?"

"It is when it hasn't been treated. Look here at this bump. The arm didn't heal straight because it wasn't set. I've checked her medical records. The only time she saw a pediatrician was when she was born. She had no contact with medical professionals. As far as I can tell she wasn't even vaccinated."

"How could she go to school without her vaccination records?"

Dr. Rogers shrugged. "I have no idea. But this child should have been taken from her home. Her entire body has signs of physical abuse." She turned back to the table.

Jess shook her head. "Poor kid. So, she was kidnapped on her way home from a community center, kept for just over twenty-four hours, assaulted, and then murdered, and then her body positioned in a public area where she would be found." She spoke aloud as she talked her way through the timeline of events so she could later retrace Jade's steps.

"I didn't see any evidence of sexual assault. There are no fresh cuts or bruises and there were no fluids or spermicides that would indicate anything of that nature. That's not to say that didn't happen; I just can't conclusively say."

Jess nodded. She knew how to read between the lines. Coroners had to be conservative in their reports, only stating what they could definitively prove. It was their job to report the cold hard facts.

There may not be definitive signs of an assault but Jess had never worked a stranger abduction case without that element present.

Jess glanced up at the clock. It was nearly five. Dr. Rogers had taken longer than she had expected with her previous autopsy and now Jess was running late. "I'm going to have to go but one last question. Did you take scrapings from under her nails?"

"Yeah and I found something."

"Let me guess," Jess interrupted, her heart picking up speed. "You found residue from blue cotton candy."

Dr. Rogers' eyes widened. "Yeah, how did you know?"

"Because that's the killer's signature."

CHAPTER TWO

Jess checked her reflection in the rearview mirror. She hardly ever wore makeup but tonight it was mandatory if she had any hope of blending in. She rubbed the corner of her mouth where the lipstick had bled over the edge. According to the tube the color was called Passion's Blush but it could have been called Prostitute Pink or Streetwalker Red because this color would not look out of place on a professional.

Between the heavy makeup, the teased hair, and the skirt that barely covered her ass, she looked like a hooker, which was exactly what she was going for.

"When in Rome," she muttered as she tossed the tube of lipstick in the glove compartment and slammed it shut.

The headlights flashed when she locked the car. She had parked in the parking lot of an abandoned warehouse. It wasn't exactly a safe or salubrious area, but it was safer than her being spotted getting out of her car.

The heel of her boot caught in a crack in the pavement as she turned the corner but she righted herself by leaning against the crumbled brick of a vacant auto-parts shop. She walked as quickly as her stiletto boots would allow because she didn't want to be loitering on K Street any longer than necessary. Lights flashed as a black BMW pulled up beside her.

Well, that didn't take long. On reflex, she stroked the gun strapped to her side. She was small so she looked vulnerable, but she had the best shot of anyone she knew. Protecting herself wasn't an issue but explaining why she was walking the streets in the red-light district would be, so she would prefer not to have to shoot anyone tonight.

The window squeaked as it rolled down. The driver, a middle-aged man, leaned across the passenger seat to speak to her. "Hey, gorgeous. You looking for a date?"

Jess scanned the car for any weapons before she stepped a little closer. She leaned in but not too close. "Hey, sugar. For you, I'm always looking. I need to meet my daddy though. Hit me up in fifteen." *Daddy*. Her stomach clenched at the term for pimp. Whoever had coined that colloquialism had a raging Electra complex going on. A paternal reference for a sexual oppressor was every shade of messed up.

"Yeah, sure thing." He pulled away even before he finished speaking. They both knew he wouldn't come back to find her. He would pick up the next woman he came across. Any female would do. He just wanted a receptacle, someone to pretend not to be disgusted as he grunted and thrusted.

Jess kept walking until she came to the string of strip clubs. Patrons and dancers lined the streets just outside, smoking. Billows of smoke hung above them like a dark cloud. She passed the strobe lights at the entrance to Bottoms Up and turned down the alley. In the distance, a siren wailed and a woman screamed, yelling a string of profanities.

She found who she was looking for standing between two dumpsters, smoking a cigarette.

"You're late." John Donato tucked a lock of thick black hair behind his ear only for it to fall again. His hair was longer now than when she had first met him and he now had dark stubble over his jaw.

"I'm sorry. I got caught up. Did you get what I asked for?"

He ground the cigarette against the wall and then tossed it on the ground to join the pile of stubs before he immediately lit up another. He handed her the pack and she took one, allowing him to light it up for her. His short, nicotine-stained fingernails had been chewed to the quick. Dark smudges of blood outlined the corner of his index finger where he had bit down too far and drawn blood.

His brow raised when he saw the scar on her hand—a permanent reminder of her last investigation. She held her breath as she waited for the inevitable question but he didn't say anything. He just turned away like he hadn't seen it because they both had their secrets and they both valued their privacy.

It hurt to hold the cigarette because her pincer grasp had been nearly annihilated with the injury to her palm, but she would be damned if she admitted defeat and switched hands because of a little pain.

She didn't smoke so she would only bring it to her lips if anyone came into the alley, otherwise she would just hold it until the glow of the tip burned its way down.

She stared down past the cigarette, to the raised skin of the jagged red scar that ran from the top of her wrist, over her palm and to the crevice between her ring finger and pinky. The skin was angry and red, puckered and twisted. It was ugly. She didn't care about the aesthetics but objectively her hand was now ugly, scary even. She hadn't realized at first how bad it was until she registered the look of horror on a cashier's face when she handed her money for her morning coffee. There was a flash of disgust mingled with fear followed by a look of pity that made her want to scream. She had survived. There was nothing for anyone to feel sorry for her about.

John reached into his leather jacket, pulled out a manila envelope, and handed it to her. She resisted the urge to rip it open and start reading the contents there and then, and instead put it in her bag. "Thank you," she said. "I really appreciate this." And she appreciated that he hadn't asked her any questions about why she needed the information or why she couldn't access the files herself.

He took a long drag of his cigarette. "It was the least I could do. It was a really decent thing you did for me. Anyway, thanks again."

"It was nothing." Jess shrugged off the thanks. She hadn't done anything special. She just hadn't been an asshole. Once she had interviewed him and ruled him out as a suspect for a case she'd been working on. She made sure his name had been taken out of all reports so that when it went to trial, it didn't become public record where his fingerprints had been found.

"Most people would have hung me out to dry. You saved my career. And my marriage."

Jess nodded. She didn't ask him if he had told his wife he frequented bathhouses and slept with men because that wasn't her business. Relationships were hard, at least that's what she had heard. She had never successfully navigated one so she had no right to pass judgement on anyone. Even if she didn't understand, she realized he had his dragons to slay just like she did.

"How's your case going?" Jess asked.

"I'm ready for it to be done. I miss my kids." He took a long drag of his cigarette. "And my wife," he added, almost like an afterthought.

Undercover work was hard. It changed people, wore them down until there was nothing left. "I need one more favor. I know it's presumptuous to even ask—"

"What do you need?" he interrupted her. His stare trained on her. His dark eyes were bloodshot. It looked like he had traded drink for sleep.

"I was at an autopsy this afternoon."

"For one of the cases I got you the files for?"

"Yeah." Jess nodded. "One of the victims, Jade Peters, was beat up pretty bad. I think it was her stepdad, Wayne Smathers.

Someone at her community center had made a report about suspected abuse but it didn't come to anything because she was kidnapped and murdered before the investigation went anywhere."

A man staggered through the alley singing the national anthem with his own less than patriotic words. A woman wearing even less clothing than Jess followed behind him laughing. She held a crumpled paper bag close to her chest like it was her prize possession.

Jess brought the cigarette to her lips. The amber end had worked its way down, leaving an ashy tip. Some of the hot ash had fallen on her palm but she hadn't felt it. It was strange the way her hand could be both excruciating and numb at the same time.

John waited until the couple had turned the corner before he said, "What do you need? Need him to go away?"

"No, nothing like that." Jess shook her head, realizing again how much it had meant to him that she had kept his secret. She hadn't done it with any ulterior motive, but nonetheless she had created an ally who was willing to make people disappear if she asked. "Jade had siblings. There are other minors in that home. I want them safe. Can you organize a wellness check on the down-low? I don't want it traced back to me. The kids should be interviewed at school and the house searched. They need to be out of that house. It's not safe."

He nodded. "Yeah, I'll make that happen."

"Thank you." The knot between her shoulder blades loosened a little.

"Anything else?"

"No. I'm good."

John took another long drag of his cigarette. "Are you hungry? I know this is a shithole but they do decent wings."

Part of her was tempted to say yes because buffalo wings sounded a whole lot better than what she had planned for the evening. "Nah, I'm okay. I have another meeting I need to get to. But thanks."

"Busy lady. Raincheck?"

"Yeah," she said because she could hear the loneliness in his voice. "Sounds good. And thank you again for this."

CHAPTER THREE

Jess took a deep breath as she scrubbed at her closed eyes. "Okay, let's do this." She rubbed at her mouth to make sure she had removed the last remnants of her lipstick.

"Excuse me?"

Jess looked up at the receptionist, realizing too late her silent pep talk had been spoken aloud. "Sorry. Nothing. I didn't say anything. I mean, I wasn't talking to you." She clamped her mouth shut to stop herself from any more incoherent rambling. She just wanted to get this over with.

The receptionist smiled, sympathy softening her sharp, hawk-like features. "These things are mostly a formality. I'm sure it will be fine. Would you like a glass of water?"

"No, thank you."

"Okay, he should be ready to see you in a few minutes. He's running a little late tonight. Are you sure you don't want something to drink?"

"I'm okay. Thanks." Jess looked down at the pile of tattered glossy magazines. They were all a good six months old. She didn't care what cooking tips the Kardashians had to offer—the article was just an excuse to show off their state-of-the-art kitchens and give the writer an opportunity to comment on each of the sisters' respective ass sizes—but it gave Jess a legitimate reason not to talk. She was shit at small talk at the best of times but her hand was in agony right now and her pulse would not slow to anything short of tachycardia so polite conversation was just not a viable option. No matter what the receptionist said, this was not a routine appointment; her career depended on the next fifteen minutes.

"Agent Bishop?"

Jess looked up at the man standing in the open doorway. His sandy hair brushed the top of his ears, curling up at the ends. He looked young, too young to be a doctor. He was probably recently recruited fresh from medical school, thinking the FBI would be a stable gig so he could pay off his student loans and maybe give him a few good stories to tell.

Jess stood up. Her eyes narrowed as she studied him: the scuffed shoes, the stethoscope that was so new the metal still glistened when the light hit it at the right angle, and the crispness of his lab coat with his name, Owen Rhys, embroidered on the pocket in cobalt thread. It was probably a gift from his mom. She probably cried at his graduation when she gave it to him, remembering how it seemed like yesterday when she'd dropped him off for his first day of kindergarten.

Everything about him screamed green. She could use that to her advantage.

She reached out her hand to shake his, knowing it would surprise him and hopefully knock him off his stride.

He stood completely still for a fraction of a second, examining her mutilated hand like someone had pushed pause on the video of his life, before he offered his hand in return.

Jess smiled to herself as the tight knot between her shoulders loosened. He was just a kid. "Good afternoon. I'm Special Agent Bishop. How do you do?"

He blinked before he cleared his throat. "Good, yeah." He shifted from one foot to the other.

Jess didn't wait to be invited into his office; instead, she walked past him and took a seat, leaving him at the door. She waited for him to return to his desk before she said, "I just need you to sign off on my medical so I can get back to work. My surgeon and physical therapist have already signed me off." She didn't mention the pitifully low bar the other health professionals had set: a healed wound and the ability to hold a glass.

Dr. Rhys sat down at his desk. "Okay, remind me, why were you signed off work?"

"Remind me" was code for "I've not read your file so go ahead and fill me in." Jess reached into her briefcase and produced the supporting documentation for Dr. Rhys to add to her file. "I had surgery on my hand at the end of September. I completed my six weeks of physical therapy today so I'm good to go." Her hand cramped and the envelope dropped to the floor. "Um-uh-sorry," she stammered as she bent over to pick up her notes, praying he hadn't noticed that her hand did not completely close.

Dr. Rhys's eyes widened at the slash across her palm. "Oh God, it's you. You're the agent who found that serial killer. The story was all over the news."

The look of awe and bemusement on Dr. Rhys's face made her look away. "I'm actually hoping to start back to work tomorrow so if you could sign my medical release that would be great. It's really just a formality as I've been cleared by my surgeon." Jess pointed down at the form.

Dr. Rhys nodded, but instead of taking the ballpoint pen she offered, he said, "Okay I just need to take a look at your hand and see how it is healing."

"Healed," she corrected. She wanted there to be no doubt in the doctor's mind that she was ready to go back to work. "My hand is fine. I have complete mobility and no pain." She lied without blinking. If anyone were watching her, there would be no subtle tells in her demeanor. It was easy to lie because she was as fine as she was ever going to be and she was determined to come back to work.

That was all that mattered.

Dr. Rhys turned her hand over to examine her mangled palm. "Wow, the damage was extensive. On the news, it just said there had been a physical altercation between a female agent and the killer, and that a male agent had been shot. I had no idea it was this bad. He really did a number on you."

She didn't correct him when he assumed the injury had been inflicted by the killer because the truth would lead to a conversation she was unwilling to have. She closed her eyes so she didn't have to see him poking and prodding her hand. Her instinct was to pull her hand away, to cover it and protect it from further pain and scrutiny.

"Can you feel this?"

Jess opened her eyes to see Dr. Rhys poking the base of her pinky. "Yeah," she lied. If she hadn't opened her eyes, she would have had no idea he was touching her hand. The nerves had been severed, completely destroyed; she was never going to feel that finger again but she wasn't about to tell the doctor that.

"What about here?" He poked the pad of her hand just below her ring finger.

"Yes," she lied again. Her surgeon was cautiously optimistic the feeling would return to that finger given that electric sensation shot through it from time to time. Jess wasn't sure she wanted it to. Those two fingers were the only part below the wrist that did not throb in continuous eye-crossing pain.

Dr. Rhys moved to the next finger. Jess sucked in a ragged breath when he ran his finger along the raised purple skin of her palm.

"Does that hurt?" A single brow raised, disappearing under the side-swept curtain of sandy hair.

"No," she blurted. "Your... uh..." For a moment the pain robbed her of the ability to think. "It's just your hands. They're cold. It gave me a chill."

Dr. Rhys's expression relaxed. "Okay good. And sorry about that. I get told that a lot." He reached across his desk for a pink stress ball.

Jess had to bite back a groan. Those sand-filled rubber balls were the bane of her existence. Her physical therapist had always wanted her to work with one to help her regain her flexibility and strength, but the pain associated was never met with results. Her hand was no stronger now than the day she'd come out of surgery, and she wasn't willing to torture herself when she knew there was nothing to gain, so eventually she told the physical therapist to put the ball away and sign her off because she wasn't going to play. The woman had blinked several times and then acquiesced. Unfortunately, she could not use the same tactic with this doctor.

"Okay. I need you to squeeze this so I can have a look at how everything is working together. I assume you've tried holding a gun to make sure you feel comfortable with the grip."

Jess nodded as he handed her the ball. Without thinking, she turned her hand palm up so she would not have to squeeze it to keep it from falling. "Yeah, it's all good. I'm going to the shooting range first thing in the morning." The lie rolled off her tongue. Once upon a time she had prided herself on her virtue, but then lying had become a necessity. She would do or say almost anything to be cleared to go back to work so she could investigate this case properly.

"Good. Now can you squeeze?"

Jess held her breath as she closed her fingers over the ball and Dr. Rhys probed the tendons along her forearm. A searing pain shot through her hand and radiated up her wrist. The excruciating heat intensified with each staccato beat of her heart.

"I need you to squeeze harder. Pretend like you're trying to burst it open. It won't break, I promise."

The pain was already unbearable. It felt like the muscle and tendons were being ripped clean from the bone. She couldn't physically squeeze it any tighter.

But she could not lose her job.

If she failed the physical, she would be assigned a desk job, probably stuck in records in the basement. She couldn't let that happen. Hunting criminals was what she did, and who she was. There was no point to her life if she couldn't do that.

Jess bit into the side of her mouth to keep from screaming out as she forced her hand to close further than it had in two months. Her fingers vibrated under the intensity of the pressure but she forced herself to keep going, pushing herself harder all the time, biting into her mouth so she would not unleash the scream that tore at her throat. She kept going even after a metallic taste filled her mouth. Tears formed behind her closed eyes but she would never let them fall.

"Good. Everything looks great."

Jess let go of the breath she was holding; all the air left her lungs in an audible whoosh. The room spun as she tried to breathe through the pain.

"Your mouth is bleeding. Are you okay? What happened?"

Jess wiped away the warm trickle of blood that pooled at the corner of her mouth from where she had bit into her own flesh to keep from screaming out in pain. Her mind could not immediately find the words to formulate an excuse so she sat for a few seconds in stunned silence before she said, "My lips are really dry. I keep forgetting to buy chapstick."

Dr. Rhys accepted her excuse and handed her a tissue. "That cut on your hand was obviously very deep. How exactly did that happen?"

The corners of her vision darkened in protest at the lack of oxygenated blood reaching her brain. "I... uh." It was impossible to concentrate on not swearing and consider her response at the same time. "I wedged a piece of shattered glass into my hand to use as a weapon against him." She didn't need to specify who she was talking about; they both knew. That case would follow her now forever.

"You did this to yourself?" His voice rose in surprise.

Her back stiffened at his tone. "I didn't have a choice. I was trapped in his basement without my gun. He outweighed me by a good eighty pounds. My options were limited. It was die or fight back with whatever I could find."

"Okay, I see. I get it now." It didn't look possible for Dr. Rhys's eyes to widen any further. "That makes sense why Dr. Cameron requested to see you right after this to complete your psych evaluation."

Jess shook her head with enough force to snap her neck. "What? Today? That's not scheduled. It's almost eight already. Surely he will have gone home by now." Her voice betrayed her by breaking. She was not prepared to talk to a shrink today.

Jess had spent her entire childhood being interviewed by mental health professionals. She knew how to play them but she needed time to prepare, practice her responses, anticipate every question. This was not something she could do blind.

Dr. Rhys shrugged. "Dr. Cameron was very clear. He said to text him as soon as you were finished here then send you straight up to his office."

She had no doubt this Dr. Cameron had intentionally kept the appointment secret from her so she couldn't prepare. Asking Dr. Rhys to text him when she left was to make sure she went straight to the evaluation. She clamped her teeth together until her jaw throbbed with a dull ache. She was being played. This was an ambush.

CHAPTER FOUR

A golden haze churns around a single filament bulb, illuminating particles of debris in the seedy light as they swirl in slow motion, drifting like the gentle rock of a boat before they land on the black lacquered bar.

Everything about the bar is dingy, from the cracked leather stools to the moldy dishrag the bartender uses to sop up the overflow from the taps. The moment the musty smell hit the back of my throat, I knew this was where I wanted to be. It is the kind of place where no one wants to be noticed.

I reach into my pockets, searching for the cash.

"Scotch on the rocks. No straw."

A quarter bounces off the bar and onto the floor. The bartender doesn't immediately reach to get it but if he wants the full amount he is going to have to bend over and get it because I'm not going to move. There is exactly enough for one shot. If I had brought more, I would drink more, and one has to be enough.

He swings the dirty dishrag over his shoulder and reaches for the wad of folded-up bills. The cash register chimes as it opens.

He turns around to measure out the shot. God forbid I catch a break and he gives me a little extra.

A leggy blond at the end of the bar looks over at me. She is all tits and teeth but under the thick lathering of orange-hued concealer, there is a car crash of a woman. She's hiding it, but I see it, lurking there just below the surface.

Her smile broadens, like she wants to talk, so I look away. She's not my type and I'm not here for that.

The bartender turns and hands me my drink. My skin warms in anticipation. A black straw pokes out of the glass, anchored between ice cubes to keep it erect. I take it out and then slowly bring the glass to my lips. My hands tremble as it gets closer. Slow down. Enjoy it. Make it last. But as soon as the cold liquid hits my mouth, I'm gone. I chug it back in a great, burning gulp. The sting only intensifies the experience. I want to slow down but I can't. I'm lost to it.

The empty bottom of the glass stares back at me, mocking my self-control. There are a few precious drops of golden liquid clinging to the ice cubes so I fish one out to suck on.

I wish I had brought more money for a second drink. Two wouldn't be that bad. I glance down the bar at the blond, who is now stroking the chest of the guy that pulled up a stool beside her. He looks like a vagrant who has panhandled just enough to get his fix, but no doubt she would fuck him to get hers too.

That's why I'm only having one. I'm better than that.

I glance over my shoulder to make sure no one is watching before I pull out her picture. A crease mars her features where I folded it to shove in my pocket but my God she is beautiful. So young and fresh and innocent. She's the one. I know she is. My heart flutters, almost giddy.

"She's cute. Is she yours?"

My head snaps up. Heat spreads over my neck and chest, creeping up my face, tightening my throat. "Yeah, yeah, she's mine."

She isn't yet. But she soon will be.

CHAPTER FIVE

Jess took the stairs rather than the elevator to postpone the inevitable or at least give herself time to think. Her heart pounded violently against her ribs as fear wrapped its thorny tendrils around her veins and squeezed. This was like every anxiety dream she had ever had: a make or break test and she hadn't prepared. She always knew she would have to have a psych evaluation before she came back but she was under the impression she would be issued with an appointment the same way she had been for her physical. She had counted on being able to prepare, to read up on the interviewer and look again at the criteria for post-traumatic stress disorder to make sure she would answer the questions in a way that made it clear that was not an issue for her.

Her mind reached back into the recesses to the course work from grad school. Never had she been more grateful for her master's in forensic psychology. They had touched on all aspects of psychology from developmental to abnormal. If this were a written test, she would pass it because she never failed tests. It was only in her real life that she failed.

She told herself to calm down but her body refused to comply. She shouldn't be this nervous; she knew what the psych evaluation would entail. She just had to prove she was not a danger to herself or the community at large and that she was competent to do her job, which clearly she was. She was good at her job; that asshole hadn't taken that from her. She just needed to show she did not have post-traumatic stress. She could do that.

She paused for a second at Dr. Cameron's door and took in a deep breath in an attempt to slow the frantic beat of her heart. Thank God this was not going to involve taking her blood pressure because that would be a dead giveaway. She used her good hand to knock on the door.

"Come in," a voice called from inside.

She opened the door to his office. The walls were standard issue government white with no adornment other than his degrees in brass frames.

"I'm Jess Bishop," she said. She had never formally met Dr. Cameron but she knew him to look at. He was mid-forties, average height, with enough of a paunch to tell her it had been more than a few years since he had passed the physical fitness requirement test. He had a full head of mousy brown hair. The only gray was peppered at the temples.

"Yes, please sit down, I've been expecting you."

They both knew that she was fully aware that he had intentionally withheld the meeting time so she could not prepare. If he were anyone else, she would call him on it, but she was relying on him to clear her for work so it was best not to antagonize him.

He waited for her to take a seat on the leather couch across from his desk. "So, Jessica, can I call you Jessica? How have you been?"

"Yeah, that's fine. I'm good, thank you. I'm eager to get back to work. Ideally, I'd like to get back tomorrow morning. My team is down two members."

He nodded without saying anything. His stare was heavy on her as he watched her. He was hoping to create a vacuum and compel her to talk but Jess preferred silence to talking.

Jess glanced at the framed picture on his desk, angled so the person on the couch could see it too. A curvy blond woman, presumably his wife, was laughing on the beach. A smaller version of her in a matching sundress, maybe three or four, was at her side, their feet buried in the sand, only the red polish on their toes poking out like ripe cherries. All of the therapists she had been forced to see as a child had a picture of their family on their desk too. Maybe it was in the therapist's handbook or something but she always found it odd. As a child, she had actively despised being forced to look at a happy functional family. It only reminded her that she had once had a happy family too before her life turned to shit.

Jess sat in silence for a few more minutes, waiting for Dr. Cameron to start the assessment.

"I've read the report on your last case. There is a lot the media doesn't know about."

Jess's spine straightened as she wondered what exactly he was referring to. She relaxed only when she realized he was being provocative, fishing for information, but Jess wasn't going to bite. Her boss, Jeanie Gilbert, had done everything in her power to keep Jess's identity out of the press. No one had made the connection between her last case and the one she had spent a lifetime trying to forget, and that was all down to Jeanie. She had made a promise to Jess that even within the bureau that information was on a strict need-to-know basis.

"It is pretty harrowing stuff, just reading about it."

"Yeah, I suppose it was one of my more difficult cases, but ultimately we had a positive outcome. That's what it's about, isn't it? I'm just grateful we found the killer and stopped him."

Dr. Cameron tapped his pen on the desk. "You didn't just stop him. He's dead. You killed him."

Jess stared down at the discolorations on her hand as she realized the course the conversation was going to follow. He could just present her with the DSM screening for PTSD but instead he was trying to upregulate affect to see what she would do when she was emotionally roused. He would keep pushing her until she cracked because he wanted to know what she looked like when she snapped.

At least he was being straightforward with his manipulation. Perversely, the trauma of her childhood had prepared her for this, made her stronger, helped her anticipate people's next moves. "That's right. The killer was apprehended. A struggle ensued, my life and the life of my partner were in danger, and I deemed it necessary to use lethal force. As you may be aware, Agent Briggs and I were both awarded the FBI Star," she added to make sure he knew the bureau supported her actions 100 percent. "Now that my hand is healed I'm eager to return to work."

"Are you ready?"

Finally, a question she didn't have to think about. "Yes, 100 percent."

"Even though you shot your partner and he nearly died of his injuries."

If he had really read the report, he would know the shot she had fired was not the one that had nearly killed Jamison. The warm, salty taste of blood filled her mouth. She had bit into her cheek again as a flash of that night played in her mind. She blinked to dislodge the image but it refused to budge. Her skin burned as memories of that night flooded her. All she could hear was the whoosh of blood in her ears. Every part of her wanted to run from this conversation but she couldn't, not without tipping him off. Jess stared at him blankly, giving him nothing he could read. "That's not the case. If you want to reread the file, I can give you a few minutes or I would be happy to tell you how it happened."

Dr. Cameron gave her a long stare. "People with PTSD avoid talking about the traumatic incident."

Jess shrugged. "Do they?"

"Yes, they do. But you know that."

"Of course. I read up on it as soon as I got out of the hospital. All the signs to look out for, the same way I looked for signs of infection in my wound. You have to look after your mental health the same way you look after your physical health. Too often we overlook the importance of self-care."

Dr. Cameron nodded but the small furrow that formed between his pale blue eyes told her he was dubious. They both knew she was bullshitting but she would keep saying what she needed to until he cleared her.

"What were you on the lookout for?" he asked.

"Well, based on the reading, I knew to look out for changes in sleep pattern, problems with emotional regulations, avoidance of people or situations that trigger memories, exaggerated startle response." She stopped herself from reciting the entire checklist. That would be overkill and tip him off that she had memorized the criteria.

"So, you haven't had issues with any of those things?"

Jess made a show of pausing to look to the side like she was trying to access a memory. "Um no. I mean at first I was a little worried because I was sleeping more than usual and a bit agitated when I was in the hospital, but then I realized it was the morphine and I switched to ibuprofen because apparently opioids don't agree with me. I'd never had them before and I won't again. If I ever need another surgery I'll tell my doctor I want a non-narcotic painkiller." Jess smiled inwardly, pleased with her response. She had managed to sound reflective and work in that she was not addicted to painkillers, which was always a possibility after an injury.

"Excellent, it sounds like you're handling things well. Almost perfect textbook recovery. Some would say better than could be expected."

Jess ignored the unvoiced challenge. They had already established she was bullshitting; now they were just going through the motions. Dr. Cameron was a bright guy. He could see through her act but he would be hard pressed to challenge her without calling her a liar.

He cleared his throat. "Why do you think it is that you've come out of the incident unscathed?"

Jess could almost laugh. "Unscathed?" She held up her hand, palm out. "I have scars. This won't fade and I'm glad it won't because every day I see it and I'm grateful that I survived, that we stopped a brutal killer, and we got answers for all those families. And yes, I am doing better than I have any right to, but that is a blessing I'm not even remotely worthy of. I rejoice in His grace and mercy. I will be forever grateful that the Lord protected me. I don't know His plans for me but I am honored to serve Him." Bile rose in the back of her throat. Of all the lies she told that was the hardest to stomach. She wasn't religious at all. How could she be after what she'd seen, but she would gladly fake it to convince him she was ready to go back to work. You want the parole board to think you're sorry about the three people you killed when you held up a convenience store? Find God, it doesn't even matter which one. You want to win an election? Find God. And if you want to convince a therapist you're okay, go ahead and find God because if you are the only one talking to an invisible sky God, you're crazy, but if lots of people have the same delusion, you're religious and that is a good thing.

"Hmm." Dr. Cameron continued to tap his pen on the desk, the tempo increasing until it matched the same frantic speed of a hummingbird flapping its wings. "What part of God's plan was being born the daughter of one of America's most infamous child murderers?"

Jess's mouth dropped open. She blinked several times, unable to fully comprehend what she had heard. He knew. He knew her father was The Headmaster. She tried to swallow but her mouth was too dry. Her chest ached, sharp and acute like a knife straight to her heart. Her shoulders dropped as her body tried to fold in on itself. If there was a pillow on the couch, she would use it to cover herself. She wanted the earth to open and suck her down.

"He wasn't just a murderer though, was he? Isn't that right?" Dr. Cameron pressed.

Jess tried to speak but nothing came out. She couldn't breathe. The room was closing in on her. She pulled at her collar. It was too tight.

"He was a sexual sadist just like the man who attacked you. The parallels must have been unnerving. It must have been like history repeating itself, coming face to face with evil in someone you cared about and trusted, seeing all that depravity up close."

Jess's lip shook. She put her hand up to her mouth to stop it but it didn't help the tremor because her whole body was shaking, vibrating from the surge in adrenaline her body had produced, willing her to run, take cover, get away from this. When she pulled her hand away, the tip of finger was covered in fresh blood where she had bit into herself again. "I… I can't," she gasped with what little breath she had left in her body.

She stood up and ran from his office without looking back.

CHAPTER SIX

Jess ran to her office. Her legs buckled under her. She pressed her back against the wall to keep from falling but all it did was slow her descent. She pulled her legs to her chest and willed her body to stop shaking.

Nearly thirty years later and someone mentioning her father could still bring her to her knees. Time had not healed that wound; it had given it time to fester. The shame and guilt were still as strong as they were then. When? When would that go away? When would she stop holding her breath every time she met someone, worried they would recognize her?

She filled up her lungs until they burned and then held her breath as she slowly counted to ten and then exhaled at the same protracted pace. She repeated the cycle until her body stopped shaking.

"Fuck," she said aloud to the empty room. She stared at the four monitors on her desk. She wanted to turn on her computer and lose herself in a case. She wanted to hunt bad guys and slay dragons but she had messed it up by not holding it together. She slammed her hand against the floor, inviting the inevitable searing pain.

A scream formed in the pit of her belly, desperate to be unleashed, but if she started screaming she would never stop. Voices in her head taunted her, telling her she would never outrun her past. She had nearly killed Jamison, her partner and the only man she had ever genuinely cared about, because she was so messed up in the head that she believed a serial killer over him.

"No." Jess shook her head. She couldn't go down this rabbit hole. There was no room in her life for regret or introspection. She could only go forward. She needed to push everything back down where it belonged and then she would be fine.

She needed to get numb. Only one thing did that for her.

She stood up and smoothed her hair. She lowered her head as she walked down the steps and out through the rotating door into the night. A gust of cold air burned her cheeks.

The keys ground against the steering column as she struggled to get them into the ignition. She swore as she tried again. This time her fine motor skills worked and the car started.

The traffic gods smiled on her and every light she hit was green, which was a small mercy because she didn't need any more time to reflect or feel.

She turned and drove down 12th Street to a club called Nomad and parked in the alley behind it. There was a line out front, mostly groups of guys waiting to get in; some were smoking, others played on their phones, only a few were involved in actual conversations.

Jess walked past the line and straight to the bouncer, who stood with his arms folded. His large frame filled the door. His skin was dark against his white shirt. The sides of his head were shaved but the top was covered in short dreadlocks. She recognized him from the last time she'd been there. He was the reason she chose this club. It was freezing but he wore jeans and a thin T-shirt that strained over the pronounced bulge in his biceps. "Do you have a break coming up?" she asked.

The slight curl of his lip told her he remembered her. She didn't know if he would because it had been a few weeks. "I can make time for you, baby. Just give me a minute to find someone to cover the door."

"Cool. I'll get a drink. Meet me at the bar."

Jess ordered a Diet Pepsi. There was no need for alcohol. She didn't need to pretend to be drunk to justify her decisions. Jess took a drink and then had a look around the club. The dance floor was packed, filled with people gyrating and rubbing against each other to the primal beat. The pulse of the bassline vibrated almost painfully in her ears. She didn't have to worry about being recognized here. It was too dark and people were too drunk.

"Hey." Large hands circled her hips and pulled her back against the flat plane of a solid chest. "Same place as before? Or we can go to my car. It's parked around the corner."

Jess took a long swig to finish her drink and sat her glass down on the bar. "The alley is fine. I need to be quick. I have stuff to do."

"Baby, you ever going to tell me your name?" He took her hand and she followed him through to the alley to a spot hidden between two dumpsters. The privacy made up for what the smell took away.

Jess ignored his question. He didn't need to know her name because they weren't going to be friends. This was the third time she had come here and she probably wouldn't be coming back again. She would have to find someone else because her rule was to never have sex with the same person more than three times. After that it started to look like a relationship.

"Do you have a condom?" she asked. She always carried them but if he had his own that was fine. The question was actually a statement, to let him know he would be wearing one. She made a lot of shitty decisions in her life but unsafe sex had never been one of them.

"I told you before, baby, I'm clean."

"You have no idea if I am. Put the condom on or we're not having sex."

"You're feisty. That's what I like about you." He pulled her against him to kiss her neck.

Presumably he left her mouth free so she could compliment him; say what she liked about him. But she didn't say anything because she doubted that he wanted to hear that she liked having sex with him because he quieted the voices and reminded her of someone else. She unzipped her coat so she could reach the button on her suit trousers. She undid her zipper before she reached for his.

She shivered when the hot air of his breath hit the slick skin of her neck where he had just licked. She took a condom out of her inside coat pocket and used her teeth to rip open the foil packet.

She stroked him a few times to make sure he was hard enough and then rolled the thin rubber down his length.

"Baby, your hands feel good. But this will feel better." He pressed her against the wall as he thrust into her. With the first thrust, the tension in her shoulders eased, and by the third the voices had quieted. There was nothing but fullness and sensation. Each stroke took her closer to numb. She was almost there.

The rough edge of a brick caught her back as he thrust into her again. She closed her eyes. She didn't want to see him or hear him. She just needed someone, anyone, to make her feel good.

CHAPTER SEVEN

Jess opened the lid of her fish tank and dropped in a pellet. As it dissolved, tiny thread-like worms wiggled in the soft current created by the splash. The fish swarmed, pushing each other out of the way to get their fill. They would eat each other if given half a chance. Actually, they had eaten the face off one of their tank mates. When she bought him, he had billowing golden bubbles around his eyes but forty-eight hours in the tank with her scaled psychopaths and his face was mutilated. The only things left of his beautiful bubbled eyes were dangling strings of pulverized flesh.

Obviously she had some sort of strange affinity for psychopaths. That's what Dr. Cameron was getting at when he compared her last case to her father; that she hadn't seen the warning signs because her childhood had conditioned her to normalize abnormal behavior. Jess shook her head to push the thought away. He was full of shit. He knew nothing about her. She was fine.

She stared down at her phone; two days and still no message to tell her that she hadn't been reinstated. It was obvious she had failed; she hadn't even made it through the entire interview. They should just tell her now so she could launch an appeal. This time she would be prepared. Now that she knew his line of questioning she would practice. She had been blindsided before. Now that she knew what to expect, she would be fine.

Her phone vibrated on the table as it rang. Her pulse spiked when she saw it was Jeanie. She tried to grab the phone but ended up knocking it to the floor because her hand refused to close around it. "Shit." She used her other hand to scoop it off the floor.

"Jeanie?" She wasn't sure why it came out as a question.

"Hello, Jessica. I just came out of a meeting with Dr. Cameron."

Jess scrunched her eyes together as she prepared herself for the blow. "Uh huh."

"Yes. He said he has some real concerns about you coming back. He is worried about how you are processing what happened. He would like to see you once a week for the next three months."

She sucked in a sharp breath. Even though this was what she expected, hearing the words still felt like someone had punched her in the face to knock her over and then stomped on her chest for good measure.

"I told him we could find time in your schedule during the workday so you don't have to take personal time for it."

Jess blinked. "Wait what?" Workday? If she hadn't been cleared she would have nothing but time.

"You've been officially reinstated. You can come back today but if you want to take a few days to get yourself organized that would be fine."

Jess shook her head as she tried to make sense of the words. She had been cleared? How? That didn't make sense. She hadn't even let herself hope for it because it was so far out of the realm of possibilities. "Today? I can come back today?"

"Yes, but take your time."

Jeanie kept talking but Jess didn't hear any of it. The only thing that mattered was that she had been cleared to go back to work. Her hand shook as a tidal wave of adrenaline hit her all at once.

"Okay, I'll be right in." She said goodbye and hung up the phone before Jeanie could change her mind.

"I'm back!" she screamed at the top of her lungs. Joy and relief flooded her. If she left now, she could still make the team meeting.

She ran to her bedroom and stripped off the black yoga pants she had put on for a run, exchanging them for suit trousers and a white button-down shirt. She slipped her holster on over her shoulder, slid her Glock into place, and then put her binder into her bag.

Usually she took the Metro to work but she couldn't wait to get in so she drove. She hugged her arms to her chest as she walked to the underground garage below her building. She should have put on her winter coat. The weather had turned. There was a crispness in the air that told her the first snow would not be long.

She parked down the street and ran back to the office. Her heart picked up speed when she walked under the line of American flags above the J. Edgar Hoover sign and through the revolving door. This office was her home, her life. There was no place in the world she would rather be.

She sighed in exasperation when she saw the line of people waiting to swipe through security. There was a woman rifling through her bag for something. For a fraction of a second Jess considered flashing her credentials and saying it was an emergency so she could move the woman's purse off the conveyer belt. But she didn't. Instead she tapped her fingers against her leg to the same frantic beat as her heart.

Once she was cleared, Jess bolted for the stairs. The loud whoosh of blood pounded in her ears and her cheeks burned. Part of her felt like if she didn't start a case that instant, Dr. Cameron would change his mind.

She ran past her office to the conference room. There was a glow of light around the closed door. The meeting wasn't over. Jess went in without knocking.

Tina Flowers, the team's cyber agent, was standing pointing at the projection on the wall. Jeanie was sitting at the head of the table, with Alex Chan beside her and David Milligan beside him. The chair on the other side of Jeanie was conspicuously empty.

"Jess," Tina squeaked. "You're back!"

Jess couldn't speak. She was too fixated on the empty seat: Jamison's seat. He should be here. Her vison clouded. In her mind, the sound of sirens blared and all she could see was a sea of red, growing by the second, covering his shirt and pants, creeping across the floor, sinking between the grooves of the worn boards. Her throat tightened like hands were wrapped around her neck, squeezing like they were that night. She couldn't breathe. She tried to push past the constriction but all she managed were small pathetic pants like an overheated dog. She blinked to chase away the vison but it refused to leave her.

"Jessica?" Jeanie said. "Are you okay?" There was a note of concern in her voice and a deep furrow between her olive-green eyes.

"Sorry," Jess said. She could physically feel the weight of stares on her. "I… buh… I…" She struggled to come up with an excuse, wondering how long she had been standing looking aimlessly into the abyss. It felt like seconds but she knew it had to have been longer. "I was just trying to remember if I turned off the oven before I left my apartment."

Jeanie frowned, clearly unconvinced. Even Chan, who took zero interest in other people's lives, looked worried.

She cleared her throat. "Sorry," she said again. She was fine. It was normal to occasionally think about what had happened. It wasn't a big deal. She wished everyone could just accept that.

She chose the seat opposite Chan and sat down. "Please carry on. I need to get back up to speed." She was desperate to ask about Jamison, where he was and if he was okay, but that would mean admitting that she had not spoken to him since that night. She should have reached out but she hadn't, she couldn't. She didn't even know where to begin. An apology would never be enough.

"I'm afraid you missed most of the meeting. We were just going over the new protocols for securing files after—" Tina's eyes widened as she realized what she was saying.

Jess shook her head. "It's okay. You can talk about it. You can say his name. You don't have to walk on eggshells around me. I'm fine. Really." She wondered how many more times she would have to tell people she was okay before they believed her.

Tina looked from Jess to Jeanie and back again. From the corner of her eye, she saw Jeanie give her head a single shake. Jess's skin burned. She was tired of being treated with kid gloves. She hated the look on Jeanie's face, like she was fragile and needed coddling or she would shatter into 1,000 pieces. She had first seen that look almost thirty years ago from the arresting officer who'd pulled her away from her father when she wouldn't let go of his hand as they tried to handcuff him. She hated that look of pity then and she hated it now. *I'm fine!* She wanted to scream it from every rooftop in the city until people finally accepted that bad shit happens but strong people get over it. And she was strong.

Tina smiled. "That's okay. We just finished. I can send you the presentation and you can read it over at your leisure."

"Sure. That's fine."

"Well, then. That is us finished for the morning," Jeanie said.

Chan and Milligan pushed back from the conference table, ready to leave.

"Actually, before you all go there is something I want to show you." Jess opened her bag and took out her binder. The metal brackets snapped as she undid them and passed out the photocopies she had made from the files John Donato had given her.

She stared blankly at the extra copy, confused as to why there were too many before she realized she must have made one for Jamison. A stabbing ache pierced at her chest but she ignored it and shoved the extra copy into her bag. She gave everyone a few seconds to look at the packet she had just given them before she said, "When I was off, I started looking into unsolved cases. As you all know, at any given time there are between twenty-five and fifty active serial killers operating in America. Too often we don't even know they are out there because we don't link the murders. Even when we are aware of a killer there are often victims we don't know about. Look at our last case. We knew he had killed three women but there were ten others that we didn't know about. They were completely forgotten about. That's not okay. We need to be looking for all the victims. Linking the cases together."

Jess paused for a second while the vision of the victims' lifeless bodies came into her mind. She was used to the vision now. She knew now after two months not to fight it, to just accept that those forgotten women were now her constant companions. "The key is identifying patterns early on. We need to be looking for similarities in unsolved crimes. If we connect them earlier, we can catch killers sooner."

Jeanie pulled her bifocals down from her head and examined the papers Jess had handed her. She turned to a page of graphs. "Where did you get all this information?"

Jess swallowed hard. "I still had access to all but the most classified databases. I went through all unsolved cases from the last five years. I created a spreadsheet based on victimology, geography, etcetera for every case and then cross-referenced them." She left out the part about calling in a favor from an undercover police officer.

"This is what you did with your time off?" Chan asked, clearly unimpressed. "If I had had two months' paid leave, I would have spent all of it on a beach in Hawaii sipping Mai Tais."

Jess ignored his comment. Most of the time Chan just spoke to fill the silence or to be provocative. It was best not to encourage him. "When I was reading coroner reports I found something that stuck out. It's on page six, the left-hand column. You can see that in the last two months there have been three murdered children in or around the DC area. Each of them died of an opioid overdose and they all had blue cotton candy under their fingernails. We have Shaniqua Jackson, Amber Cross, and Jade

Peters. They are between the ages of nine and twelve. I think this is the work of a serial killer."

Silence descended on the room as everyone looked over the presentation Jess had provided.

After five minutes Agent Milligan looked up, his gaze going from person to person like he was waiting for someone to say something. "Fine. Okay, I'll just say it: I don't see it. Look, I know you put a lot of effort into this. And I'm really sorry about what you went through." He held up the papers and waved it around. "But this is all coincidence. You're seeing what you want to see here. Cotton candy? Next you'll be saying they all have skinned knees and their stomach content revealed hot dogs. They're kids. Kids eat cotton candy. This is not a signature. It's a coincidence. Sorry, I said it."

"It's not just the cotton candy. The cause of death was the same and at each scene there were blue triangular fibers consistent with carpets found in cars. And the positioning of the—"

"Really?" Milligan sighed in exasperation. "A murder victim transported in a car? Because that never happens? Come on, you're grasping at straws now."

"I think if we tested the fibers we might find they were all from the same vehicle. Plus, if you look here at the crime scene photos you can—"

"Again, I'm sorry about what happened to you but—"

"Stop. Stop bringing that up. This has nothing to do with that. I can't have you throwing that in my face every time you disagree with me. If you don't think this is a viable case, say that, but at least hear me out and stop dismissing me." Jess winced as she tried to close her hand into a fist.

"Fine." Milligan tossed his copy of the report into the middle of the table. "I don't think these deaths are related. For starters, opioids in their systems doesn't indicate murder; it indicates that they overdosed. This country is in the middle of an opioid epidemic. I just read that ninety-one people die every day in America from opioid overdoses. Some of those people are kids."

"None of these girls had a history of drug use," Jess countered.

"People die the first time they take drugs because they have no tolerance. You know that." The tinge of annoyance had gone from Milligan's voice, replaced by pity.

"Fine." Jess looked around the room. Everyone was looking down, trying to avoid eye contact with her, even Jeanie. Her shoulders slouched. "Do any of you see it?"

No one spoke.

Jess shook her head as anger mounted in her. The urge to scream tore at her. They were dismissing her outright. All of them. Two months ago, they would have investigated further simply because they knew she never went on her gut. This wasn't some hare-brained conspiracy theory. She had spent every waking hour going over open cases. She hadn't pounced on every similarity. She was logical and measured in her approach like she had always been, but that meant fuck all because apparently she ceased to be a competent agent the moment she was dragged into his basement. *I'm not a victim.*

"Thank you for compiling this, Jessica. I'll have a proper look at it later." Jeanie pushed up her glasses, a clear sign that the conversation was over. "Everyone has a lot to do this morning. I think we should all get started on the day."

Jess sat silently seething as everyone got up to leave. The cases were connected. She knew it and she could prove it if her team would take her seriously and give her ten minutes to talk them through her methodology. A decade of loyal service should at least buy her a few minutes to state her case. She stared down at the red and purple mottled skin on her scarred hand. She hated the injury and everything it represented. Before it happened, she had been well respected. Her opinions mattered, her ideas carried weight, and then that asshole took that from her. The whole time she was in the basement, she was fighting to get back to this, back to doing the only thing she knew how to do, and now she wasn't even being taken seriously. She tried to close her hands over the scar but she didn't have the dexterity to cover the hideous reminder.

With her good hand, she pushed away from the table to leave.

Jeanie looked over at her. "Jessica, do you have a minute?" Jess knew it was a demand rather than a question.

Jeanie waited for everyone to leave before she said, "I'm worried about you. Are you sure you're ready to be back?"

Her skin heated—not Jeanie too. She couldn't take one more person questioning her competence. More than anyone, Jeanie's opinion of her mattered. She could disregard the judgements of most people, but not with her. Jeanie was more than her boss, she was her mentor. So much of what Jess knew about being a good agent and a good person she had learned from her. Her career was based on emulating Jeanie's bridled strength so it stung that she was questioning her. "Yes, ma'am. My hand is healed. There is no reason for me not to be here. I can still be of service to the team."

Jeanie gave her a small smile. "No one doubts that. Least of all me. I do, however, think Dr. Cameron may have been correct in his initial assessment."

Jess's eyes narrowed. "What? What do you mean?"

Jeanie sighed. "His initial report said he wanted you to be in counseling for at least the next three months before you started to integrate back into the team. He suggested coming back part-time for a few months to see how you did."

Jess shook her head. She could not do her job on a part-time basis. That was impossible. Jeanie knew that as well as she did. During an active investigation, she gave herself completely to the case, only going home long enough to sleep and change clothes. Going part-time was the same as resigning from her team. And Jeanie supported that recommendation. Ignoring her instincts about a case was one thing; thinking she no longer deserved a spot at the table was another. The betrayal stabbed at Jess; her heart ached with it. She had to look away for a second to keep her composure. "Why did he change his recommendation?"

Jeanie's mouth flattened into a tight slash. "I'm not at liberty to say."

"Obviously, something or someone changed his mind." As she spoke she realized who. "Lindsay," she said aloud. Of course it was Lindsay. Her role as an FBI psychologist meant she was one of the few people in a position to pull strings to get her back on the team. Plus, she was her best friend of over a decade, her only friend really, and the only person in her life who had consistently believed in her.

"I can't speak to why Dr. Cameron changed his mind."

Jess nodded. That was as much of an admission as Jeanie was going to give.

CHAPTER EIGHT

Jess forced herself not to run to Lindsay's office. The door was closed, which meant she was probably in a session. Jess paused for a second before she knocked on the door.

"Come in," Lindsay's cheery voice sounded. Even through the closed door, Jess could hear the smile in her voice.

She walked into Lindsay's office and closed the door behind her. Lindsay was seated behind her desk with a stack of papers in front of her, at least an inch thick. "Welcome back. Are you here to save me from report hell? Please tell me it is six o'clock and it's time to go get a margarita at El Cartel because this day can just suck it."

"Did you have to convince Jeanie and Dr. Cameron to let me come back to work?"

Lindsay let out a stream of air as she pushed back from her desk. Her bangs blew straight up from the strong gust. "I swear to God people these days can't keep their mouths shut. This is the goddamned FBI and people still struggle with confidentiality. Really, what hope is there for the nation if our best and brightest can't keep their lips sealed?" When she smiled, her blue eyes brightened, almost like they were lit up from behind.

"Just be straight with me. What did he say?" Jess pushed.

"Now I really am sad it's not leaving time because this conversation requires nachos and tequila."

"Please, Lindsay, just tell me. I'm getting really fed up with people questioning if I should be here."

"What do you want to know?"

"Everything."

"Okay, sit down."

Lindsay waited for Jess to take a seat on the leather sofa across from her desk. Jess picked up the sequined throw pillow and hugged it to her chest as she readied herself for some home truths.

"Yes, Dr. Cameron recommended to the committee that you not be reinstated."

Jess sucked in a sharp breath. She knew that was the case but hearing it aloud was still a blow. "And then what?"

"And then I told him he was wrong, that I had known you in a personal and professional capacity for the last ten years and you are bar none the most devoted agent we have working for us."

Jess tried to smile but her mouth would not comply. "And then he just changed his mind?"

Lindsay tapped her fingers on her desk like she was deep in thought, trying to determine how to phrase what she said next. "No. He still wasn't convinced. So I told him that bringing up your father was neither therapeutic nor relevant and that if he really thought you were as vulnerable as he was making out, it was a real dick move to trigger you the way he did."

"You said that?"

"I did. Of course, I did. You're my best friend. I will always go to bat for you; that's my job as your friend. I know you would have done the same for me. If our roles were reversed, you would fight tooth and nail for me, no questions asked."

This time Jess did manage a smile, the first in over two months. "Thank you."

"You don't need to thank me."

"I do. Not just for this, for being my friend through everything. You know I don't trust very many people."

"Really? You? Shocking." Lindsay feigned surprise.

Jess wasn't great with expressing her feelings, she could barely identify her emotions at the best of times, probably because she spent most of her life running from them and numbing the ones that she could not bury deep enough. She never ever wanted to be seen as weak but with Lindsay she could let the mask slip. "Thank you. I really appreciate you having my back."

"You're welcome. In the spirit of full disclosure, I should tell you that I'm the one who recommended you have weekly sessions with Dr. Cameron."

Jess shook her head. "What? You just said he was a dick. Why would you—"

"No, I said that intentionally trying to wind you up when he had no therapeutic relationship with you and no idea how you would respond was a dick move. He's actually a decent guy and a pretty good therapist. I think you could um…" Lindsay paused to weigh her words, "make some great progress with him."

Jess's back stiffened. She pulled the cushion hard against her chest, like a wall, protecting herself. She swallowed against the lump in her throat. Emotions, familiar and yet unnamable, pressed against her lungs, crushing them from the inside.

"Do you think I'm ready to be back?" She wasn't sure she was prepared for the answer but she needed to know. Lindsay had admitted she would always fight her corner. Jess appreciated that but she could fight her own corner; what she really needed was someone to believe in her again, just one person to say, "Hey, that was fucked up what you went through, but you got this."

"You want me to be straight with you, or make you feel better? Because I can play this either way." Lindsay smiled again, trying to add a little levity.

"Give it to me straight."

"You took a hit, a big one. That on top of all the other shit life has thrown at you, most people would be a sniveling mess right now, but you're not. But that also doesn't mean you got off scot-free. You have some stuff to work through," Lindsay admitted.

Jess's shoulders slouched. That was not the answer she wanted to hear. She bit into the side of her mouth. This time it wasn't to keep her from speaking; it was to give her some pain to focus her. Just one person, that was all she wanted. One person to not question her and just accept she was fine.

"You'll get there. I know you will, but you do need help, Jess. I think Dr. Cameron can help you, if you give him a chance."

CHAPTER NINE

No one even noticed me as I walked in. My job taught me that: to blend in, be inconspicuous. Or maybe people's heads were so far up their own asses they wouldn't have noticed anyone. Either way: I'm in.

There are two nurses at their station. One is typing something on her phone while the other one is filing her nails and talking about wanting to book her honeymoon in Bora Bora. I doubt she could find Bora Bora on a map but it gives her something to brag about: She found a schmuck to marry her and she is going on an exotic vacation.

Her room is at the end of the hall. I know because I have visited her before, always late at night when the security guard is half-asleep or on a cigarette break. But this time it's different. I'm not just here to look at her asleep in her bed.

Tonight, I'm going to take her.

CHAPTER TEN

Jess's heartbeat pounded in her ears as she ran. She concentrated on the steady thump, timing her stride to the rhythm. It was the only melody she needed. She didn't listen to music anymore when she ran. She needed to make sure she could hear someone approaching. She would never be caught out again or lured into a false sense of security. Her earphones were still in as a force of habit and to keep anyone from trying to speak to her, not that there were many people out at this early hour. Most people would still be in bed, getting their final hours of sleep before they had to attack the day.

Sleep didn't come easily to her. If she managed four hours before her alarm went off, that was a good night. There was a temptation every morning to turn off her alarm and return to the sleep she had fought so hard to achieve, but her morning run was sacrosanct. It was the only healthy coping strategy she had, so she would sacrifice being well rested to keep her daily date along the Potomac.

Jess's arm vibrated. Without slowing her pace, she held up her arm to look at the phone strapped around her bicep. She stopped when she saw Jeanie's number flash up on the screen.

"Hello?" It came out like a question because she wasn't sure why her boss would be calling her at 5 a.m. She was pretty sure they had both said all they needed to say the day before.

"Good morning, Jessica. I hope I didn't wake you."

"No, it's fine. I'm out running."

"I thought you would be. It's a nice morning for it. A great way to clear your head at the start of the day."

"Yeah," Jess agreed as she looked over the expanse of dark water.

"I really need you in the office as soon as possible this morning. I just got off the phone with the director and there is something I would like to speak to you about."

Jess's stomach cramped. The concerned tone in Jeanie's voice made her want to keep running. But there was no place far enough away where she could outrun her feelings. Her mind raced thinking of the plethora of things it could be but it always came back to one: They had reconsidered her place on the team. Maybe Lindsay going to bat for her wasn't enough.

"What is it?" Whatever it was, Jeanie could tell her then and there. Being tortured with worry before the inevitable served no purpose.

"Do you remember hearing about the Ava Marsden case?"

Jess's brow tightened as she wondered where this conversation was going. What was she talking about? "No. Should I have?"

"It's a big case. It's been all over the news."

"A murder? Here in DC?" Jess didn't own a television but she read the crime section of three major newspapers every morning and the case didn't ring a bell. "When was she killed?"

"No, Ava is not a murder victim. She is an eight-year-old girl. She has terminal bone cancer. She is an only child and her parents are locked in a bitter legal battle about her treatment. Her dad wants her to enter hospice and her mom wants to take her to Prague for an experimental treatment."

Jess blew out a stream of air. Instantly the buzz of endorphins she had gotten from running evaporated. "No, I hadn't heard. That's really sad. That poor family."

"Yes, it's tragic. I'm calling you because I found out this morning that Ava was kidnapped from her room at Children's

National Hospital last night. According to her hospital notes, her nurse administered a dose of morphine at 3 a.m. When she went to check on her later, she was gone."

"If she's on morphine, it sounds like she's end-stage."

"Yes, she is. She was receiving oxygen when she was at the hospital. Her doctor said she has less than a month."

Ah shit. Jess closed her eyes. A shooting pain stabbed at her palm when she tried to close her hand into a fist. "It's one of the parents. They need to find the mom and dad and bring them in if they want to find Ava before it's too late. My money is on Mom kidnapping her to get treatment for her. If Ava is already on morphine at the hospital, there is no need to move her to hospice because her pain is being managed and the parents can spend time with her there. Hospitals are pretty good at accommodating for families when children are involved. Obviously, whoever is investigating will need to check Ronald Reagan and Dulles but if she is smart she might have flown out of another airport, maybe even a chartered flight because there will be too much heat here. I don't think she will have gone far though. She is a mom: Her first priority is the safety and comfort of her child. I don't think Ava is at risk." Jess paused as sadness crept over her. "I mean from this."

"That was our initial thought too."

Jess paused for a second as she considered her words. What she was about to say was technically illegal and Jeanie was already questioning her judgement. "Maybe the mom shouldn't be prevented from taking her to Prague. Ava is going to die and then that poor woman is going to endure the most horrific thing that can happen to any human being. For the rest of her life she will have to deal with the loss of her child, her only child. It seems immoral to rob her of what she thinks is a viable chance to save her daughter. If you called me to ask how we should proceed, I think we should let her go and save her the guilt. Guilt eats people up from the inside." She was speaking from experience. It was one of the few emotions she had no problem identifying, and the only one she could never fully numb.

There was a long silence at the other end of the line. For a second Jess thought the call had been dropped but then Jeanie sighed. "Yes, there doesn't seem to be a clear answer here and even fewer winners. Both parents are at the hospital now and both claim to have nothing to do with it. Neither were at the hospital last night because the court order has set out prescribed visiting hours for each parent. Technically it was the father's time, so he could have spent the night, but he went home at midnight to get some sleep. He doesn't always stay over at the hospital."

Jess shook her head. That didn't make sense. "The mom would want to be with her. I don't see any parent trusting anyone else to take their child overseas for cancer treatment. Mom would want to be there." A pain squeezed at her chest and she considered the heart-wrenching decisions that would go into orchestrating something like this. "Unless she knows it would be impossible to get Ava out of the country if she accompanied her so she let her go with someone else knowing it was her only chance. They need to look into the mother's closest friends and family. She may have trusted them to get Ava out of the country."

"That's… um… definitely a possibility. The case has been assigned to CARD. I'm sure they'll follow up on everything," Jeanie said.

There was another long pause. If the Child Abduction Rapid Deployment team was already involved, Jeanie didn't need her advice. They were the best of the best at finding missing children. There was something else.

"What aren't you telling me?"

Jeanie cleared her throat. "It's probably nothing, we'll soon know, but there was something that stuck out and it would be remiss for us not to at least look into it so we can move on. As you have suggested, the parents are currently the focus of our investigation given the contentious case they are involved in over the end of life care for their daughter, but there was something at the crime scene that needs to be looked at further. There was a bag of blue cotton candy left on Ava's hospital bed."

Jess's heart stopped with a painful thud. For a moment the world stopped, all colors and sounds ceased to exist. All Jess could do was breathe.

"Both parents have denied bringing it in. We need to interview hospital staff but it seems unlikely since Ava recently had a feeding tube put in."

"It's him. It's our guy. He uses the cotton candy as a lure. When he saw Ava couldn't eat it, he just tossed it because it wasn't necessary. I need to see the crime scene and pull any CCTV the hospital has. There are cameras everywhere. They will have picked him up."

"I'm going to call Tina as soon as I hang up with you. As I said before, this could be entirely unrelated to the cases you were looking at."

Jess turned around and started running toward home. "We need the room sealed off. I want to see it before CARD sends in anyone. We need a list of all the hospital staff. We should focus on men, anyone who could have known that the parents would not have been there. Not just health care professionals, we need to look at delivery people and janitorial staff, anyone who has access." Jess's brain fired into action. There was a serial killer on the loose and Jess wouldn't stop until she brought him to justice and saved that little girl.

CHAPTER ELEVEN

The smell of bleach burned the back of her throat and made her eyes water. The hospital buzzed in a low hum of beeps of medical equipment. When Jess was hospitalized for her hand, the only time she had been able to sleep was when she was sedated and rendered unconscious to the tinny cacophony of machinery.

She pulled out her badge and presented it to the uniformed officer guarding the door to the oncology unit. He was a slight man, middle-aged, with thinning hair combed straight back. The gelled comb marks were severe enough to create the illusion of black and silver grooves. "I'm Special Agent Jessica Bishop. I'm here to investigate the disappearance of Ava Marsden."

"Officer Hastings." He reached out his hand to shake hers. When she offered her hand in return he looked at the bright red scar and his expression changed. His smile slipped, replaced with surprise and concern.

For a second she thought he might refuse to shake her hand. Maybe he thought he would hurt her, or catch something, but either way she was glad that his focus on her scar meant he didn't give her face a second thought. At least there was no worrying about him recognizing her.

"Your colleagues are already inside speaking to the parents. Someone from Forensics is in the hospital room now."

Jess nodded. "Thank you."

Officer Hastings punched a code into the keypad and the door slid open. Jess followed him down the hall. The nurses she passed were all dressed in lavender scrubs. Each one had a different brightly colored stethoscope, all shades she had never seen in a medical setting.

Jess paused at the closed door of a room marked "Family Area." Someone was crying, wailing actually.

"The parents are in there with your colleagues," Officer Hastings said, answering the question she was about to ask. "At least they have both stopped screaming."

She continued to follow him to the end of the corridor. Jess opened her bag and snapped on a pair of latex gloves. Black powder covered the door handle and the glass panel of the wall where the Forensics team had tried to pull prints. As you would expect from a public location, the door was covered in prints. It would take a while to scrub the door clean again.

The white hospital room was accented in bright decals: balloons, a rainbow, and a smiling clown riding an oversized tricycle. All of the cheery décor and everything else in the room was now covered in fine black powder. They would be checking fingerprints for the foreseeable future.

A technician from the bureau looked up when Jess entered the room. She had worked with her before but couldn't remember her name. "Good morning," Jess said, offering a generic greeting.

"Good morning, Agent Bishop."

Jess smiled, wishing she could remember her name. She thought it might be Sally but it was better to not say anything than use the wrong name. "Have you found anything?"

"Yes." She held up a plastic bag. "I found it on the pillow. According to the notes, the nurse changed the sheets just after midnight because the victim had an accident. Dad had already left for the night so it shouldn't be his."

Jess had to squint to make out the single strand of short dark hair. "Excellent. Juries love DNA. I was also told you found cotton candy."

"Yeah." She pointed to the chair beside her. It had already been bagged for evidence but the label was still clearly visible: Miller's Blueberry Surprise. The red block writing looked old-fashioned, as did the boardwalk scene below it.

Jess took out her phone, snapped a picture, and sent it to Tina to track down the manufacturer and find out what outlets supplied it. "If you find anything else, can you let me know, please? And can you cc me in directly on any lab reports? Here's my card." Jess reached into her pocket.

"That's okay, I already have your details."

"Great. Thank you." Jess wished again that she remembered her name. She really should keep a file or make flashcards because it was rude not to remember people's names. If the woman were a suspect or a victim, Jess would remember her name, age, social security number, and any other pertinent information that would help her solve a case but everything else was filtered out.

She closed the door behind her and went back to the family room. The sobs had turned to the hushed tones of a heated argument; clipped voices hissed their disdain. Jess took a deep breath. Victims' families were by far the hardest part of her job. Their pain radiated from them, so fresh and visceral. It was impossible not to feel their distress. She barely managed her own emotions, she couldn't even begin with other people's. In a sick way that few people could understand, she preferred spending time with rapists and killers because they were more straightforward and she didn't give a shit what they felt.

She looked down at the names she had written down for Ava's parents before she knocked twice and then went in. Chan and a man, presumably the father, Ryan Marsden, were seated on a blue vinyl couch. She could not make out his face because it was buried in his hands but she noted his short brown hair. Only a DNA test could confirm if it was a match for the sample found, but the shade could not be far off.

Ava's mother, Stacey, stood pacing. Her body vibrated with frenetic energy, desperate to do something, anything, to find her daughter. Her hair hung around her face, limp and lifeless. The dark roots of regrowth spoke to a time when she had had the time and energy to get her hair done.

Chan smiled when he saw her. Relief showed on his face. He was possibly the only person worse than Jess at dealing with victims' families. At least Jess had empathy.

"Where's Milligan?" she asked.

"Talking to hospital security."

Jess nodded. Knowing the acrimonious nature of the parents' relationship, Chan and Milligan should have separated them to be interviewed. She kicked herself for not getting there quicker.

"Hello, I'm Special Agent Bishop." She introduced herself. Ryan Marsden glanced up at her, his eyes red-rimmed and bloodshot. He'd been crying but that meant nothing. People cry for all sorts of reasons, many of them self-serving.

Stacey stopped pacing long enough to ask, "Have you found her? Have you found my baby?" Her eyes pleaded with her, begging Jess to answer in the affirmative.

"We're doing everything we possibly can. Forensics are here and we've already found some trace evidence. So that is positive."

"So that's a no? Just say no. Why can't people just say what they mean?!" Stacey screamed. Her face contorted in barely controlled rage.

"Don't do that!" The red undertone of Ryan's skin darkened a shade with anger. "Don't lash out at people. The world is not your whipping boy."

"I think it's okay to lash out at incompetence. But of course you don't agree, you just roll over and take everything even if it means sacrificing your daughter's well-being."

"There you go again. I'm not going to apologize for being civil. You really should try it some time. But that would mean controlling yourself. And that's not going to happen. You're hurting so you get a free pass to be an asshole to everyone, right? That's how it works in your world."

The argument felt well-travelled, almost like a script—most arguments were.

"Mr. and Mrs. Marsden, I know this is an incredibly stressful time for both of you. I fully appreciate that. But please know we are doing everything we can to find Ava. I think it would be best to separate the two of you to be interviewed. Agent Chan, maybe you could take Mrs. Marsden down to the cafeteria for a coffee," Jess said. "But first I need to get fingerprints and a DNA sample from both of you."

"Why do you need our DNA?" Ryan asked.

"We have found a hair in Ava's room. We need to rule you both out," Jess said.

Ryan shook his head. "Or rule one of us in. No. Nope. This is her. This is about her crazy plan to torture our child further. You did this, didn't you, Stacey? Did you plant one of my hairs to deflect attention while one of your cult-member friends takes Ava overseas to do something that has zero medical evidence behind it?" He seethed, the anger palpable.

"Now who is lashing out? And a cult? That's a new low even for you."

"What do you mean cult?" Jess asked.

"It's not a cult. It's an online prayer group. We support and pray for each other," Stacey said.

"Yeah, because inspirational memes and likes on your posts cure cancer. I'm sure Jesus is monitoring that shit very closely." The disgust dripped off him.

"How many people are in the support group?" Jess asked.

"I don't know, like 500, but not everyone is active. Some people's loved ones have transitioned so they're not—"

"They're dead! You can't even say the word. Dead. They haven't transitioned, or passed, or gone to a better place. They're dead. Just like Ava is going to die soon. Why can't you just accept it and let her last days be as pain-free as possible, not tied up to a machine, tubes everywhere. That's not living. We should have stopped treatment after the last round of chemo. We could have had time together as a family, finally taken her to Disney World, but no, you can't grow the fuck up and do what is right for our child."

Stacey's shoulders jerked as a retching sob tore through her, the sound more animal than human.

Jess stared down at her hand, not knowing where to look or what to say. The display of primitive emotion seemed too intimate for her as a stranger to observe. She felt like she was violating Stacey further, seeing her so raw, her core completely exposed. She wished there were words to comfort her. But there was nothing to mitigate that kind of pain.

"Chan, can you please take Mrs. Marsden for a coffee while I talk to Mr. Marsden?"

"Yeah." He got up off the couch.

Stacey offered no resistance when he touched the back of her arm and guided her through the door.

Jess waited for the door to close behind them before she let go of the breath she was holding. She opened the cap on a bottle of ibuprofen. She had only just taken two but her hand was pulsating with searing flashes of pain like someone had taken an iron and pressed it to her palm.

"I'm sorry about that. You are the third group of investigators we have spoken to this morning. That's not an excuse. Christ, maybe it is. I don't even know what I'm saying anymore," Ryan said. He was holding his face in his hands again.

"Yes, the DC Metropolitan Police fielded the 911 call. Once they realized Ava was missing they called in CARD." Jess realized after she said it, Ryan Marsden might not yet be familiar with the acronym. "By that I mean the Child Abduction Rapid Deployment team or CARD for short. They are the part of the FBI devoted to child abduction cases. They are the ones leading the investigation into your daughter's disappearance. If you haven't already met Special Agent Claire Ayres, you will soon. She's in charge of the DC team. She's very experienced. You're in good hands."

"Tall woman, short purple hair?"

"Yeah, that's her. You will also be assigned a liaison officer who will stay with you and answer any questions. You can also call me." She reached into her jacket and handed him a business card.

He examined it for a few seconds. "Why are you here? What does your office do?"

Without flinching she said, "We're here as an extension of the CARD team. In incidents like this, we want all boots on the ground. As I said before, we are doing everything we can to bring Ava home safe." There wasn't a chance in hell she was going to tell him she was there because she suspected his child had been taken by a serial killer.

"Thank you." He wiped away the wetness from his eyes with the back of his hand. "And again, I'm sorry for before. The way we acted."

"It's fine. You don't need to apologize to me. But maybe you… um…" She stopped before she could offer unsolicited advice. She was the last person on Earth who should give advice to anyone about anything. She had no idea what these parents were going through, not really.

He looked up. "What? What were you going to say?"

"Just that maybe someday you will both want to apologize to each other. That's all. Sorry, it's really none of my business."

"No, that's fine. You're right." He breathed out a heavy sigh. "Believe it or not, we were nice people once upon a time. I can barely remember it now. But we were and we loved each other. We had a good life and then Ava got sick."

"I'm sorry."

"Yeah, me too. Stacey has never been able to accept there was a possibility that Ava might not get better. From the beginning, it has always been about fighting. She even made shirts that said "Ava's Army." I hated that, promoting the idea that cancer was a battle to fight. That's bullshit. It is a horrible, insidious disease that doesn't give a crap about your moral fortitude or who is praying for you."

"Tell me more about the prayer group Stacey is part of."

Ryan sighed in exasperation. "I'm not even convinced half of those people have family members with cancer. And their name: Christians Against Cancer. How asinine is that? Everyone is against cancer. Might as well call themselves Humans for Breathing. Absolute morons."

Jess texted the name of the organization to Tina to check out.

"I swear that group is just to swindle people. That is where Stacey found the guy who claimed to have insider information on clinical trials. She went behind my back and maxed out our credit cards to pay this guy to look for treatment for Ava. There are no hidden treatments. Every single study in America is public; the government is not hiding a cure from us to make us dependent on big pharma. That shit isn't real but it allows monsters to prey on vulnerable people."

"Is he the one who found the treatment in Prague?"

"Yeah. There is no treatment in Prague. There is a doctor who is working with computer models. That's it. Treatment is years away but he has agreed to see Ava. Why?"

The question was rhetorical but Jess answered anyway. "I guess some people just need hope right until the end. Maybe that's what he is trying to offer. Or maybe he just doesn't want to be the person to take it all away." She wondered if that is what she did. When she told families she was doing everything in her power, was she just offering false hope like every snake oil peddler?

Sometimes she knew that by the time she was called, there was very little hope left, yet she always told people the same thing, that she was doing her best. She blinked to dislodge the thought.

"Can you think of anyone who could have taken Ava?"

"Other than my wife and her Bible-thumping friends?" He shook his head. "No, no one I know of. This was the best place for her. Her pain was under control and we got to spend time with her. No, there's no one else I can think of." He shook his head again.

"Where were you last night?"

"I was here and then I went home to go to sleep for a few hours before I had to go back to work."

"There is a cot set up beside Ava's bed, why didn't you sleep here?" She hoped she didn't sound critical, because there was no judgement behind the question.

He rubbed his eyes with the pads of his hands. "Because I was tired. I needed a break. Not from Ava, never from Ava. I just needed to black out for a while so went home and had a Scotch and a sleeping pill. I don't have a prescription for them, if that's your next question—a friend hooked me up."

Jess understood the need to get away and get numb better than most. She had no right to judge anyone for how they coped. Things only became her business when people were being hurt; until then she was quite happy to let people do whatever they needed to get through the day. "Are you willing to give me a DNA sample? It's a simple mouth swab."

Ryan looked up, his ice-blue stare fixed on her. "No. I didn't take Ava. This is where she needs to be. I'm fighting with everything I have to keep her here. You may well have found one of my hairs—I'm here every day. But I'm not going to let you railroad me."

"I can get a court order."

"Fine. Do that. But make sure you're looking for my daughter too."

CHAPTER TWELVE

Jess walked into the conference room and put her bag down, and Chan and Milligan followed her in. Jeanie, Tina, and Claire Ayres were already seated at the conference table.

"I'm sorry we're late." It was nearly seven before she, Chan, and Milligan had finished at the hospital and got back to the office. "Good to see you again, Claire," Jess said, remembering her manners.

Jess had meant it when she told Ryan Marsden that his daughter's case was in safe hands with Claire. Every time they worked together, Claire impressed her with her thoroughness and dedication. Nothing went unnoticed with her and no stone went unturned.

Claire smiled as she tucked a lock of purple hair behind her ear. "That's all right. I just got here too. I was at Dulles looking at CCTV footage."

Jess took out her bottle of ibuprofen and took two. "Did you see anything useful?"

"Unfortunately not. We had a possible sighting of Ava—a girl in a wheel chair, around the same age and build, but it was a British tourist. We tracked them to Heathrow and confirmed it's definitely not Ava."

Sadly, there would probably be a lot of tips that led nowhere. That was the nature of the beast. But they had to chase down every lead because one of them would be the one that led to Ava.

"What about you? What have you guys found?" Claire asked.

"Mom is heavy into a Christian prayer group. Dad thinks one of the members might have helped Mom take Ava. Tina is looking into that."

Tina looked up from her computer at the mention of her name. "Yep, that's me, I'm on it. I'm currently making my way through the group list. There are 486 people in Christians Against Cancer but only about fifty or so post regularly. Jess asked me to look for pedophiles in the group. I have found six registered sex offenders; all are lurkers, i.e. not regular posters, and none of them are in the DC area but I am verifying their whereabouts now."

"He might not be a registered sex offender yet. Less than half of all cases of child sexual abuse are reported. Offenders can be at it for years before they are caught so I wouldn't recommend narrowing your parameters based on criminal history alone," Claire explained. "Also, at this point we don't know if there is a sexual component to this case. We aren't even sure it is a stranger abduction. Statistically that is the least likely. Half of kidnappings are perpetrated by family members, and another twenty-seven percent are committed by acquaintances. So, most likely Ava knows her abductor. My team will focus on the people Ava has had contact with: family, teachers, health care professionals, etcetera."

Claire looked around the room. "Where this gets tricky is the possible link with open homicide cases. That's where your team comes in. The victims that have been identified have no known commonalities. That would indicate a stranger. With stranger abductions, the average age of the perpetrator is twenty-seven. They're likely to be male, and likely to be unemployed or underemployed, usually menial labor. They likely live alone or with their parents."

The keys clicked as Tina noted down the information. "Okay, that should help narrow things down a little. Also, something interesting I found when I started going through the group lists is that several of the women do not have cancer, nor do any of their immediate family members. I don't know if that helps the case at all but I thought it was weird."

Jess nodded. "Ryan Marsden suspected that."

"What kind of sick people pretend to have cancer?" Chan asked.

"Lonely people, compulsive liars, sociopaths, take your pick," Jess said. "I'm not surprised, to be honest. The internet is a goldmine for fantasists. You can live any life you want from your keyboard. And there are a lot of people who get validation through real or feigned illnesses. They get attention and nurturing they're not getting anywhere else. It's a leap from malingering or even Munchausen's to murder, but I'd like to see a list of the people faking cancer."

"I'll keep looking into them but so far I'm not seeing any red flags. I'm waiting for Facebook to release all the private messages between Stacey and the other members. We've also pulled her cell phone records. We should be able to tell pretty quickly if she did this and who, if anyone, helped her," Tina said.

"That's great. Thank you. Have you had any luck with the manufacturer of the cotton candy?" Jess asked.

"Yes. They are based in New Jersey. Good news is that Blueberry Surprise is their least popular flavor and so stocked in the fewest stores. Bad news is that it is available all up and down the East Coast at several amusement parks and arcades. And it is also available online, direct from the manufacturer or from an eBay storefront that specializes in regional candies."

It wasn't quite the smoking gun Jess had been hoping for. "Is there any chance you could check if any of our Christians Against Cancer members have ordered any Blueberry Surprise?"

Tina winked. "You know I can read your mind, right? I'm already on it. I'll let you know as soon as I find anything."

Jess smiled. Tina was possibly the friendliest person she had ever met. At first Jess was taken aback by the constant smiling and cheerfulness, convinced it must be an act or an angle she was playing, but eventually she realized there were just genuinely nice people in the world and Tina was one of them. "Thank you."

"Did you find anything else at the hospital?" Jeanie turned to Chan and Milligan.

Milligan nodded. "Yeah, I got something." His blue tie now had a reddish splodge of what looked like ketchup or marinara sauce, or whatever he had had for lunch. Most days she could guess what he had eaten because he sported a stain somewhere on his person, usually his tie or his sleeve. "I spoke to hospital security and several members of staff, and most of them saw nothing and know nothing. The usual you get in any investigation. But three people did report seeing a man carrying what they thought was a sleeping child to a car. He was wearing a dark coat and a hat. They only saw it because the car was parked near the designated smoking area. At that point, Ava hadn't been reported missing, so they didn't think anything of it at the time."

"What kind of car?" Jess asked.

"There's a bit of confusion over that. One of them said it was a black two-door, another said it was a blue four-door. The closest I got to a description was the nurse who said it looked like the funny European car her pretentious ex-boyfriend drove. You know what eyewitnesses are like."

"Yeah, useless," Chan said.

He wasn't wrong. Eyewitness testimony was notorious in its inaccuracy. One hundred witness could easily have one hundred different accounts of the same event. "It's still worth checking it out."

"I agree," Jeanie concurred. "Call them tomorrow and invite them to sit down with a sketch artist. We might be able to find the make and model of the car. What about the man they saw?"

Milligan shook his head. "None of them saw a face. I don't even have a race. They all think white but they just saw from the back. I couldn't get them all to agree what kind of hat he was wearing but they all agree they saw a child's legs dangled over his arms, and he got in a blue or black, two- or four-door, maybe foreign car."

"The mind fills in arbitrary details," Jess said.

"I know but it's not really helpful."

"What about CCTV footage? The hospital has cameras everywhere, surely they were picked up?" Jess asked.

Claire shook her head. "If only." She held up her hand. "Don't even get me started on that antiquated system they call security. The long and the short of it is half of the cameras are only for show, and the other half were down for routine maintenance. The first Wednesday of every month, their security is offline for about an hour to do system checks and updates."

The hairs on the back of Jess's neck stood taut. "That's not a coincidence."

"Nope," Claire agreed. "Our kidnapper knew those cameras would be down. He knew when to strike."

"Who would have that information?"

Claire shrugged. "It's not exactly advertised but everyone within the hospital seems to be aware that is the protocol."

"Including parents?" Jess asked.

"Yes, it appears even some parents are aware."

Shit. Jess closed her eyes as she remembered Ryan Marsden's tears and his heartfelt apology for lashing out. He seemed genuine. She didn't get any read off him to indicate he was involved. Then again, he wouldn't be the first man who had fooled her. She shuddered. "Have you looked into Ryan Marsden's alibi?" Jess asked.

"You mean the whiskey and Quaaludes?" Claire asked. "Did he tell you that one too? Nice touch, don't you think, admitting to a petty offence to make us think, 'Aw shucks, this guy is so honest he is admitting to crimes we don't even want him for,' and at the same time get us thinking how rough he has it. If he is involved, I'm going to give him his due, that was well played."

Jess blinked. Is that what he was doing? Did she miss something? No, she knew how to read people. She was good at her job. There were enough people questioning her, she wasn't going to start questioning herself.

But a voice deep inside whispered that she had gotten it very wrong before. Jamison had nearly died because she had gotten it so wrong. She pulled at her shirt collar. It was too hot. The small amount of air that made it past her tight throat was like acid on her lungs, burning her. The edges of her vision went black and all she could see was blood everywhere, Jamison's blood, and she couldn't stop it. She tried but then she was dragged into the basement with all the other victims.

"Jessica!" Jeanie shouted.

Jess shook her head to dislodge the last remnants of the macabre vision. She turned to see Jeanie staring at her. Her brow was knitted together in concern. Suddenly she realized she had never heard Jeanie shout, not in all the time they had worked together. Even in the most heated conversations, she remained even-tempered.

Everyone was staring at her with bemused expressions of concern. Mortification crept along Jess's skin igniting everything on its path. They had been trying to get her attention for a while, she realized now. The quiet whispers she had heard calling in the far distance were not his victims calling for help; it had been her colleagues.

She opened her mouth to speak but nothing came out.

"Jessica, are you all right?" Jeanie asked.

Still nothing would come out. She was like a fly stuck in tar, desperately trying to flap her wings. All she could do was nod.

Jess pushed back from the table. "I'm sorry," she said, finally able to speak. "I forgot to eat today. I think my blood sugar is low. I'm going to get some food." She didn't wait for a response before she picked up her bag and left.

CHAPTER THIRTEEN

A siren blares on the street, getting louder as it gets closer. I jump at the shrill sound. My nerves are shot to hell. I need a drink but I won't risk having one and ruining our time together. I can't keep her forever so every minute counts. Later I can get blackout drunk but right now I want to be present.

I wish I would have gone for her sooner. I could kick myself. I should have gone months ago when she was still conscious so she could enjoy it. It would have been so much better if she were awake. This was supposed to be beautiful. It would have been. I would have made it perfect for her.

The water splashes as I lower her into the bath. "Not long now," I whisper against her ear.

CHAPTER FOURTEEN

Jess stared at the screen of her computer monitor. All of the names blurred together. She blinked several times to clear her vision but it only worked temporarily. She was exhausted in a way sleep couldn't touch, not that sleep was an option.

There was a knock on her door.

"Come in."

Jeanie opened the door. Standing in the doorway she looked more a timid grandma than fearless leader, but pity the fool that made that mistake. "What happened just now?"

"I told you, I was just hungry. I'm fine now."

"Did you eat?"

"I'm about to order something."

"No." When she shook her head, her glasses slid down her nose. "You're going to go home—it's almost nine. You need to go have dinner and get some sleep."

Jess rubbed the scar on her hand. Jeanie was in charge of the team; whatever she said, went. Jess would never disrespect her authority by disobeying her. But for the sake of the investigation she had to point out the obvious. "The clock is ticking. It's almost twenty-four hours since Ava went missing. Every minute is critical. We both know that."

Jeanie was silent for a long time as she studied her. Jess's skin burned at the scrutiny. Finally, she said, "CARD is leading the search. You can trust that people will be working around the clock to find Ava. We're only here to explore how this might be connected to the other cases you found. No one is going to forget about her if that's what you're worried about."

"What? No, I'm not worried. I know everyone is doing their best."

"Do you remember when you were in the hospital?"

Jess's back stiffened, immediately uncomfortable with the direction of the conversation. In the hospital, she was out of her mind on painkillers. There was no filter to keep things hidden where they belonged.

Jeanie didn't give her time to answer before she said, "I sat with you when you were coming out of anesthesia. You probably don't remember, but your doctor let me sit with you when you were in recovery. You repeated two things, over and over. Do you want to know what you said?"

Jess clenched her jaw to keep it from shaking.

"You said, 'Tell Jamison I'm sorry,' and, 'What are their names?' I didn't know who you were talking about at first but then I realized you wanted to know the names of all the victims you had seen in the basement. You wanted to make sure they were named."

"The next time you came to see me you had a list of all of them," Jess said. She didn't remember asking for it but she was glad Jeanie had given her that information because it had allowed her to research every woman she had seen, to get to know a little bit about them and in a small way thank them for giving her the energy to fight when all hope was gone. She was connected to them now. She couldn't admit that out loud, but she was.

"You blanked out in the conference room tonight. That was the second time. I—"

"I'm just hungry, that's all. I forgot to eat," Jess interrupted her. It's not like she had disassociated, she was just distracted. It wasn't a big deal. She was fine and she really wished people would stop trying to tell her she wasn't.

"I'm very worried about you, Jessica. You're a fine agent. You know that. And though I don't say it often, I care for you. That is why I'm telling you, if that happens again, I'm going to have to speak to Dr. Cameron and reassess things."

Jess looked away. She couldn't bear to see the disappointment in Jeanie's eyes. She tried to think of something to say, an explanation or an excuse, but nothing came.

"Good night, Jessica. I'll see you in the morning."

Jess waited for Jeanie to leave before she grabbed her coat and left. She took the Metro home and grabbed her car keys. She slid them into the ignition. She had promised herself she wasn't going to do this again. Every time she promised herself it would be the last, and it was until the next time. Now was the time to stop if she was going to break the habit. She looked at the dark circles staring back at her, then slammed the visor back up and reversed out of her parking spot.

"Last time," she made herself another promise.

Jess drove through the congestion of downtown traffic, past the monuments, and then further out of the city where bungalows and trees replaced apartment blocks and traffic lights. She knew the route now by heart because even though she promised not to come back, she always did.

She pulled up at the end of the street, on the red line just beside a fire hydrant. It was her spot, always free because it was illegal to park there. She wasn't going to get out of the car and she would move if an emergency service vehicle needed it, but until then it was her spot, hidden in the darkness.

She turned off the engine and then set the timer on her phone. She had fifteen minutes. That was all she allowed herself. And then she was going to drive away and not come back. This time she meant it.

Her heart pounded hard against her ribs; it beat so quickly it felt like the hum of a motor in her chest. It made her feel dizzy and lightheaded.

Her gaze darted along the street, settling only when it got to the arched porch on the corner. The curtains were drawn and the lights were out. The entire house was dark except for the periodic flicker of light from a television. She willed the lights to go on and a silhouette to appear. That's all she wanted, just an outline. That wasn't too much to ask for.

The timer sounded. Jess jumped in her seat at the sound of the alarm. She clamped her hand over her mouth when she realized she had screamed. The fifteen minutes couldn't be over yet. It was too soon.

"Damnit!" She slammed her hand down onto the steering wheel, inviting the rush of pain that shot through her. She wanted to sit longer, but she wouldn't because she had made a promise to herself, so she turned on the ignition and pulled away.

Now she needed to go get numb.

CHAPTER FIFTEEN

Jess bent over and pulled up her underwear. There was a hole in the seam she hadn't noticed before. She needed to buy some new clothes. Other than her work clothes, which were always immaculate, her stuff was threadbare and all of it was loose now.

"You want a drink? I get them half price," the bartender asked.

She didn't even know his name, not that it mattered because she would never see him again. Up close she could tell he was younger than she initially thought, early twenties maybe. There wasn't even a hint of lines around his blue eyes. He had sandy hair and his jaw had a ginger glow of patchy stubble that he was trying to pass as a beard. "No, I'm good. Thanks."

"Cool."

She didn't wait for him to finish getting dressed before she opened the door. The beat of the music pulsated through her. The club specialized in the kind of music with no words or discernable melody, just a whine of electronics. A red strobe light flashed along with the bassline. It made everyone look like they were dancing in slow motion as they descended into the depths of hell. She liked this place because it was dark so there was no danger of being recognized and the loud music assured no one tried to speak to her.

She walked across the dance floor. There was a crowd around the bar because she'd taken one of the bartenders out of rotation for the last fifteen minutes. People were now lined up three deep holding up money in an effort to be served first.

Someone touched her arm, pulling on her to stop, but she kept walking.

"Jessie," a deep voice boomed over the music.

Jess stopped dead in her tracks but she didn't turn around. Only one person called her Jessie. She shook her head. It couldn't be him. She was hearing things.

"Jessie," he said her name again.

This time there was no mistaking the dark timbre of his deep voice. She spun on her heel to turn around. Her heart stopped when she saw him, all the blood in her veins stagnated in place, frozen. All she could do was blink. Her gaze swept over him, taking everything in, studying every familiar feature, his towering height, his dark skin, short cropped hair, the angular set to his jaw, his broad shoulders, and his solid chest. The last time she had seen him they had been in the back of an ambulance and he had been bleeding out. She'd had no idea if he was going to live or die.

Her skin tingled as relief washed over her again like it had that day when the nurse had finally told her that he had survived. And then the magnitude of what she had done to him hit her, sucking all the oxygen from her lungs. For a few seconds she could not breathe; all she could do was stare while tides of emotions she could not even identify tore at her.

So many times, she had wanted to call or knock on his door but something stopped her. She realized now what it was: shame. She had nearly killed him, her partner. He had nearly died because of her stupidity, her mistakes and lack of judgement, and because she didn't trust him.

"Jamison," she whispered, though her voice was hardly audible. There was so much she needed to say to him but the words refused to come. She couldn't look away from the spot on his shoulder where she had shot him. She winced as she clenched her hand to keep from reaching out to touch him. For the last two months, she had wanted nothing more than to see him, to be the way they were, to pretend the last case hadn't happened.

But it had and she no longer had a right to want anything from him.

"I thought tonight might be the night you would knock on my door. But you didn't. You came here instead." There was no denying the sadness or the disappointment in his deep voice. He knew why she was here, what she did to numb herself. They had been partners for a decade. He knew all her secrets, even the ones she kept from herself.

"You knew? You saw me?"

"Yeah, Jessie. I'm an FBI agent. I know when someone sits outside my house watching me. Every night I wondered if that would be the night you would be brave enough to knock on my door and come in and say the shit that needs to be said."

Shame pressed hard against her chest, an invisible weight of her own creation, crushing her. He was a stranger now and she had done it. She had fucked them up and then she hadn't even had the courage to apologize. Jamison had lost everything—his wife and unborn child—and she couldn't even get it together to tell him she was sorry.

But she could say it now. She had practiced what she would say to him. All the hours she couldn't sleep had given her time to think about what to say. "Jamison. I'm so—"

"I'm coming back to work. I've been cleared. I start in the morning. I followed you here tonight because I didn't want you to be blindsided. I thought, well I don't know what I thought, maybe that you would give a shit but obviously you're good. You've moved on. You're back to," he looked around the dark club, "doing what you do. I shouldn't be surprised though, should I? This is what you do." He rubbed the stubble on his chin with the back of his knuckles. There was no emotion in his voice. His large frame was an impenetrable wall of ice.

There was obviously so much more he wanted to say but he was keeping it in because that's what Jamison did: He was always cool and in control of his emotions.

"Say it. Say what you need to say," Jess pushed.

He looked past her, to the bartender who had just taken his spot behind the bar. The flash of annoyance in his dark eyes told her he knew he was the one she had just been with.

"Nah, Jessie. I'm good. I don't think we have a lot to say to each other anymore."

"I'm sorry." They were the only words she had. So many emotions roiled beneath the surface, fighting to escape. She was ashamed, of herself and how she had doubted him. Jamison had always had her back and she paid him back with betrayal.

For a long moment, silence reigned. Finally, he opened his mouth like he was about to speak but he just shook his head.

"Say something. Anything. Yell at me. Tell me you hate me." She fought the urge to make excuses. There was nothing she could say to mitigate the betrayal.

"Please, J. I know I fucked up. Please just speak to me," she begged. She was ready for whatever words he had for her, no matter how harsh, as long as he spoke to her. She loved him. He had been her best friend. She slept with lots of men but he alone was the only man she could call a friend. Losing that was what stung.

"Go home or go back to what you were doing. There is nothing left for either of us to say." His arm brushed hers as he pushed past her and walked away.

His words, the finality of the sentiment, ricocheted off her, stinging as they hit. Her lungs tightened like someone had reached into her chest and squeezed. She tried to take a deep breath but her body refused to comply.

"I'm sorry," she whispered again but he was already gone.

She stood frozen, locked in place by shame and embarrassment and something else, something she couldn't even identify but it hurt. Her chest ached with it. She wanted to run away, or find another guy to make it stop but it wouldn't stop. Nothing could make it go away.

The room started to spin. She closed her eyes and willed it to stop. She felt raw and naked, vulnerable and exposed. The need to numb herself overwhelmed her. She closed her eyes and tried to push down all the emotions she fought to contain but they wouldn't stop. The relentless voices refused to be quieted.

She could find another bar, another stranger, but then what? As soon as he pulled out, the reality of who she was and what she had done would return. She wanted to be numb but there were not enough men in DC to fully anesthetize her.

Make it stop. She pulled out her phone and pressed the first name in her favorites. She needed to speak to Lindsay. She would know what to do. She was the only person Jess trusted to let in and see her like this.

After three rings Lindsay answered. "Hello," she said.

Jess couldn't say anything past the screams of condemnation coming from inside her own head.

"Hello? Jess are you there?"

She nodded even though Lindsay couldn't see her. "I messed up," Jess whispered.

"Oh, Jess. Where are you? What's going on? Are you okay?" There was an urgency in Lindsay's voice. "Where are you? I'm coming to get you."

Jess shook her head. "I have my car."

"Then I'll take a cab and meet you. Where are you?"

"I'm at the Opal Lounge. You don't have to get me. I just needed to… I don't know." She couldn't think what to say, she just had to say it aloud to someone, admit that she had made mistakes she was scared she would never come back from.

"Stay there. I'm coming to get you."

Jess shook her head. "No, I'm okay."

"I love you but you're not. I'll be there as soon as I can."

She should tell her again not to come, but the truth was she wanted Lindsay to come. She needed to be around someone who didn't resent her or think she was incompetent. She needed her friend. She hated how vulnerable that made her feel. She shouldn't rely on anyone for anything but at least she knew she was safe with Lindsay.

A gust of cold air hit her when she walked outside into the dark night to wait for Lindsay. She looked up at the yellow light of the street lamp. The first flurry of snow swirled around like a gauzy halo.

Winter always reminded her of her childhood, sledding down the hill with her father, building snowmen and drinking hot chocolate with marshmallows—he always picked out the pink ones just for her. She closed her eyes and pushed the memory away. It wasn't normal to still love her father. She shouldn't still miss him.

But she did.

She loved him as much as she hated him for everything he had done, the boys he had killed, the families he had destroyed, and she hated him for teaching her to look for the monster in every man.

She wrapped her arms around herself and watched as the snowflakes drifted down and splatted on the ground where they melted instantly, like they had never really existed.

"Jess, are you okay?" Lindsay asked.

She looked up. Lindsay's hair was arranged in loose curls. Her thick lashes were coated in mascara. She was even wearing lipstick. "Shit, you were on a date. I'm sorry. I'm such an asshole."

"Don't you be talking about my best friend like that. I'm serious." Lindsay's face split into a broad smile.

Jess tried to smile. "You had a date tonight. I messed it up."

"I finished dessert before you called so it's all good. I was just there for the chocolate decadence."

"I'm sorry," she said again. "Call him. Go back now. You like this guy." It had been a while since Lindsay had been excited about seeing anyone. She didn't want to ruin that for her. Lindsay was the happiest she had been in a long time. Jess didn't want to suck her into any of her shit. "Go. I'm not going to be good company anyway."

"Stop. I don't want to be anywhere else. You called me for a reason. You don't have to tell me why. We don't even need to talk but we both know you shouldn't be alone right now. So, I'm going to drive you home. And when and if you're ready to talk, I'm ready to listen."

Jess closed her eyes. She didn't deserve to have someone be nice to her, not after everything. It wasn't fair the way she kept taking when she didn't have anything to give back. If she were a better person she would insist that Lindsay go back to her date, but she wasn't.

CHAPTER SIXTEEN

Jamison was already seated at the conference table beside Milligan when Jess walked into the morning meeting. He glanced up and nodded a hello. It was like nothing had happened, no time had passed, no wounds inflicted. He was a consummate professional. Jamison was the only person who could compartmentalize better than her. He would never let his feelings or personal relationships impact a case.

"Good morning," Jess said.

"Morning." Jamison smiled but it didn't reach his eyes.

Chan and Tina were seated at the other side of the table. Chan was in the middle of a story, his arms outstretched. Tina caught her gaze and smiled as she rolled her eyes. Everyone knew Chan was desperate to sleep with her in the way he was desperate to sleep with everything with breasts and a pulse. It was never going to happen because Tina had self-respect but that didn't stop him from trying.

"Good morning, everyone," Jeanie said from the doorway. "As you can see, Jamison is back. I know I can speak for the entire team when I say, you have been missed."

Everyone voiced their agreement except for Chan, who sat stone-faced. There was no love lost between them. Chan was all blustery bravado, pretending to be alpha, but Jamison was the real deal, he didn't have to force it; everything about him commanded respect and Chan resented him for that.

"I've just got off the phone with Claire Ayres. Early this morning we were able to secure a warrant for Ryan Marsden's

DNA. We both agree that CARD should not be the ones that execute it. We need to keep the integrity of that relationship intact, so our team will be doing it and searching his property. Chan and Bishop, I want you speaking to Mr. Marsden. Milligan and Briggs, I want you coordinating the search of his apartment."

Jess's head snapped to look at Jeanie. She was being partnered with Chan. She shouldn't be surprised. It was the logical choice. They had worked together before. He was a good partner, he just wasn't her partner. At some point her mind needed to accept that Jamison wasn't her partner anymore. Or her anything else for that matter.

"Tina, can you send everyone Mr. Marsden's address? Let's get this started. Once we have sent the DNA to the lab we can meet again with any updates from CARD and also get the investigation rolling into the victims Jess has identified."

Jeanie adjourned the meeting. Jess went back to her office to get her coat and gloves.

She found Chan waiting for her outside the door. "Do you like him for this?" he asked.

"Let's see where the evidence takes us." She wasn't ready to commit to anything.

"What do you think, is it his hair we found in the bed?" Chan asked.

Jess walked past him to the stair. Most people thought Chan was just an asshole, which admittedly he could be, but a lot of the time what looked like callousness was a shitty coping strategy. She knew all too well about those. The more uncomfortable he was, the more cavalier he became.

"I don't know, fifty–fifty," she indulged him by playing along.

He nodded, seeming happy with the odds she had given.

The drive across town took forty minutes thanks to construction works, which meant she got the best part of an hour of the Alex Chan show. She only had to nod occasionally to show she was listening; other than that he was quite happy to carry the conversation single-handedly. That was probably why she didn't mind being partnered with him: She never had to make small talk when he was around.

They pulled up in front of an eight-story red brick apartment building. Chan had to circle the block three times before a parking space opened up. "God, I hate the traffic in this city," he said as he reversed into the parking space.

"He's on the top floor. Want to take the stairs?" Jess asked. She always took the stairs, no matter what floor she was going to. She liked the exercise and she didn't love confined spaces.

"No, let's take the elevator."

Jess flashed her ID to the doorman. He nodded and let them in without any questions. He would be accustomed to having agents coming and going at all hours now. It was probably the most action the apartment complex would ever see.

They took the elevator to the eighth floor. A uniformed officer from the metropolitan police stood guard at the door. Again, Jess pulled out her ID to be inspected before she knocked on the Marsdens' door.

A few seconds later a blond woman in a charcoal suit opened the door. She looked late-twenties. She had a dusting of freckles across her upturned nose. Before Jess could introduce herself, she extended her hand and said, "I'm Agent Welsh. I'm from CARD. I've been assigned to stay with Mr. Marsden."

"Hello. I'm Agent Bishop, this is Agent Chan."

Agent Welsh's eyes flashed with surprise when she saw Jess's palm but she quickly recovered and shook her hand before she opened the door fully to the apartment. On the gray walls were framed pictures of the Marsden family in happier times: a black-and-white wedding photo, another picture of Ryan standing behind Stacey cradling her pregnant belly, and half a dozen pictures of Ava as a baby and toddler. Each of the glossy black frames held a memory, perfectly preserved in time.

"He's across the hall in his study."

"Thanks," Jess said.

She found him sitting at his desk staring at the blank monitor of his computer. His office, like the rest of the apartment, was gray with walnut floors. Chan was still in the living room chatting to Agent Welsh. Odds were that he was probably hitting on her because that was what Chan did. Sometimes she wondered if he even realized he was doing it. His fiancée had recently broken up with him which meant that now he was not even a little bit subtle about it. It was unprofessional but Jess would ignore it as long as he didn't let it interfere with the case.

"It's like a fishbowl," Ryan said. "I'm constantly being watched. I don't even have to open the door anymore. People just come and go as they please." There was no rise and fall to his voice. He had the flat affectation of someone in the downward slide of depression. She reminded herself that that meant nothing. It could be a genuine depression because he feared for the safety of his daughter but it could also be despondence because he thought the noose was tightening.

"I have a warrant for your DNA. We also have a warrant to search your house. My colleagues will be here in a few minutes for that," Jess said.

He did not move or speak; he just stared straight ahead like he hadn't heard her.

"I said—"

"I know. I heard you," he said, clearly annoyed.

"I need you to turn and look at me. I need a swab from the inside of your mouth."

The chair creaked as he turned to face her. His eyelids were speckled in a dusting of purple pin-prick-sized bruises where capillaries had burst from crying so hard. His shoulders slumped like he didn't have the strength left to hold himself up. Again, she had to remind herself that it was possible, probable even, that he had been crying for himself. She had learned her lesson the hard way. She had looked into the eyes of a psychopath and not suspected a thing. She was good at reading people but evil was even better at hiding.

"Please don't stop looking for her," he begged.

"We won't," Jess promised.

"I read that eighty percent of children that are kidnapped and murdered die within six hours of being abducted. There are golden hours for finding children alive and we've missed them, haven't we?"

Jess took a deep breath, torn between the false hope of a lie and the cruelty of the truth. "Every case is different. Children have been found months, even years, after they go missing." She cited the exception rather than the rule because it would be cruel to tell him the truth right now.

Ryan opened his mouth. Jess opened her bag and took out a swab. She opened it and then scraped the soft bristles on the inside of his cheek. She put it back in the paper case she had already written on and sealed it in a larger clear plastic evidence bag.

More voices joined in the discussion in the living room. Jess assumed it was Jamison and Milligan but the addition of a female voice made her turn.

Stacey Marsden ran into the study.

"Why are the FBI searching our apartment?" she demanded. She was still wearing the same yoga pants and stained sweater that she had been when Jess had first interviewed her at the hospital. Her hair looked darker now because the roots were greasier. She had not bathed or changed her clothes. She probably hadn't eaten or slept either.

"It's not our apartment anymore. You moved out. You ran away to your sister's house in Arlington, remember?"

"What did you do?" Her body vibrated with anger. "Where is she? Where is Ava?"

Agent Welsh came in, followed by Jamison, Milligan and Chan. "Mrs. Marsden, I asked you to come here this morning so I could speak to you both at the same time. Please can you both come into the living room and sit down," she said.

"I don't want to sit down!" Stacey screeched. "I want to know where my baby is."

An uneasy feeling crept up Jess's spine. There was only one reason to get the parents together: There was a major development. She closed her eyes for a second and willed the news to be that they had found Ava alive and well, or as well as any terminal cancer patient could be.

"There you go again, screaming at people. They are just trying to help us and you're being a bitch."

Jess held up her hand to stop him. Name-calling wouldn't help anyone. She understood the need to lash out but now was not the time. They needed to keep their focus firmly on finding Ava. "Mr. Marsden, please, let's hear Agent Welsh out."

"Would you please come into the living room and sit down?" she said. Her voice was calm and practiced. She had done this before, given this speech.

Oh shit. Jess knew where this was going.

"I don't want to sit down. Just tell me where Ava is!" Stacey screamed.

Agent Welsh didn't even blink. She had been down this path many times. She knew the reactions to expect. "Okay, you don't need to sit down. As I promised you both before, I will keep you abreast of every development in the case. Remember we discussed there was likely to be lots of hoax calls and false sightings? We need to bear that in mind with any report. Remember, until they are verified, they are just rumors." She paused to allow the Marsdens to take it in and respond if they wanted but neither moved. "I have just received a call from Metropolitan PD. A child's body has been discovered on Skyline Drive in the Shenandoah National

Park, we haven't yet confirmed that it is Ava. A park ranger made the discovery this morning."

"No!" A guttural scream tore through the silence of the room. "No." Stacey Marsden fell weeping to the ground. Her entire body convulsed in wracking sobs.

Ryan knelt beside her and held her as she screamed. She thrashed and wailed but she did not fight her husband's embrace. In grief they were united, if only now in this moment.

Jess couldn't bear to watch the outpouring of grief. An anxious heat prickled her skin and warmed her cheeks. She didn't have a right to see this. She was a stranger to them. A voice in the back of her mind reminded her she was a murderer's daughter. Her father had done this to people, killed children and destroyed their families, made them weep with pain. The families of his victims must have screamed and cried like this. What right did she have to be here now, to see this? Every muscle in her body coiled, ready to run, but she couldn't move.

She didn't know where to look so she looked over at Agent Welsh, who stood in the doorway watching. Her face was calm as she watched the parents sob. She didn't offer any platitudes or tell them everything was going to be all right; she just stood, taking it all in, a physical presence so they knew they were not alone. Most people would try to tell the person crying that it was going to be okay, but the reality here was that it wasn't going to be all right; nothing about this situation was all right.

Agent Welsh might be young but Jess had to admit she had the maturity and fortitude for her job. Jess couldn't do it. She had enough self-awareness to know she would be a disservice to these families. They needed someone better than her, someone less broken.

Minutes stretched on to what felt like an eternity of sobs and tortured screams but eventually, the tears slowed to a soft trickle and the shaking turned to dead stillness. It was a break in the storm but the hurricane would return. It would hover above them, striking at will until they took their last breaths.

Jess was the first to speak. "I'm going to go to the Shenandoah Valley." She needed to be at the crime scene. Jamison and Milligan could stay and interview them once they calmed down enough and find out why the killer targeted Ava, but she needed to get out of there. She could deal with death and decomposition but the oppressive weight of grief was crushing her from the inside.

Stacey looked up. Her face was a mottled shade of red and purple. The sheen of tears and bloodshot eyes made her blue irises sparkle like marbles at the bottom of a swimming pool. "I want to go too. I need to see her."

"We don't know if it is Ava. We need to let the Forensics team do their job. As soon as we know anything I promise you will be the first to know. We will never keep anything from you," Agent Welsh promised her. Her voice was so calm and comforting. Even Jess felt reassured.

Stacey wiped the tears from her eyes with the pads of her hands. "I'm not deluded. I know it's her. And I knew she was going to die. I know my husband thinks I'm crazy but I'm not. I just wanted some control over all this, for Ava. I fought hard to keep her alive because when I held her for the last time I wanted to be able to tell her I had done everything for her. I wanted her to know I had fought for her."

Ryan's chest rose and fell in a rapid cycle. He didn't say anything or interrupt his wife. It was like he was finally hearing her.

Fresh tears streaked down Stacey's face, following the same worn path down the contour of her hollow cheek and over her chin, collecting in a pregnant drop before falling to her chest. "I read a lot, everything I could, to prepare for the end, about the afterlife and the transition. I don't even know if I believe in God or heaven but I know that there is a transition that happens between life and death. We don't just die. The brain can take a few hours to shut down; the whole time the person is aware. I wanted to be there for that. I wanted to hold her hand and explain everything and tell her how much I love her and how my life started the moment the doctor put her in my arms." She tried to say something else but the words were lost to tears.

Her husband put his arms around her and they wept together.

CHAPTER SEVENTEEN

Chan drove the hour to the Shenandoah Valley. He tried to speak to Jess a few times but she could only manage the occasional nod. She turned on the radio to a classical music station and watched as the horizon turned from houses to a sea of orange and red leaves on a deep green backdrop as the road curved into the natural bends of the landscape. This part of Virginia was beautiful, especially this time of year, right before the leaves fell. It was hard to believe there was so much untouched natural beauty, so close to the city.

Chan pulled over behind a police cruiser. The lights flashed on the parked car, a strobing beacon to tell everyone a crime had been committed here. Forensics were already at the scene, snapping pictures and collecting trace evidence. Jess got out of the car and walked over to the hard shoulder where a park ranger was talking to two uniformed police officers.

"Hi, I'm Special Agent Bishop, this is my partner Special Agent Chan." She turned to point to Chan, who was a good ten feet behind her, fiddling with the locks on the car, the headlights flashing on and off. There was no need to lock the car: They were in the middle of nowhere with half a dozen law enforcement agents. He was making a show of doing something, a viable excuse to hang back and not deal with a dead body. No agent liked dealing with death and decomposition but most did a better job of hiding it than Chan.

She waited for everyone to introduce themselves before she turned to the park ranger. For better or worse the ranger had moved himself to the top of her suspect list by discovering Ava's body. In her experience killers often injected themselves into investigations by offering information. It gave them the thrill of reliving the crime and they got to feel superior as they watched law enforcement scramble for clues.

The park ranger looked like he was nearing retirement. He was older than the average abductor but that didn't mean much. Statistics could not offer concrete answers in criminology because people had a bad habit of not doing what was expected.

She gave him a hard stare, taking in every feature, his thinning hair, slight frame, and the liver spots on his weathered face. She glanced down and examined his hands for any scratches before she remembered Ava had been comatose when she was abducted. She would not have been able to fight her killer. Jess noted the absence of a wedding ring. Being unmarried would give him the privacy required to kidnap and murder a child.

"Are you the one who found the body?" she asked.

"Yes, ma'am."

"Can I please get your full name."

"John Paul O'Reilly."

She wrote the name in her pad so Tina could do an enhanced background check. "Okay, Mr. O'Reilly, can you tell me exactly how and when you found the deceased?" Jess closed her notebook. She glanced over at Chan, who had finally joined them. She held up her hand to waist level and pretended to write something in the air to tell Chan she wanted him to transcribe the conversation. She needed to watch Mr. O'Reilly, read his expressions and his body language, look for any telltale signs of deception.

"Well, I got to my station," he pointed to the structure in the woods that looked like a small log cabin that she would have made out of Lincoln Logs as a kid, "at around six o'clock this morning. At approximately six twenty I heard a car starting. We don't usually get people that early at this time of year because it's too dark to hike so I came outside and had a look around and that's when I found her." He pointed to the white Forensics tent. "She was just right there like he wanted her to be found."

"He? Did you see the man who dumped the body?" Jess asked.

O'Reilly shrugged. He looked to the side like he was trying to remember. "No, I don't think I saw him, maybe the back of his head. Actually, yeah, I did see him. He was wearing a hat, you know the kind… Ah I can't remember the name."

Jess intentionally did not offer any suggestions. She didn't want to influence his recall. "It's okay. We can show you pictures of hats later."

"This is really going to bug me. Why can't I remember? It has a funny Spanish-sounding name. What are they called?"

"Fedora?" one of the officers asked.

"That's it! He was wearing a black fedora."

Jess glanced at the officer and then back at Mr. O'Reilly. "And what kind of car was he driving?"

He shrugged again. "I don't know. It was dark, blue or black. I think it was one of these fancy foreign cars. Maybe there was a snake on the logo."

"Was it a—?" the officer started.

"Actually," Jess spun to face the officer before he could finish the sentence. "You know what would be really helpful? Could you and your partner go look for tire tracks? Those could really help ID the car. I don't know why I didn't think of it before." She held up her hands and gave her best I'm-just-a-girl-and-I-have-no-idea-what-I'm-doing look. Through her many years in the FBI she had learned the key to avoiding confrontation with other law enforcement agencies was to always make them think she was deferring to their expertise, make them think that she needed them. She was willing to play dumb when it was needed. It didn't even phase her because there wasn't a lot she wouldn't do to solve a case.

"Yes, ma'am," the older of the two officers answered for them.

Jess waited for them to get out of earshot before she continued. "My partner is going to show you some pictures of cars, different makes and models, to see if you can recognize the car the perpetrator was driving." Jess gave that job to Chan so he didn't have to deal with examining the body.

Jess put a pair of plastic protective booties over her shoes and then entered the tent. There were two crime scene technicians working, a man who was taking pictures and a woman who was on her knees examining the debris around the body.

Jess's eyes narrowed in confusion when she looked at the body on the ground and she saw a cascade of cornsilk blond curls tied with a blue satin ribbon the same shade as her dress. "This isn't our victim. Ava Marsden lost all her hair from chemo."

"It's a wig. That's definitely Ava," the man said.

Jess's shoulders slumped. "How can you be sure?" She realized she was still holding out for a miracle which didn't even make sense because Ava was terminally ill, but she wanted what little time she had left to be spent with her parents. They deserved that time.

"She had a feeding tube and an IV port in her chest. She also has scars that match her surgeries."

Jess blew out a stream of air. It was Ava. She closed her eyes for a second to let herself process the information. All hope was gone.

She swallowed hard and pushed away all emotion before she opened her eyes to examine the body. She looked like she was sleeping on a bed of pine needles. Her hands were folded across her stomach and her head was propped up slightly on a rock. In addition to the blue satin party dress, she was wearing white ruffled socks and black patent leather shoes. The soles were pristine. They had never been walked in. A white autopsy bag lay unzipped beside her.

She noted how he had dressed and posed the body, taking in every aspect of the scene to compare it to the other victims. She had no doubt now that they were dealing with the same killer. In those cases, the victims had been dressed in new party dresses as well. Their hair had also been styled with a satin ribbon. That was his signature. The placement of the body was key to him. He also dumped the bodies where they would be found quickly. He didn't want them to decompose before people saw his handiwork. This was a show and he needed an audience.

"We're almost done here. We're about to transfer her to the morgue," one of the technicians said.

Jess stood for a second, watching them transfer her into the body bag and reliving the conversation with Mrs. Marsden, remembering what she said about the new research that indicated that brain activity did not immediately stop when the heart did. She hoped for all the victims she had seen this wasn't the case, and death had been an immediate release for them. But if it were true… She rocked from one foot to the other as she tried to decide what to do. *Screw it.* People already thought she was crazy. "Do you have an extra set of gloves?"

"Yeah sure, did you see something?" The male technician reached into his bag and handed her a pair of blue surgical gloves.

Jess snapped them on without answering his question. She went to the body and knelt down beside the unzipped bag. The heat of their stares was hot on her back but she ignored it. She was wearing gloves so there was nothing they could really complain about. This might be unorthodox but it wasn't against any rule. She didn't give a shit if they thought she was crazy. She was doing this for a mom, to give her what little piece of mind she could.

She reached out for Ava's hand. Her small hands had not yet stiffened in rigor mortis. Her arms were so light like a bird. Her tiny nails were perfectly rounded like crescent moons. Jess closed her eyes. Her throat tightened as she tried to speak. "Ava, my name is Jess. Your mommy asked me to be here for you to tell you that everything is going to be okay. She loves you so much and she tried so hard to keep you safe. We are going to take you to a special doctor right now and she is going to have a look at your body so we can understand what happened to you. Don't be scared. I'm going to be with you the whole time until your mommy can come and say goodbye." Gently, Jess laid Ava's hand down and then stood up.

Both of the technicians stared at her wide-eyed but she just walked away.

CHAPTER EIGHTEEN

Lying on the autopsy table, Ava Marsden looked smaller and frailer than Jess thought she would be. The wig had been taken off—maybe that was why she looked so small now.

Jess looked at her hands again. There was no telltale blue dye under her fingernails from cotton candy because she could not feed herself. She had not even been able to eat. "What did you find in her stomach contents?" She looked up at Dr. Sumner. They had worked several cases together including her most recent. She was middle-aged with wiry salt-and-pepper hair which she wore in a sharp bob that came just below her ears. Even when she moved her hair stayed in place.

"Nothing. She had not been fed anything in the twenty-four hours before she was killed."

"How did she die?"

"We are still waiting on toxicology but I can say there was no trauma. As you can see there are no wounds anywhere on her body, defensive or otherwise," Dr. Sumner said.

Jess looked over her frail body. There was nothing to her, no chubby softness of youth, just bones covered in translucent skin. It was obvious that she had been in the final stages of death before she was taken. "According to her doctor, she had been unconscious for several days before she was kidnapped."

"Yes. She was in the end stages of cancer. I don't think she would have survived the week."

"Are there any signs of a sexual assault?"

"None." Dr. Sumner shook her head. "Nothing consistent with any sort of abuse. We've taken swabs from everywhere and all are negative."

Jess shook her head. That didn't make sense. "The most likely reason a kidnapper murders a child is to prevent an ID and cover up a sexual assault."

"Not in this case. I did find something interesting though. She was bathed recently. There was soapy water in her port from bubble bath."

"He gave her a bath? Maybe to wash away trace evidence. Maybe he abducted her with the intention of assaulting her and wasn't able to perform for whatever reason but he was able to leave trace on her."

Dr. Sumner pursed her lips in an expression that said that it was a possibility but she wasn't entirely convinced. "Or he wanted to wash off the sand."

Jess looked up. "She had sand on her?"

"Yes, in the wig. We're testing it now for diatoms and I'll be able to narrow down which beach it came from. Oh, and one more thing." Dr. Sumner pointed down at a patch of skin near Ava's hip. The skin was red and speckled. "That is an allergic reaction. Something she was allergic to was applied topically before death."

"Did it kill her?"

Dr. Sumner shook her head. "The reaction appears localized. No signs of anaphylaxis."

"Okay. Can you please call me once you get the lab results?"

"Sure." She glanced up at the clock. It was nearly 7 p.m. "The parents are coming in half an hour. Do you want to stay and speak to them?"

Jess sighed. She would rather bathe her eyes in acid but this was her job and it needed to be done. "Yes."

CHAPTER NINETEEN

"You look like shit," Chan said from the doorway to the conference room. He came in and handed her a styrofoam cup from the coffee kiosk.

"Thank you," Jess said. "I mean for the coffee not the commentary on my appearance. You can go to hell for that but coffee is always appreciated." Usually she just ignored Chan's inane comments but today she had very limited tolerance for anything or anyone.

"I'm serious. You look bad. I mean I still would, but yeah you look rough." His face split into a smile like he had just cracked the funniest one-liner ever.

Jess didn't respond. He said shit just to be provocative. He wasn't really interested in her, he just couldn't help himself. His auto-setting was sleaze. If she were ever to green-light him, he would run a mile in the opposite direction because he wouldn't know what to do with himself.

"Is that what you were wearing yesterday?" he asked.

"Jesus, Alex. I didn't know we were doing auditions for *America's Next Top Model*."

"I'm serious," Chan pressed. "That's the same shirt. Did you go home last night?"

"I was with the Marsdens at the morgue until midnight and then I came back to do some work. The time must have got away from me." She left out the part where she went to a bar and picked up a guy because she didn't know how to deal with the grief she had seen. Chan didn't get to know anything about her private life. She wasn't ashamed but she knew not to give anyone ammunition they could use against her.

She opened her laptop and pretended to work on something so she could end the conversation.

"And what was that praying over a dead body about yesterday? When did you find Jesus?"

Jess's head snapped up. "What? Who told you that?"

"Kristi told me she saw you praying."

"Kristi?"

"The redhead from the Forensics department. She was at the scene yesterday. We hooked up last year. We still talk. She's not that great-looking but she—"

"You're an asshole."

Jamison opened the door at that exact moment. "The woman speaks the truth." A slight curve of a smile pulled up on his full mouth.

Chan scoffed. He opened his mouth to say something but snapped it shut when he thought better of it. He was no match for Jamison on any level.

An awkward silence fell on the room as they waited for the rest of the team to arrive. Finally, Jeanie came in with Tina and Milligan.

"Good morning, everyone. As you are all aware, last night we received formal confirmation that the body found in the Shenandoah Valley was indeed that of Ava Marsden. I know it's not the outcome that any of us were hoping for but now we need to refocus our energy and remember this is now an active investigation to find a serial killer targeting children." She glanced up to look at Jess.

That was as much of an acknowledgment as she was going to get. She had been right, and Jeanie was admitting it, but there was no satisfaction in it because she hadn't saved Ava Marsden.

"Where are we now?" Jeanie asked.

"I spoke to the lab this morning. The DNA from the hair we found on Ava's hospital bed is not a match to Ryan Marsden. We can confirm it belongs to a man of European descent," Jess said.

"So, a white dude," Chan said.

"That doesn't narrow it down much, does it?" Tina said.

"No, unfortunately not, but we also know the hair was recently dyed. The man we are looking for has gray hair but dyes it Natural Medium Brown," Jess said.

"Do you think he is older or he is prematurely graying?" Milligan asked.

Jess shrugged. "I don't know. We can't say with certainty either way but if we pair the hair dye with the fact that there was no sexual assault of Ava Marsden, I'm thinking he is older and has possible erectile dysfunction. That is why there was no evidence of sexual assault as you might expect in a case like this."

"Yeah, that would point to an older man," Jamison agreed.

"Were the other victims not sexually assaulted either?" Jeanie asked.

"There wasn't definitive evidence of perimortem assaults. But remember this wasn't our case so I didn't have access to everything—I don't know any more than what was in the file I put together." She wasn't trying to make a point; it was just how it was.

Jeanie cleared her throat. "Now that this is an active investigation, there will be no restrictions on what you can access."

Jess nodded. She opened up her binder and passed out the copies of the report she had given to everyone initially, when her idea was rejected. And then she stood up and taped a picture of each of their victims on the whiteboard. She wanted to make sure the team remembered every victim. Each of the girls had something to say that could add to the case, and each of them had had value and meant something in their short lives. She didn't want anyone to forget that.

"Starting from the beginning with what we do know. Shaniqua Jackson was abused before her death, probably over a sustained period of time. Same for Amber Cross and Jade Peters. They had all been referred to social services at some point for suspected abuse but in all the cases there was no evidence that a sexual assault took place around the time of death."

"So, all of our first three victims were abused previously but they weren't when they were murdered? Is that normal?" Tina asked, shaking her head. "Obviously none of this is normal behavior but what I mean is, wouldn't you expect an abuser to abuse his victim the day he kills her?"

"No, it's not normal at all and yes I would have expected to find evidence of an assault. That is what is telling me that this guy is impotent and he is taking out his anger on these girls."

"Check Viagra prescriptions," Chan said. "Trust me, if he is having a problem getting it up, he will want to do something about it."

"But if he was on Viagra he would be able to get an erection so that doesn't make sense," Tina said.

"Good point." Jamison nodded.

"Our guy is unmarried," Jess said. "He lives alone. All the girls were kept between twenty-four and thirty-six hours. He would need privacy to do this."

"What do you think about the park ranger who found her?" Jeanie asked.

"I haven't had time to run a full background on him because I have been tracing fibers," Tina said apologetically.

"That's okay. I've looked into John O'Reilly. He's unmarried but he lives with his widowed mom and his disabled brother. Both are housebound. He couldn't have kept Ava there. I've checked if he owns other properties and he doesn't. And he has a clean record. There is nothing to indicate it's him."

Jeanie looked up at her over her bifocals. "When did you have time to look into him?"

Jess cleared her throat. "Last night. I came in to do some work."

Jeanie's face remained impassive but Jess could see her formulating follow-up questions. Jess interrupted the train of thought by adding, "I spoke to the lab this morning. The toxicology report came back and the rash on Ava's leg was caused by a reaction to a fentanyl patch."

"What's that?" Milligan asked.

"It is an opioid-based pain medication. It's for severe and chronic pain. It's pretty heavy-duty."

"So…" Milligan's head cocked to the side like he was trying to understand. "It was just a rash from her medication?"

Jess shook her head. "No. I spoke to one of Ava's oncology nurses. Ava was allergic to the adhesive. She couldn't even use Band-Aids. She was never prescribed fentanyl patches for that reason. Also, she had a port, so all of her medications were intravenous."

"You think the killer put the patches on her?" Jamison asked.

"Yes, I know he did. Ava died of an overdose of fentanyl. That was the cause of death. The other girls also died of opioid overdoses. We don't know if it was fentanyl patches because they weren't found on any of the victims. We wouldn't know with Ava if it weren't for the allergic reaction she had."

"All of the victims died of opioid overdoses?" Chan asked like he was hearing the information for the first time.

It took all of Jess's strength not to roll her eyes. She had given her team all of this information in detail, complete with graphs, and they had ignored it. "Yes." She took a deep breath. "The lab also got a hit from the sand in Ava's hair. It is from Ocean City, Maryland. Ava, or at least the wig she was wearing, was at the beach in Maryland. I've checked, and there is a candy store on the boardwalk there that sells Blueberry Surprise. Tina, can you show them the map I emailed you this morning?"

Tina tapped on the keys. A screen opened on the whiteboard with a map of Ocean City, Maryland. She clicked again and the map filled with bright white and blue pinpoints of light. "There you go."

"Thank you. Okay, let's assume our perpetrator is from Ocean City. He is comfortable with the area if he took Ava there. Even if he doesn't live there he knows the area well enough to avoid detection even after an AMBER Alert was issued. My gut says this is where he is from."

Jamison nodded. "I agree. This is his comfort zone."

"Every dot on the map represents a man on the sex offenders register. Even though there is no obvious evidence of assault there could still be a sexual component for him. These are our best suspects for the moment. The white dots are for men between eighteen and thirty-five; the blue dots are for men thirty-six and older. Given that we now know our guy has gray hair, I think we check the older men first. Obviously, we will work through everyone until we find him but this will give us a more systematic approach."

Milligan stared at the map. "Dang. There are a lot of sex offenders in Maryland."

"There are a lot of sex offenders everywhere," Jeanie said, her tone glum. "Sadly, that is why we are all gainfully employed."

They all nodded their agreement.

"Where is he getting the fentanyl patches?" Tina asked.

"You can get those on the black market, no problem. A fent patch would cost you about twenty bucks. They're not pricey. Shady family members steal them from terminal relatives and use them or sell them on. They're easy to get a hold of," Jamison said. If anyone on the team would know the going rate of narcotics, it was Jamison. He had only recently come back from two years undercover deep in the meth scene.

"I don't know..." Jess shook her head. "Remember how the security cameras were down at the hospital for routine maintenance? And our guy knew to take Ava at that exact time? That tells me that he works at the hospital. He might be medical, and that's how he had access to fentanyl patches, or he could be in maintenance or security and have stolen them."

"You just said you thought he lived and or worked in Ocean City. That's a three-hour drive. You can't have it both ways," Jamison reminded her. There was no malice in his voice just the gentle challenge that had been emblematic of their partnership. He had trained her, pushed her to be better, forced her to always take a second and third look, to go over information time and time again until it revealed all its secrets.

Her chest constricted painfully. She had missed that, missed him. Working with him made her a better agent. "True. We need to go back to our original victims. They'll tell us more."

"Good idea. What else do we know?" Jeanie asked.

"All of our victims, including Ava Marsden, had the same triangular fibers on their clothes," Jess said. "It appears they were all transported in the same car."

Tina's eyes lit up. "Finally, something I can contribute. I think we are finally getting somewhere on the car. I have sent you the three makes I think it is to narrow it down for the witnesses. And on a side note, I am going to start paying more attention to these things because some of our eyewitnesses were worse than useless. Blue is not a make of car."

"Okay, Chan and Bishop, can you re-interview the witnesses and see if we can get a definitive ID?"

"Actually…" Jess cleared her throat. She had never been one to question authority. Organizations thrived on structure, everyone pulling their own weight and doing what they were supposed to do. She knew her place, where she added value, but she also knew that Ava Marsden was fresh in everyone's mind. They all had a dog in that fight. But Shaniqua and Amber and Jade needed someone to fight their corner. "I think Chan and I should look at the historic cases, find out what connects them."

Jeanie pushed up her glasses and looked over at Jess. For what felt like an eternity, Jeanie silently scrutinized her. She wished she knew what she was thinking. An anxious heat prickled her skin as she waited for a reply.

"I agree. Let's see what we can find out about our other victims."

CHAPTER TWENTY

Jess's eyes stopped on her best friend's name as she reread the passage in *Psychology Now*. She picked up the journal and walked down the hall to Lindsay's office.

Jess knocked on the open door.

Lindsay looked up from the stack of papers on her desk. If anything, it had gotten bigger since the last time Jess had been in her office. "My God, how many forms do you have to fill out? I thought my job was bad."

Lindsay made an exasperated sound. "You have no idea. I feel this level of busy work must be a breach of my human rights. It's really not humane. If I die under an avalanche of forms, please adopt Stan and raise him as your own. He likes you, you're one of the only people he doesn't try to bite."

Jess smiled. "All dogs like me. It's my thing. It's just people that don't like me."

"I like you," Lindsay reminded her.

"Thank you." She could always count on Lindsay.

"So, what's up? Are you just here to talk about my lethal paper mountain? Because I can talk forms all day."

"No, actually, as riveting as that is, I'm here because of this." Jess held up a copy of the article she had just been reading. "I was researching for interviews and I found you co-authored a paper with one of my witnesses. She was the court-ordered therapist for one of the victims, Shaniqua Jackson."

"Ooh, which article? I don't know if you know this but I'm kind of a big deal in the obscure journal circuit. All the ones with less than 1,000 readers—those are my jam."

"It's an article on ethics. You wrote it with Pamela Reid."

Lindsay laughed. "Wow, now you're going way back. I wrote that in grad school. I think that might have been the first thing I ever had published. It's all coming back to me. My Yale days. I wore clogs and overalls. It was not a good look. I still see Pamela at conferences from time to time. She lives here in DC."

"Yeah, I know. Chan and I are scheduled to see her to get information about Shaniqua's past."

"While you're there, go ahead and have Pamela diagnose Chan. I have my suspicions, but it would be good to get a second opinion." Lindsay laughed. "No, but seriously, tell her I say hello. She's great. She has somehow managed to stay idealistic even after being in practice for fifteen years. Paperwork has left me bitter and jaded but she is still as passionate as ever."

Jess stared down at her hand. Her painkillers were refusing to kick in and the throbbing had turned into an acute burn that refused to shift.

"You didn't come to talk about Pamela Reid. What's up?"

Jess blinked. "What?"

Lindsay didn't say anything, she just left the question hanging.

Jess shrugged. "No, I don't need to talk. I'm okay."

Still, Lindsay didn't say anything. Normally the technique didn't work on Jess because she wasn't much of a talker anyway, so silence didn't bother her, but today it made her think. "I'm sorry. I guess that is what I wanted to say—I'm sorry about the other night, you know ruining your date and um…" Jess sighed. She didn't know what else to say. "So yeah, I'm sorry."

"First of all, you didn't ruin my date, we're going out again tonight. I think the leaving early thing made me look mysterious and alluring. Little did he know. Second of all, you don't need to be upset because you relied on me. That's what friends do. Third of all, that's not what you're upset about. Do you want me to tell you why I think you're really upset, or should I ask lots of insightful probing questions until you get there on your own? Just tell me which way we're going to play this."

Jess shifted from one foot to the other. She loved how smart and insightful Lindsay was, but she also hated it a little, that Lindsay had insight into her that she didn't. Jess preferred to keep her emotional microscope trained outward, reading other people, so she didn't have to look too hard at herself.

"I'm just going to tell you because ain't nobody got time for the therapeutic process today. You're upset because I saw your vulnerability. You think if people see the real you, they will run away. Well, I see you, and I'm not going anywhere. You would rather be seen as an asshole than weak any day, but it's okay to struggle sometimes and it's okay to rely on other people. Remember last year when my house was broken into and I called you at two in the morning? You came over no questions asked and stayed with me all night until the police came to take a report, and then you stayed in my guest bedroom for the next five nights, on that shitty mattress that I still need to replace. I couldn't be alone in my own house because I was so scared. I was a mess and you showed up because you're a good person. So now you're having a shitty time and it's my turn to show up for you."

"Is that what I'm thinking?" Jess asked because she honestly didn't know. She didn't want to think about any of this too long. Maybe she had wanted reassurance but all she wanted now was to get into the killer's head and out of her own.

"Yes, that's what you're thinking. I usually charge for this kind of insight and here I am giving it away for free. For most people, this would be the part where we hug but you've got that tactilely defensive thing going on so instead you can tell me I'm brilliant and right as usual."

Jess smiled. Lindsay knew she hated to be hugged; actually she hated physical contact of any description except for sex, and even then she wasn't thrilled about the idea of being hugged or kissed, but that was part of the deal. So instead of hugging her, Lindsay would just tell her that it was an opportune time for a hug. It had started as a joke but now it was their thing.

"You're brilliant and right as usual."

CHAPTER TWENTY-ONE

"Do you smell that? What is it? Like patchouli or something?" Chan wrinkled up his nose like a bloodhound on the scent of a trail. He had moved chairs three times since they arrived at Dr. Pamela Reid's office.

Jess looked up from the *Country Living* magazine she was reading, or rather looking at the pictures and wondering where the fascination with distressed furniture came from and why people would pay more for an armoire with the paint chipped off. "Were you diagnosed with ADHD as a kid?"

"What?" He shook his head so quickly that his black hair rose from his forehead. She hadn't seen his hair move the entire time they had worked together.

"You can't ever just sit. Even when you're reading on a computer you highlight sections with the cursor. You need constant stimulation."

"No, I wasn't. Were you diagnosed as weird as a child?"

Jess let out a single-note laugh. "Yes." If only he knew the half of it.

He made a *pfft* sound and then picked up a magazine. He tried to read it for thirty seconds before he put it down and grabbed another. He was about to put it down to pick another when he caught Jess's stare. When she smiled at him, his back straightened like an errant schoolboy who had just been caught.

Jess glanced up when the door opened. An androgynous-looking teenager, wearing head-to-toe leather and chains, came out of Dr. Reid's office. The musky scent of patchouli tickled the back of her throat as he or she walked by.

Chan glanced over and gave her an I-told-you-so look when he smelled the patchouli.

Dr. Reid waited for her patient to leave before she greeted them. "I'm sorry I'm running a bit behind schedule. I would like to say it's an anomaly, but I would prefer not to lie to you." When she smiled there was a small smear of coral lipstick on her front tooth.

Jess stood up. "That's all right. We understand. Thank you for meeting with us, Dr. Reid."

"Please, call me Pamela. Dr. Reid is my father."

"Okay, Pamela. I'm Special Agent Jessica Bishop. This is my partner, Special Agent Alex Chan." Even standing, Jess had to crane her neck to look Pamela in the eye. She was taller than Chan, who pretended to be six feet but was actually closer to five ten.

Pamela had brown hair that fell just above her shoulders and mossy-green eyes. The sharp angles of her face gave her features that were more striking than beautiful but she was none the less attractive.

Pamela's eyes narrowed in question when she looked at Jess. Recognition flashed across her face. "Did you say Jessica?"

Jess sucked in a ragged breath. Panic shot through her. Of course she would be recognized today. She had been too focused on her case and forgotten to worry about people discovering who her father was for more than twenty-four hours so it was time for the universe to remind her of her place with a cosmic smackdown. She closed her eyes for a moment to load the response she always had ready to be fired. *No, who's that? I've never heard of that case.*

But the question never came. Pamela glanced from Jess to Chan and then back again. She gave her a small nod, so subtle that most people would have missed it. She was telling her she knew who she was but she was not going to say anything.

Jess let go of the breath she was holding as relief eased through her, unknotting the coiled muscles along her spine. People were bound to recognize her; the case had been primetime news when it broke. As a child, she had been on the cover of a national magazine, sobbing, her hand outstretched reaching for her father as the FBI pulled him away from her to arrest him.

"Come on in." Pamela moved to the side to allow Jess and Chan into her office. The walls were painted a warm, sunny yellow. In the center of the room there was a large sand tray and a table with small child-size chairs. The walls were lined with bookcases packed with dolls and figurines. The room instantly transported Jess back to her childhood. She had spent most of her formative years in the company of psychologists. They had rooms like this. "Play therapy" was what it was called. Jess played with plastic toy animals while therapists and trained law enforcement officers asked her seemingly innocuous questions about her dad and what she knew.

Even at the tender age of eight, she knew not to disclose anything. Her instincts for self-preservation had always been strong and she intuitively knew that one question would lead to another, and with every admission her world would unravel a little more until she had nothing. So she stuffed everything down into a little box in her mind, and when she was being watched at play therapy, she would act out the plots of *The Smurfs* or *Transformers*, anything far removed from her.

"Sorry," Pamela apologized. "I specialize in children and adolescents," she said, pointing to the bean bag chair and small metal seats. "Kids are more comfortable when we get down on their level."

"That's fine." Jess pulled out a chair and sat down at the table. There was white construction paper and markers in several skin tones from a peachy beige to the darkest brown. "Is this for the 'draw a monster' exercise?" It could also be called 'draw a perpetrator' because that was what the exercise was designed to do.

"Yes. It's sometimes surprising how much freer children are when they are speaking in allegorical terms. Even for adults it is easier to deal with characters. Just that little distance is sometimes all people need."

Jess nodded like she agreed, which she did in theory, but she had never gotten to that therapeutic place personally. She had only ever told the therapists what they wanted to hear, what she thought were safe answers. "We understand that Shaniqua Jackson was one of your patients."

Pamela gave a single nod. "Yes. If you know that, you must have access to her confidential records. You will know I was her court-ordered psychologist. I really want to help you find Shaniqua's killer, but as you might know confidentiality survives the patient. I'm still duty-bound to keep her secrets. You can appreciate that?" Pamela's gaze settled on Jess. The rhetorical question was for her alone.

"Yes," Jess said. "I do know that." She had researched Pamela Reid and knew she had written extensively on the legalities and ethics in psychotherapy. "We fully appreciate your position and the constraints because of your therapeutic relationship with Shaniqua. We'll do our best not to ask any questions that could potentially violate confidentiality."

"Thank you. And I will do my best to give you any information I have. Though I don't think I have anything of value to add." Sadness pulled down the sides of her mouth.

"You reported Shaniqua Jackson missing," Chan stated.

"Yes. We had a session booked for that Friday afternoon. She had never missed an appointment before. She used to take the city bus to see me because her foster mom was unable or unwilling to drive her. At first, I didn't worry too much when she didn't show up because I thought she just hadn't come because she was upset with me, but the next day I called her foster mother to check on her and she hadn't seen her either, so I called the police."

"Why would she be upset with you?"

Pamela opened her mouth and then closed it again. "I… uh." She blinked rapidly as she realized she had said more than she had intended before she held her hand up in defeat. "I'm sorry. I have very limited experience dealing with the police. I have written at length about the ethics of patient confidentiality but I haven't had a lot of real-world experience, and apparently that is a whole other ballgame. I can't tell you why Shaniqua was upset without violating privilege. I hope you can appreciate that."

She seemed genuinely sad that she could not say more.

Chan made a click sound with the side of his mouth, the way he did when he was about to get stuck into a witness. Chan approached interviews like a performance piece, creating a character and spinning a tale. "You know what I appreciate? I appreciate that Shaniqua Jackson is dead and you have the opportunity to try to help us find her killer but you're choosing not to. Ethics? Privilege? She was a little girl who was murdered. And you can help her get justice. From where I'm sitting there's no moral dilemma."

Pamela let out a long sigh. "I don't disagree," she said. She stared past them to the rows of small figurines as she thought. "It's a fine line. Always such a balance, weighing the needs of a patient, the law, and of course the safety of the community at large. It's not easy," she admitted. "And I get it wrong, I know I have. I'm sure there were times when I should have made a different decision. Unfortunately, we can't undo mistakes."

"You're overthinking it. There are four dead girls and their killer is still at large. You have the ability to help us apprehend him."

"I wish it were that easy. I must admit privilege for the deceased is a difficult one to get your head around, even for me, especially in cases like this, when a crime has been committed, or in the cases of suicide when families have so many questions. I understand that desire to ignore confidentiality but we can't. Here is the way I explain it to my students: Privilege for the deceased is to protect the therapeutic process for the living. There are some secrets that feel so dark that people would never be able to bring them to the light if they thought their therapist or doctor could disclose them even after they died."

Jess's skin burned when she glanced up at her. Pamela's explanation hit too close to home. She had never put it into words before, but she had felt that— the fear of anyone knowing her secrets—even after she died. Maybe that was one of the reasons she had never been able to open up and be honest with a therapist.

"But—" Chan started.

"We understand," Jess interrupted. Even if she hadn't agreed with Pamela, she would have realized they were flogging a dead horse with this line of questioning. While it was frustrating that she would not disclose everything in minute detail, Jess respected her for her decision. It was time to go at it from another angle.

She ignored the weight of Chan's stare and kept talking. "As a therapist, you are a mandatory reporter. If Shaniqua disclosed that she was being abused or threatened by anyone, you are legally required to report it. That obligation is also not terminated by death."

Pamela picked up a toy cat from the table and turned it over as she spoke. "There was a lot of abuse in Shaniqua's past. I'm sure you can find court records that will lay it all out but I will save you the time. It started when she was a toddler. We can't determine the exact age but she was pre-verbal. Luckily, she had a very astute kindergarten teacher who didn't ignore her hunch that something was wrong. We all have an innate gift that senses fear and when something is off, but too often we lose it because we are trained to ignore it. Luckily her teacher didn't ignore it.

Shaniqua was withdrawn and wetting herself. Normally that would not be enough to open a CPS case but her teacher pushed and Shaniqua was appointed a social worker who discovered that Shaniqua was wetting herself because she had been abused by her mother's boyfriend. I can't say a lot more than that but Shaniqua never really had a chance."

"Do you know if the boyfriend had been in contact with Shaniqua recently?" Jess asked.

Pamela sighed. "I really want to help you. I can't answer that without violating privilege but what I can say is that you should speak to Shaniqua's foster mother Claudette Baxter. I would also suggest you not give her warning that you're coming. Sometimes unannounced visits are the most... How do I put it? Revealing." She gave Jess a hard stare, like her eyes were trying to communicate the message her words were not allowed to convey.

Jess nodded. "Thank you. We will go see Claudette today."

CHAPTER TWENTY-TWO

"Damn, this is a shithole. Is it safe to leave the car here?" Chan asked when he pulled over to park.

Jess would have liked to tell him it would be fine but looking around the street made her ask herself the same question. She hadn't driven through the Anacostia neighborhood in years. Politicians were always talking about cleaning up the historic area but it still looked as run-down and impoverished as ever. Groups of teenagers clustered on the corners, their faces obscured by hoods and puffy jackets. They were all bent over like they were deep in conversation, which meant they were probably doing a deal. Without thinking, she stroked her Glock in the leather holster she was wearing just to make sure it was still there. "You have your gun, right?"

"Yeah, but I'd prefer not to use it."

"I'd prefer you not have to use it either. Your aim is shit," Jess said.

"So, should I leave the car?"

"Chan, don't you dare pull your bullshit where you screw around with the locks so you don't have to deal with actual work. I'd rather not go into this house on my own, so you're going to have to man up and come with me. If anyone jacks the car, we'll deal with that later. It's not like it's yours and you have to claim it on your insurance."

"You know, you only ever speak to me to insult me?"

"That's not true. I also speak to you to tell you to shut up when you're sexually harassing me."

When she smiled, he smiled back. Jess got out of the car and walked to Claudette Baxter's door. She turned around when she reached the porch to make sure Chan was following her. Jess pressed the doorbell but she couldn't hear the corresponding chime that should follow so she pushed it again and then made a fist with her good hand and pounded on the door. Her knocks were met with angry barks. She pounded again. Finally, the door opened. A rail-thin thirty-something woman opened the door. Her stringy brown hair was tied up in a knot on the top of her head. Her eyebrows had been shaved and colored back in with a charcoal-black pencil. The shape looked like a seagull's wings, extended midflight. Her sallow skin was covered in scabs. She had all the hallmarks of a meth user.

"Do you mind? My boyfriend is trying to sleep. The dog's going to wake him up." She spat out the words. From behind her a baby cried in a playpen.

"Claudette Baxter?" Jess asked. She wedged her foot between the door and the frame so she could not slam the door in her face.

The woman eyed Jess dubiously. "Who's asking?"

Jess didn't bother to hold up her ID. She would rather have her hands free for her gun. "I'm Agent Bishop. This is Agent Chan. We're from the FBI. We would like to ask you some questions."

Panic flashed across her face. "This isn't a good time." She had to shout over the barking of the dog. She tried to close the door but Jess's foot prevented it.

Jess glanced over at the black pit bull confined in a cage that was too small for him. Of course she had a pit bull, because every home with vulnerable children needed a dog famed for its viciousness. "This won't take long. You said your boyfriend was sleeping? I was under the impression you were single. According to the paperwork you filed with the Department of Health and Human Services when you applied to be a foster parent, you're single. If you have an adult male living here, that needs to be reported. I'm going to have to call and report that," Jess said.

"No one else lives here." When she spoke, her lip curled to expose nicotine-stained teeth.

"See, here's the thing, if you don't let me in, I have to assume it is because there is a man in there. I'm sorry, that's just the rule. Nothing I can do about it. Rules are rules. Have a good night." She turned to pretend to walk away. By walking away there was a risk she would shut the door, but Jess didn't have a warrant so Claudette needed to invite her in. "Chan, can you call Rebecca, tell her we need to report a seventy-two thirty?"

"Yeah, sure thing." Chan pulled out his phone to play along. There was no such thing as a seventy-two thirty and Jess wasn't on a first-name basis with any social workers, but details added veracity to her implied threat.

"Wait…" Claudette looked back behind her. "I, uh, have a few minutes before I need to start making dinner."

Jess spun on her heel. "Excellent, thank you. I really appreciate your time." She followed Claudette into the house. Claudette said something but she couldn't hear anything past the barking and the baby screaming.

"Diesel!" Claudette screamed. "Quiet!"

Jess walked over to the cage. Poor dog. He could barely stand up without his shoulders touching the wire top. She would bark too if someone stuffed her in an enclosure that small. He probably just wanted to get out and stretch his legs. She put her hand out for him to sniff through the bars. She didn't realize she had offered her injured hand until he licked the scar on her palm. The sensation of his rough tongue on the tender skin felt like electric needles being poked into her in rapid succession. It wasn't the most pleasant sensation but the dog had stopped barking as he enjoyed the salt of her skin. She didn't mind a bit of pain if it gave the poor dog a bit of joy. "Hey there, buddy," she whispered to him.

"Careful, he doesn't like people," Claudette warned.

"It's okay. I'll risk it." She was tempted to tell her that perhaps if she took the dog out and gave him some proper exercise he wouldn't be so aggressive, but there were only so many battles Jess could fight in a day so Diesel was going to have to accept his fate.

Chan stood in the doorway like he was unwilling to come in; his gaze darted around the living room. If he was looking for a clean place to sit, he wasn't going to find one. The brown cushions of the velour couches were covered in overlapping stains. The floor was covered in dirty diapers, pizza boxes, and roach motels, which gave off an unmistakable odor.

Jess glanced at the table.

"It's a pipe not a bong. It's not illegal," Claudette said.

"And I'm sure the spoon is for feeding your baby not cooking up. Are there needles too? Maybe because you're diabetic?" Jess asked, her tone neutral.

"Yeah, yeah that's it."

"That's fine," Jess said. "We're not here about that. We're here about Shaniqua Jackson."

"What about her?"

"She was living with you when she was murdered," Chan said.

"Ain't like that. I didn't touch her."

"Nobody is saying otherwise," Jess said. "But we need to ask you a few questions. The man who killed her has killed three other girls."

"What you want to know?"

"Do you know anyone who would want to hurt Shaniqua?"

"Nah." Claudette shrugged. "She ain't never go out enough to meet people to hurt her. She just stayed in her room and wrote in her journal and cried."

"Shaniqua kept a journal? Do you still have it?"

"Yeah, I think so, maybe."

"I would like to see it if you have it."

"Okay. It's not like I'm going to do anything with it."

Jess and Chan followed her as she walked down the hall to a bedroom. A cockroach scurried across the brown pile of the carpet when Claudette turned on the light. There was a set of bunk beds on both sides of the small room, leaving only enough room to stand sideways between them. Housing vulnerable children was how Claudette made her money so she would stack them six-deep if she could.

Claudette bent down and tugged on the corner of a stained mattress and pulled out a diary with a lock on it. "No idea why she locked it. Ain't nobody want to read it." Claudette handed the diary to Jess. "Shit, what happened to your hand?"

"Glass."

"Looks like a bomb exploded in your hand. Did it hurt?"

"Yeah, it did. It still does," Jess admitted, although she wasn't sure why. She held up the diary. "Why was Shaniqua crying all the time? Did she tell you? Was something bothering her before she died?"

"I don't know. The electric shock therapy was supposed to take care of that but she was just sleepy after and then the next day she was back to her mopey self, crying and writing."

"Electric shock therapy? Shaniqua had ECT?" Jess's head snapped round to look at Chan.

"Yeah. I guess that's what it's called. It was right downtown at the children's hospital and she couldn't even take the bus home. I had to pick her up in a taxi because she was so out of it. I still never got my money back for that cab either."

"When did she start having ECT?"

"It was just that once. She had it on the Wednesday before she died. Dr. Reid sent her to a shrink. Said there wasn't anything more she could do for her just talking and whatnot."

That was what Pamela Reid had been talking about when she said Shaniqua had been upset with her. She blamed her for referring her to a psychiatrist for electroconvulsive therapy. That was what she wanted them to know but couldn't tell them.

"Thank you for this," Jess said as she held up the journal. "If there is anything else you can think of, please give me a call." She reached into her pocket and gave her a business card. She very much doubted she would call, but on the off chance, she would leave her details.

She walked down the hall. When she passed a bedroom door, it opened and a man came out wearing boxers and a wife beater. His chest and shoulders were covered in tattoos. His pupils were black pinpricks engulfed by glassy hazel irises and at the edge of his left eye were two teardrop tattoos.

"What the fuck?" he barked.

Before Jess could identify herself, he drew back his arm and swung. Jess only had time to blink before something hard connected with the side of her head. She stumbled back from the force of it and fell into Chan, who kept her from hitting the ground. For a fraction of a second there was no pain as the receptors in her body geared up to process the assault, and then it crashed against her all at once like lightning splitting her orbital bone. "Son of a bitch." She reached her hand to access the damage but her eye socket was too sore to allow even the slightest touch.

When she pulled her hand away, it was wet with blood.

The smell of whiskey burned the back of her throat. Shards of glass studded the stained carpet. Her vision went in and out of focus.

The man ran from the house.

"Are you okay?" Chan asked.

Jess threw the journal to the ground and then reached for her gun.

"Jess, you're bleeding," Chan said. "I think you're really hurt."

"Go!" Jess screamed, pointing at the door. She tried to speak, to give Chan directions, but the words came out garbled.

Chan bolted for the door. The man was already running half-naked toward the street. "FBI! Stop!"

The last thing she heard was the door slamming.

CHAPTER TWENTY-THREE

"Agent Bishop, we meet again. Two visits to the ER in two months qualifies you as a frequent flyer." A doctor whose name she couldn't remember smiled as she looked up from her chart. "How is your hand?" She chewed gum as she talked, smacking with every syllable.

Jess vaguely remembered her from the night she escaped the basement, the gum, and the way her blond ponytail swished from side to side when she walked.

"Yeah, it's good, thank you."

"Is that your new partner?" She gestured to Chan, who was at the nurse's station talking to a brunette with rosy cheeks and bright red lipstick. He was leaned over the desk and she was laughing at something he said. No doubt he was being inappropriate as usual but at least he had stopped touching things in the ER. He had spent almost fifteen minutes pressing the pedal on the trash can, watching it go up and down. He really couldn't sit still for any length of time.

She wasn't sure she wanted to claim him as hers but she nodded anyway.

Jess hadn't wanted to come to the hospital but the arresting officer had called an ambulance as soon as he saw her. He convinced her to come in and get checked out by reminding her that it would play better in court if she was admitted to the hospital. He also took pictures because juries loved pictures.

"Okay, let me have a look." The doctor snapped on a pair of gloves and shone a light into Jess's eye. "Pupils are equal and reactive. That's good. I don't love the way your eye is drooping though. That's probably just superficial swelling but I want to check it out."

A stab of pain shot through the left side of her face when the doctor pressed against her cheek bone.

"Sorry, I should have said that might be sore. Have you been given anything for the pain?"

"Just ibuprofen."

The doctor made a *tut* sound. "Girl, I can do better than that."

"No, it's okay. I'm fine."

"Really? Okay. If you change your mind, let me know, and I'll hook you up with the good stuff."

"I'm good, thanks," Jess said.

"All right. Let's get you in for an MRI and see what's going on."

Jess's pulse quickened. "Like in the machine?" She had never had an issue with confined spaces before. It was all in the mind, that's what she thought. But then she had done battle with a serial killer in his basement. She didn't have a phobia. She preferred to think of it as a personal preference not to freak the fuck out. "Do you have to do that?"

"Your partner said you lost consciousness."

"No, I didn't, I mean like maybe for a second."

"And you were slurring your words."

Jess closed her eyes; she was not going to win this argument. "I don't love confined spaces." She felt stupid even saying it. If she needed an MRI, she needed an MRI, and she needed to just deal with it.

The doctor stopped chewing her gum. Her face changed, the levity gone, replaced with sympathy. "Oh yeah, of course. A little anxiety is totally normal, especially given what you've been through recently."

Immediately Jess regretted saying anything. She should have just bucked up and dealt with it.

The doctor glanced over at the nurse's station. "I was going to ask Abby to get you your meds but looks like she's busy."

"Sorry." She didn't know why she was apologizing on behalf of Chan but it wasn't the first time and it wouldn't be the last.

"I guess we'll just leave them to it."

The doctor left and returned a few minutes later with a relaxant before an orderly took her upstairs. The pill could have been a horse tranquilizer for all she knew. She didn't care, it did the trick. Instead of being panicked and trying to claw her way out of the MRI machine, she closed her eyes and listened to the hum of the machinery. It was the most relaxed she had been… probably ever.

"That's some good shit," she said to the nurse who helped her into the wheelchair and wheeled her back to the ER where Chan was supposed to be waiting for her. She wasn't sure why the nurse insisted on a wheelchair; she had been hit in her head not her legs. "Tell Dr. Ponytail thank you for me."

The nurse laughed.

The ER was busier than before she went for her scan—more people bleeding and coughing. The nurses must have changed shift because Abby, the brunette who laughed at Chan's attempt at jokes, was gone. And so was Chan.

Jess rolled her eyes. Of course he was gone. He was probably getting down to it with nurse Abby by now. He had almost passed the threshold into decent human territory but he had fallen at the last hurdle.

"Jess! There you are. The nurse said you would be down in ten minutes. That was an hour ago."

Jess looked over to see Lindsay kneeling near the vending machine, her hand in the slot, reaching up to try to grab a Twix that dangled just out of reach.

"Be careful. At least two people die every single year in vending-machine-related accidents. That's twice as many as shark attacks," Jess warned.

"There's my little trivia queen. This is why the team needs you." Lindsay abandoned trying to get her Twix and stood up. "Paying for parking isn't enough. They have to rob me of all the change I have in the bottom of my purse too. I hate hospitals. Oh man, look at you." She walked over to her. The sides of her mouth pulled into a frown. "That jackass was lucky I wasn't there. I would have bust out my Krav Maga. I've been going to classes for like two months so I'm pretty much a cage fighter now. Just a little something I do." She smiled as she shrugged.

"I'm fine. It's only sore if I touch it. Why are you here?" Jess asked. She realized after she said it that she sounded rude and ungrateful, which she wasn't. If she weren't still high she would have thought of a better way to phrase it.

"Your doctor said you needed a ride home because you're doped up good. Chan promised to wait for you but he got a better offer so he called me."

"Nurse Abby."

"Is that her name?" Lindsay asked. "Let's just call her random woman with low self-esteem. I diagnosed him by the way. He has a serious case of asshat with underlying overcompensation." She held up her hand, her thumb, and pointer finger a few inches apart to demonstrate what she meant.

"Don't make me laugh. It hurts."

"Sorry. He left this. He said you would want to see it as soon as you got out." She handed her Shaniqua Jackson's diary.

"There it is. I dropped it when I got hit. Thank God Chan picked it up. He's good for something."

"Besides being the rock bottom women hit before they seek help?"

Jess laughed. "Yeah, that too."

*

Lindsay drove her back to her apartment. Luckily she knew Jess never had anything in her fridge so she had brought the ingredients to make cheeseburgers and fries.

"This is good. I never thought to put the cheese inside the burger before you cook it. Genius," Jess said.

"You're still high, aren't you?"

"A little bit but seriously this is really good."

"Thanks. The secret ingredient is A1 sauce because I'm fancy like that. I got the skills of an MMA fighter and I'm practically a Michelin chef."

"And you're humble." Jess wiped off the ketchup that had oozed out of the bun and down her chin.

"I know, right? Full package right here. Remind me again why someone hasn't put a ring on it."

"It's a mystery. Right up there with the Bermuda Triangle. Here, can you hand me a knife?"

"Is my banter that bad? You need to off yourself?" Lindsay asked as she handed her a steak knife.

"There is a lock on Shaniqua's diary. I think I can just shimmy it." Jess pointed the tip of the knife down into the lock, angling just right until she heard it click. "And there we go."

"I might be an MMA fighter but you are a world-class spy with those lock-picking techniques."

"Just a little something I do," she said, quoting Lindsay.

"You can go home, you know. You don't need to babysit me," Jess said.

Lindsay had been the same when she came home from the hospital after her hand surgery. She had been like a mother hen, looking after her and making sure she had taken her antibiotics at the right time and never on an empty stomach.

Lindsay was going to be a great mom someday. They had never talked about it but she knew Lindsay wanted kids. She doted on her brother's children. Every picture she had on her phone was of one of them performing in one of their many recitals or riding their bikes.

Jess opened the diary. A lump formed in her throat. This wasn't just evidence, it was the secrets of a murdered little girl. She closed her eyes and gave herself a second to reflect on that.

The first page was covered in doodles of stars and a Pegasus flying over the moon. She smiled. Shaniqua was talented. She hoped that when she was alive, someone had spotted that talent and praised her, given her something to feel proud about.

Slowly, almost reverently, she turned to the next page and started reading the journal entries. They had started just over a year ago. "Pamela Reid asked her to keep a journal," Jess said to Lindsay, but she was too engrossed in watching something on her phone to listen.

Jess kept reading. With every entry, her heart sank a little lower. Pamela was right: This poor girl had never had a chance. Every journal entry was a detailed account of abuse. The most devastating part was how her mom blamed her for what her boyfriend had done. Shaniqua was a preschooler at the time. There was no gray area there. This was no Lolita scenario. She had been abused and her mom blamed her; and worse yet, Shaniqua blamed herself.

Jess turned the page and kept reading. "Oh shit," Jess whispered. The abuse hadn't stopped when she went into care. Chad Schwartz, the guy who had hit Jess, had abused her too, along with a P.E. teacher at school. Shaniqua didn't tell Pamela about the abuse because she knew Pamela would have to report it. Shaniqua didn't even see it as abuse, it was just her normal. To her that was what affection felt like.

"Our list of suspects just got bigger," Jess said.

Lindsay muted her phone and looked up. "What's going on?"

"Shaniqua Jackson wrote down every man who ever abused her in here. She even put corresponding dates and times and locations. Pamela Reid asked her to write down things that she wasn't ready to disclose."

"That's really smart," Lindsay said. "That can all be used as evidence. That was a great call. If Pamela had ever convinced Shaniqua to press charges against her abusers, she would have documentation to back up her claims. That would have made prosecution so much easier."

"I know. It was a great idea. It's harder to argue false memories if the victim documented it at the time but I don't think Shaniqua was ever going to press charges against anyone else. She didn't even realize it was abuse."

"Yeah." Lindsay nodded. "We both know that's not uncommon."

"I found something else. Pamela told me and Chan that Shaniqua was upset with her. Her foster mom told us that it was because Pamela had referred her to a psychiatrist for ECT. The doctor she referred her to was Peter Reid, Pamela's father. The last entry in the diary is right before she went in for her first treatment. She was terrified."

Lindsay's eyes widened in surprise.

"What?" Jess asked.

"Nothing. It's just... nothing." Lindsay shook her head. "I'm surprised she referred her to her dad, that's all."

"That part surprised you, not the fact she prescribed shock therapy?"

"No. I mean if the procedure wasn't explained properly to Shaniqua, she would have been really scared but it is a good treatment. ECT gets a very bad rap in the media. Journalists who have no business commenting on it pass it off as cruel and barbaric, and say people are being tortured and electrocuted. That's bullshit. It's a life-saving tool. The success rate is something like ninety percent. And it works immediately, unlike medication which can take several weeks to get to a therapeutic dose."

"So, you would recommend it?"

"One hundred percent. If I had a severely depressed or suicidal patient, I would definitely refer them for ECT, especially if they hadn't responded to medication. The treatment works."

"Do you know anyone personally who has had it done?"

"Yes."

Jess didn't ask any follow-up questions. Lindsay would never violate confidentiality. Even if something was confided in her outside the therapeutic environment, it went in the vault.

CHAPTER TWENTY-FOUR

"Dang, you look even worse today than last night," Chan said when he walked in the room and handed her a styrofoam cup from the coffee kiosk. That was his version of an apology for leaving her at the hospital. He would never say the words, so this was the best she was going to get.

"Thanks," she said before she took off the lid and had a sip. "Yeah, that's what the doctor said would happen. It's going to look worse before it gets better." She had done her best to cover up the bruising with concealer but there was no covering up the swelling.

"How much worse are we talking because I can barely look at you right now," he said with a smirk.

Despite the pain in her head and her hand, she smiled. He really was an asshole but it was strangely endearing.

Tina stood in the doorway for a second. She took one look at her face and said, "Ah Jess, you should have called me. Lindsay told me this morning. Here, this is all I could find at the pharmacy down the street." She handed her a shiny gold bag with the words Happy Anniversary embossed on the side. "I'm not sure why anyone would be doing anniversary shopping at a pharmacy. Clearly it is more likely you would be shopping for your friend who was injured in the line of duty. They should have a card and gift bag section just for that."

Friend. Jess was still getting used to the idea of another person wanting to be her friend. Tina had to see that Jess was pretty shitty in the friend department but still she seemed willing to try, or maybe she was just nice to everyone.

Tina opened the bag for her. A tiny vial rattled when she took it out. "These are arnica tablets. They will help with the bruising. And, of course, I got you chocolate because that will help with absolutely everything."

Jess smiled. "Thank you, Tina. I appreciate it. I'm fine though, really, nothing broken. It looks far worse than it is. It doesn't even hurt." By that she meant it felt the same as the throb in her hand, which was her new baseline.

She glanced up when she felt a stare heavy on her. Jamison stood in the doorway; his massive shoulders filled the frame. The muscles along his jaw flexed as he clenched his teeth together. "What happened?"

"It's nothing. Just an interview that got a bit lively. He thought I was vice and he tried to get away. He's been charged. It's all good," she assured him.

"Where was Chan?" Jamison asked. Annoyance flashed in his dark eyes.

From the corner of her good eye she saw Chan glance down at the table rather than look at Jamison.

"I'm fine," she said again.

"Where were you?" Jamison asked again, this time directing his question at Chan.

Chan didn't answer. He had a retort ready for every occasion but not now.

"Nah man, that's not good enough." Jamison came in and sat down. He didn't press the issue farther. He had made his point.

Jeanie and Milligan came in behind him. Milligan had a crusted stain on his tie that looked like dried yogurt or maybe regurgitated milk from his baby. She couldn't remember seeing him without a stain somewhere on his person since he transferred to the team three months ago and today was no exception.

Jeanie took her seat at the head of the table. "I spoke to the district attorney this morning. Chad Schwartz was denied bail; he violated his parole conditions by living with minors, and of course assaulting a federal agent will never be tolerated. Ever." She glanced over her glasses at Jess.

Jess smiled. Jeanie could never be described as warm or effusive but she was protective of her agents.

"He whacked you over the head with a whiskey bottle?" Milligan asked.

"Um, yeah." Jess shifted in her seat, uncomfortable with the attention. "It's fine. I'm fine. Anyway, we've made some headway into piecing together Shaniqua's last few days. Her foster mom gave us her diary. I've made everyone copies of the relevant passages." She passed out the packets she had come in early to make. She had planned on coming back into work last night after the hospital but she had fallen asleep on the couch. When her alarm went off she discovered Lindsay had gotten her a pillow and covered her with a blanket. She had even left a lemon poppy-seed muffin on the kitchen table.

"As you can see, Shaniqua has given us a list of suspects we need to speak to. She outlines several men who have abused her in the recent past. Chad Schwartz is on the list. He's a heroin user and low-level dealer. Heroin users can develop erectile dysfunction, which fits our profile. And we've seen he is not averse to physical violence." She pointed to her face for evidence.

Jeanie nodded. "Yes, I agree."

"Chad Schwartz has been processed. I was going to interview him this morning once I've established if he has any known connection to the other murdered girls. I'm currently trying to determine if he or any of his known associates would have knowledge of the security system at Children's National Hospital."

"I'd like to interview Chad Schwartz," Jamison said.

Jess blinked, too taken aback to speak.

"Yes, I agree. I think that is a good choice. Briggs and Milligan, can you interview Schwartz and Shaniqua's P.E. teacher? And Bishop and Chan, can you…" Jeanie tapped her pen against the table like she was looking for something to say, a task to give them. "Can you interview the doctor who administered ECT? What's his name?" She looked down at the file Jess had given her. "Here we go. Dr. Peter Reid. Shaniqua's journal entries end the day she saw him. He might be able to give us some insight into what was going on with her."

Jess looked from Jamison to Jeanie. Chad was her witness. She had the hairline fracture of her orbital socket to prove it. Did they think she was incapable of handling her own interviews now? Obviously, Chad Schwartz was violent but he wouldn't be a risk to her now, and even if he was, she could handle herself. She should be the one conducting the interview but her hand and head hurt too much to immediately formulate a cogent argument.

"Tina, where are we with identifying the car?" Jeanie asked.

Jess cleared her throat. "Dr. Reid will still be bound by doctor–patient confidentiality. I don't think that is the best use of our resources because he is limited in what he can tell us." She had no desire to be disrespectful, but she didn't want to be sidelined either. She was the one who brought the case to the team's attention; they wouldn't even be investigating if it wasn't for her.

Her input was met with a stony silence. She could not remember ever questioning Jeanie's authority. Jess was many things, but defiant was not one of them. What Jeanie said, went. Jeanie was her boss and she respected her authority but this was ridiculous.

Eventually Jeanie spoke. "Thank you for your input, Jessica, but I've made my decision. We won't know if Dr. Reid has anything to say until we interview him. Now, where were we, Tina?"

Jess bit the inside of her mouth to keep from saying anything more.

Tina gave her a small sympathetic smile before she began. "Based on the most reliable eyewitness account, which was the park ranger from the Shenandoah Valley, the car appears to be an Alfa Romeo. The triangular fibers found on the first three bodies are consistent with the carpets used in their cars. The good news is only 13,000 have been sold in America. And only six of those are registered in or around DC. Unfortunately, all but one of those are blue or black so I can't narrow it down any further."

"Please tell me Chad Schwartz owns an Alfa Romeo," Milligan said.

"No such luck. Mr. Schwartz doesn't even have a valid driver's license."

"That doesn't mean he doesn't drive or have access to a car," Chan chipped in.

"True," Tina said. "I am going to look at everyone in the area with an Alfa Romeo.

"Good. I think everyone knows what they're doing. We have a lot to do, so unless anyone has a question, I think we are done."

Everyone looked at Jess to see if she would respond but she didn't; she just took out her trusty bottle of ibuprofen and took two pills with a swig of black coffee.

CHAPTER TWENTY-FIVE

"Thank you for seeing us on such short notice," Jess said to Dr. Peter Reid. Unlike his daughter's office, which was sunny and patient-centered, his office was clinical and austere. The walls were all white, and the furniture, what little there was of it, was black leather. The only small accents of color were the gold frames that held his credentials. He had the same sharp features as his daughter but unlike her, there was no carefree smile on his face.

"I'm quite busy. So, if we could hurry this along. You have five minutes." He spoke to her breasts, his glance only moving up to her eyes when he tapped his watch to reinforce his point, and then they returned again to her chest.

She fought the instinct to curve her shoulders or pull on her suit jacket to try to conceal herself. That would give him the impression she was self-conscious or that he had made her uncomfortable, and that was what he wanted. She knew his type all too well. He wanted to make her squirm because there was power in it.

She let the silence hang between them because he expected her to nod or thank him again for his time, something that would reinforce his importance, but Jess had spoken to his secretary and knew he wasn't seeing any patients until later in the afternoon.

She glanced at Chan and gave her head a small almost indiscernible shake, telling him not to speak. If Peter Reid wanted to play power games, she would show him how it was done. She stood silently, staring him down, looking at him look at her breasts.

The seconds dragged on past the point of socially acceptable pauses but still no one spoke.

"Why are you here?" Dr. Reid asked at last.

Jess smiled to herself. Point to her.

"We want to talk to you about Shaniqua Jackson," Chan said, taking a seat without being asked. He opened his notebook and pulled out the ballpoint pen he kept anchored at the top. The taut leather of the couch squeaked when he crossed and uncrossed his legs trying to get comfortable on the hard seat.

"Who? I'm not familiar with a Shania."

"Shaniqua. Her name was Shaniqua," Jess corrected him.

"I still don't know her."

"Well then, our investigation has taken a surprising direction and the FBI is going to have to investigate you for insurance fraud because you billed Medicaid for treating her." Jess smiled.

"That's hardly necessary. I treat an extraordinary number of people. I couldn't possibly be expected to remember them all."

"Because you're very busy and very important?" Chan asked. "Is that what you're trying to get at? You were pretty subtle before so I just wanted to make sure that is what you were implying. I like to be very specific with my notes. I'm sure you can appreciate that."

Dr. Reid's nostrils flared ever so slightly but he didn't say anything.

Jess pulled out her phone and showed him a recent picture of the girl. "This is Shaniqua Jackson. You administered ECT on the twentieth of September, two days before she was abducted and murdered."

He shrugged.

Jess had to shake her head at his callousness. This wasn't the reaction people normally had when learning a child had been killed. No matter how many patients she had, she would remember all of their faces if not their names. She had worked over 100 cases and she still remembered all of the victims. She would be a really shitty person if she didn't. "Your daughter referred her," Jess prompted.

Dr. Reid made a tutting sound. "Oh yes, another one of Pamela's failures. Perhaps if she had applied herself more she could have gone to medical school and been able to provide comprehensive care to all of her clients and not have to refer them for appropriate treatments. At least she recognized her limitations so that child could get adequate help and support."

Jess's eyes widened, surprised by how mean-spirited and dismissive he was of his own daughter. She had thought he was a lecherous old man but she could not shake the feeling that there was something more sinister going on here. Since she had walked into the office, the reading she got off him was clear. There was something predatory about him. She could feel it. "Do you dye your hair, Dr. Reid?"

"Excuse me?" he said, clearly annoyed by the question.

"It looks like you do," Jess continued. "What color would you say that is, Agent Chan? It looks like Natural Medium Brown to me. What do you think?"

"I really don't know what this has to do with anything." Subconsciously he stroked the limp strands of his matte brown hair. The color had a red undertone that didn't match his dark brows. It was a dye job and not a very good one.

Rather than answer him she said, "Where were you on the twenty-second and twenty-third of September?"

"What? Where are you going with this?" Dr. Reid demanded.

Chan looked up from his notepad. "I'm glad I'm not the only one who likes to have things spelled out for me. She is implying that you have something to do with Shaniqua Jackson's murder; or was she inferring? I can never keep those two straight."

"You can't possibly think I have something to do with that poor child's death."

"Poor child?" Jess scoffed. "Thirty seconds ago you could not remember ever treating her and you weren't entirely sympathetic when you learned that she had died."

"As I said before, I treat an incredible number of patients."

Jess noted his lexical choices: extraordinary and incredible. Those were the word choices of a narcissist. Even if he did not meet the diagnostic criteria, which she was confident he would, he certainly thought very highly of himself. "I know you're a very busy man. Very important. We established that earlier. What I want to establish now is if you have an alibi."

"This is absurd." His face went from a sallow hue to a worrisome shade of red. The vein in his neck bulged under the strain, pulsing with the increased pressure.

"I need an hour by hour detailed account of where you were on the twenty-second and twenty-third of September."

"Honestly, I have never been more offended in my life," he ground out between clenched teeth.

"A simple DNA test can rule you out as a suspect," Chan offered.

"I won't even dignify that with a response."

"Wait what? Now I feel really stupid because from where I'm sitting, it seems like the easiest option for you, Doc. You can clear yourself with a simple mouth swab. I mean, I would do that. Unless, of course, all the righteous indignation is just for show. If that's the case, yeah, don't give us your DNA because that will nail your ass," Chan said.

Dr. Reid's nostrils flared again but this time he could not begin to cover his annoyance; it was written on every feature on his face. "Your hypothesis is predicated on the assumption I have confidence in the judicial system."

Chan made a show of holding up his hands. "You're going to have to use smaller words with me, Doc. Break it down for me. What's the problem?"

"I don't want to speak for him but it sounds like he is saying he is worried we will fabricate evidence against him. Is that what you're saying, Peter? Can I call you Peter? Or do you prefer Pete?" Jess asked. "And the word you're looking for, Chan, is paranoid. Pete is showing clear signs of paranoia."

"That's it! I knew you would know the word. She always knows the right word. She's really smart," Chan told him.

"I'm done with this conversation. Unless you have a warrant, you need to leave now. I won't be insulted in my place of business."

Chan gave him a dubious look. "Dude, this can't be the first time you've been insulted. Look at you, I doubt it's the first time this week. No offense."

"That's enough!" Dr. Reid's body vibrated with barely controlled rage.

Jess pointed at Chan. "Can you write down anger issues for me? Thanks." She smiled as she stood up and made her way to the door. "This has been a truly enlightening conversation. Thank you so much, Pete, for your candor."

As soon as Jess was out of the office, she pulled out her phone. "I'm telling you, he has something to do with Shaniqua's death. Did you see his hair? That was his hair we found on Ava's hospital bed. It's the same color."

Before he could answer, she had called Tina.

"I literally just picked up the phone to call you," Tina said when she answered the phone.

"Please say you called to tell me Peter Reid owns an Alfa Romeo. Chan and I just met him and he is a real piece of work."

"Sorry, no. He's never owned an Alfa Romeo. But there is another psychiatrist in DC who does. Dr. Martin Schofield has a blue Alfa Romeo. And another tidbit you might find interesting is that Martin Schofield and Peter Reid are colleagues. They have been in practice together for almost thirty-five years."

Jess's heart picked up speed. That was indeed an interesting new bit of information. "That's awesome work, Tina. Thank you."

"It gets better. Martin Schofield reported his car stolen last week. He claims he doesn't know when it was stolen because he was on an extended vacation. He was on a cross-country trip in his RV. He did Route 66. When he got home, he realized his car was gone and reported it. And this is the part where you're really going to love me. I have found it in Ivy City."

Jess squeezed the phone until her hand ached. "You found the car? And because it was reported stolen, we don't need a warrant to search it. You're right, I do love you."

CHAPTER TWENTY-SIX

Jamison and Milligan were already at the scene when Jess and Chan got there. The apartment building was set between two abandoned warehouses. Gang tags covered the dilapidated buildings in layers of color.

A Forensics team was searching the car. A tow truck was on site, ready to take the car back for further tests.

Jess had to step over a used condom and a hypodermic needle to reach them, reminding her that Ivy City was one of the most dangerous areas of DC. Despite the incongruity of a run-down inner-city dump site and a Rolex-wearing doctor, Jess had no doubt Peter Reid was involved.

"They found three bags of Blueberry Surprise cotton candy in the trunk," Jamison told her. "There is also sand. It looks like it belongs to our guy."

"It's Dr. Reid, the psychiatrist who treated Shaniqua Jackson. He has privileges at Children's National Hospital. He would have known when the cameras were down when he took Ava Marsden. We need to get a warrant for his DNA," Jess said to Chan.

"I'll call Jeanie," he responded.

Jess glanced at her clock. It was almost five, still early enough to canvass the area and speak to residents. "We should go door to door and see if anyone can place him with the car."

"I'll go with you," Jamison said, glaring at Chan.

"You don't have to." If she didn't know better, she could have been tempted to believe he still cared. But that was just Jamison.

He offered because he thought it was the right thing to do. "I have Chan. We'll take the even-numbered apartments, you take the odd."

"Jessie, you're—"

"I'm fine," she cut him off. Whatever he was going to say, she didn't want to hear. "Chan, let's go."

Chan held up his arm and pointed to his wrist where a watch would be if he wore one. "I'm starving. It's dinner time and I skipped lunch. I saw an IHOP down the street. Can't we let Forensics do their thing and we can come back in the morning? Everyone knows eyewitnesses are shit witnesses. I mean, they couldn't even agree on the color of the damn car. And these people are going to be high. I don't want to deal with high people today. Look at your face. That's what high people do."

She just shook her head, turned around, and started walking to the first door. She didn't have to check that Chan was behind her; Jamison would make his life unbearable if he wasn't.

She squeezed her good hand into a fist and pounded on the door but there was no answer. She tried again before she moved on to the next door and then the next until finally there was an answer.

"Who's there?" a frail voice called from the other side of the closed door.

"Ma'am, this is Special Agent Jessica Bishop. I'm from the FBI. I'd like to speak to you for a few minutes." She held her ID up to the peephole so the woman could inspect it.

There was a thump of the deadlock turning followed by the rattling of the door chain before the door opened. An elderly woman opened the door. She had wiry white hair, cut inches from her scalp. She was wearing a winter coat on top of a robe to try to keep warm.

When Jess stepped closer to shake her hand, she saw that behind her thick glasses were the hazy sheen of cataracts. Her vision was probably too poor for her to make a reliable eyewitness but they would speak to her anyway.

When the door opened fully, a pungent smell assaulted her sinuses. It smelled like rotting meat. Her stomach clenched at the assault on her olfactory nerve. She had to take small steady breaths to keep from being sick. From the corner of her eye, she saw Chan cover his mouth as he dry-heaved. He had always had a delicate stomach. Any sort of organic decomposition set him off. Sometimes she wondered why exactly he had gone into law enforcement, what skillset in particular had led him to believe it was a good match, but right now she was concerned about where the smell was coming from.

"Ma'am, my partner and I would like to ask you a few questions, if you wouldn't mind."

"Is it about those boys who come round with their spray paint? They're not bad boys really. I know they get up to no good but they leave me alone. Never give me no bother."

"No, ma'am, we're not here about those boys." The boys she was talking about were undoubtedly gang members but good to know they had a bit of humanity and were leaving her alone. "We're here about the car parked just over there." Jess pointed across the parking lot. Forensics had finished and the car was now hooked up to the tow truck ready to be taken to impound.

"Ain't been here long, I can tell you that." The woman looked to the wrong side of the parking lot.

"Can you see the car I'm pointing at, ma'am?" Jess asked.

"Nah, but ain't nobody taken it yet so it can't have been there long."

Jess smiled. Her logic was sound even if her vision wasn't. Jess paused to look around the apartment. The living room was clean even if the décor was suspended in the seventies. The walls were covered in peeling brown wallpaper with large clusters of orange and mustard-colored flowers. The carpet was a matching shade of russet. At one point, they would have been the height of sophistication but that time was forty years ago.

Jess kept looking around for the source of the smell but there was no rotting food or litter box to explain the foul odor. "Ma'am, can I ask you your name?"

"You can call me Nettie but I like ma'am too. Ain't nobody called me that in a long time."

"Okay, ma'am it is. It's very cold in here. Do you have heating? Is it broken? Can I help you turn it on?" Jess asked.

"Ain't worked since last winter. Landlord said he would fix it when he could. It's been almost a year now and he ain't seen fit to fix it."

"Well that's not good enough, is it?" She turned to Chan, who was still standing in the doorway. "Alex, can you call Adult Services? I think it's too cold for Miss Nettie and someone should do something about that."

Chan rolled his eyes but he still took his phone out of his pocket. Thirty seconds later he said, "It went straight to voicemail. Everyone has gone home for the night. Or to IHOP because they're hungry."

Jess ignored him. She tapped her foot on the floor as she thought. The radio had been forecasting all week about imminent snowfall. It was too cold to leave Nettie in the apartment. "Ma'am, would you like me to have a look at your heater and see if we can get it working?"

Chan tutted. "Are you serious? Now you're a social worker and a plumber?"

"No, just a decent human. You might want to try it sometime." Jess smiled. "Ma'am, if you want me to look at your boiler, I'm happy to."

"Well, if you wouldn't mind. It's pretty cold."

"Yes, ma'am, it is. You shouldn't have to wear a coat inside."

Jess and Chan followed Nettie down the hall. With each step the putrid stench intensified until it was almost unbearable.

Jess paused as she considered how to broach the subject. No one wanted to be told their home smelled like raw sewage. "Do you have a pet? A cat or a dog?" Jess looked down at the orange and brown linoleum for signs of an animal but there wasn't anything.

"No, it's just me."

Jess sighed. She had no idea how to phrase the question in a polite way. She was tempted to call Lindsay and ask her. Lindsay always knew how to word things without offending people. But a phone call would mean being subjected to the smell even longer and she wasn't sure her stomach would hold out. Chan's certainly wouldn't. He stood behind her, one hand wrapped around his waist, the other clamped over his mouth as he dry-heaved. His entire body convulsed with each involuntary spasm.

Jess cleared her threat. "Miss Nettie, can you smell that?"

"Oh, sweet Jesus, of course I can smell it. It's my eyes that are the problem, not my nose. The smell's getting worse every day. I called my landlord at least a dozen times. I told him I think it's coming from upstairs but he don't want to come and see to it until he gets another tenant. He said no reason to be coming twice."

"So, no one lives upstairs?"

"No, the last people moved out this summer. We was supposed to be getting someone new but he never showed up. I reckon from what the landlord said he is being housed by the state now instead, if you know what I mean?" Nettie said.

"You mean he is in prison?"

"Yes, that's what I be saying. I'm just guessing like, but I've been around awhile. I know how these things go."

"Well, we can't have you living in here like this. If you give me your landlord's number, I'll be happy to call and chase it up with him. I'll make sure he sends someone out tomorrow," Jess assured her. Even without Nettie's blessing, she had every intention of calling the owner and putting the fear of God into him. If she needed to, she would ask Jamison to pay him a visit. She had no doubt that would get it sorted.

"Well, if you wouldn't mind, that would be nice. The smell was bad enough, but now I can't use the bedroom because of the leak."

Jess shook her head. This guy was clearly a slumlord. This flat was uninhabitable. "You can't use your bedroom? Then where do you sleep?"

Nettie pointed to the living room. "I have my chair. It's one of them fancy recliners."

Jess pulled out her phone to take pictures and document the situation. Leaving an old woman in this predicament was unacceptable. She was going to be writing some very strongly worded letters tonight. "Ma'am, can I see your bedroom? I want to take a picture of the leak. That'll help me convince your landlord to come and fix it."

"All right, if you think it will help," Nettie said.

"Jess, don't open the door. It stinks. I can't take anymore," Chan begged her. The color had faded from his cheeks.

"Fine. Go outside and wait for me."

He made a *pfft* sound. "And have Jamison kick my ass for leaving you? I don't think so. I don't get it. You shot him and he still has it bad for you. You must have some mad skills or—" He tried finish the sentence but he had to hold his mouth as another wave of nausea hit him.

Jess shook her head. Jamison didn't have any feelings for her; he had made that very clear. He was only protective of her because they had been partners for so long but now was not the time or place to explain that to Chan, so she said, "I'll be two minutes. Just keep your mouth covered and breathe through your hand."

Jess opened the door. Nothing could have prepared her for the smell. The stench was overwhelming. With each breath she tasted the disgusting odor as much as she smelled it.

Her ears buzzed as insects flew past her head. She brushed them away only for another one to take its place. She looked up at the dark patch in the ceiling. Thousands of flies swarmed at the center.

Jess peered to examine their winged forms. "Oh shit." Her heart rate spiked. "Those are blowflies."

"What does that mean?" Nettie asked.

Before Jess could answer, Chan threw up on himself. Vomit dripped between his fingers where he tried to catch it but there was no holding it back. He bent over as another powerful spasm wracked his body.

"It means there is a dead body above us."

CHAPTER TWENTY-SEVEN

"Do you think this is our guy?" Jamison asked when he got to the door. Slushy drops of frozen rain rolled off his jacket.

"I don't think so. We'll check it out but our guy left all his victims in public places. He wanted them to be found quickly. Based on the paraphernalia I saw outside my money is on an overdose."

"Makes sense," Jamison agreed.

"Can you wait with her while I check on Chan?"

"Yeah, of course."

"Miss Nettie, this is my colleague, Jamison Briggs. He is going to look after you for a minute and help you pack a bag."

"Well, he's a handsome fellow, isn't he?" Nettie looked from Jamison to Jess.

"Yes, ma'am, he's easy on the eyes." The old woman's vision must not be that bad if she noticed that Jamison was good-looking, though to be fair even if she were completely blind, his appeal wouldn't be lost on her. There was just something about him.

Jess walked out to the street where Chan was standing, wiping down his coat with wadded up tissues he had found in the glove compartment. She didn't remember putting them in there so God only knew how long they had been there and why they were stuck together.

The crisp fresh air had done him some good. The color had returned to his cheeks and he no longer looked like he might pass out.

"How are you feeling?"

"Like I just threw up on myself. I might have to burn this coat to get the smell out."

It was a safe bet that the coat was more expensive than her car payment. Chan took great pride in his appearance; everything he owned was top quality, usually imported. "It'll be fine. Just get all the chunks off and take it to the dry-cleaner. Go home and get cleaned up."

"You don't have to ask me twice. I don't want to have to tell you I told you so, but this wouldn't have happened if we had gone to IHOP."

Jess shook her head. "Go home. I'll take you to IHOP tomorrow. Seriously, sometimes I feel I'm partnered with a child. Though if you were my child I would medicate the fuck out of you."

"Aren't you going to come with me? We can let the police handle Miss Havisham and the dead body. It's got nothing to do with us; we got the car. We're good."

Jess glanced back at the apartment building and then down at the spoon on the ground that someone had used to cook up some heroin before they shot up. "Her name is Nettie Lawrence and I want to make sure she is housed somewhere safe. She can't stay here tonight. You saw that place. I wouldn't leave a dog in there."

"You know you're not a social worker, right?" Chan asked. "It's okay to leave shit the way you find it. Not my problem: That's my motto."

"You're so noble, especially covered in your own vomit. It adds a little something," Jess said. "Good night, Chan. I'll see you in the morning."

Jess wrapped her arms around herself to keep warm as she watched him drive away before she took out her trusty bottle of ibuprofen and swallowed two tablets. She had only just taken two at Dr. Reid's office but the pain had not subsided. She stroked the scar tissue on her palm. Her head would heal in a week or two but there was no telling when or if the stabbing pain in her hand would go away or the feeling would return to her fingers. She couldn't think about the possibility that she might never be healed so she pushed down the thought and hid it away in a dark corner of her mind with all the other shit she would need to numb later.

She shoved her hands into her pockets and went back inside. Jamison was holding two plastic bags filled with clothes. Nettie was in the bathroom packing up more of her things.

"She has a suitcase but it was in her bedroom so that's a write-off. It's going to take the trauma and crime scene cleanup guys at least a week to get this place livable," Jamison said.

Jess nodded. "Milligan is still waiting upstairs for the police. I'm not sure if Jeanie has convinced the landlord to let them have access yet or if they're going to need a warrant to get in."

"Yeah he wasn't cooperative at first but Jeanie gave me his number and we got it squared away. He's going to drive over with keys tonight. It's all good. He's also going to put Miss Nettie up at the Best Western until her apartment is cleaned up and the heating is fixed."

"Funny how people are always in a super helpful mood with you," Jess said.

Half of Jamison's mouth rose up in a lopsided smile.

"All righty now. I got all my things." Nettie came out of the bathroom holding a plastic bag. "I think I got all my pills sorted. I'll know if I got it wrong if I wake up outside the pearly gates."

"Yes, ma'am, that is one way to tell. Do you have everything?" Jamison asked.

Nettie nodded. "I even have my Bible, ain't no way I'm leaving without it. It's protected me so far."

"Good. Then let's go get you settled in." Jamison took the bag from her and then laced his arm through Nettie's to help her down to the car. The woman looked even smaller and frailer next to Jamison.

Red lights flashed as two squad cars pulled into the parking lot. Even after they turned off their engines the lights continued to flash. Four uniformed police officers got out.

"Evening folks," a lanky, redheaded officer said. "I hear you reported a possible DB."

"Yes, it has started to liquefy; there are fluids coming through the ceiling," Jess said. "Is there a Forensics team coming?"

"No, ma'am. It's a busy night. We can't be pulling people off cases for every bad smell."

She bristled at the dismissive statement. She had an answer to fire back but then she remembered Chan's motto: Not my problem. They would soon find there was a dead body in apartment nineteen but they could deal with that on their own because as soon as she verified this had nothing to do with her case, she would go home. She would be having dinner while they worried about how to get the stench of decomposition out of their uniforms. Nothing to do with her. Who knew she would be taking advice from Alex Chan? "Hmm, all right then." She smiled.

More lights shone as a Mercedes S-Class pulled into the parking lot. A middle-aged man got out wearing a wool jacket and leather driving gloves. The gold wristband of his watch glistened in the glow of the headlights. Everything about him looked out of place here.

"Good to know he's got the money to put her up until he cleans up her place," Jamison said.

"Mr. Spiro?" Jess asked the man when he walked up to them.

"Yes. I believe there has been a problem with one of my rental properties."

"Yeah, you could say that," she said. "Did you bring the key?"

"Yes, of course. I'm really surprised that this has happened. My rental company maintains the strictest of standards." He pulled out a metal ring with at least fifty keys on it, all labeled and color-coded.

"Nettie Lawrence has reported the smell over a dozen times."

He shook his head. "No, if she had, we would have sent someone out to investigate within twenty-four hours. That's our policy."

"Really? Because I've pulled her phone records. I can give you the exact time and date of each call," Jess lied. She hadn't looked at her phone records but she would first thing in the morning, and she was confident Nettie was honest when she said she had reported it—she had no reason to lie.

"Well... um... in that case, it must have been a clerical error. This will be investigated. I give you my assurance I personally will look into this and make sure all faults in our system are rectified."

Rectified meant if he needed to, he would fire someone to cover his ass. He was setting up his defense, passing the buck. No doubt he would blame his secretary or some other low-level employee who couldn't afford to lose their job.

Jess sighed. She didn't have the energy for his crap. She was tired and cold, she hurt, and her tolerance for bullshit was at an all-time low. "You closed your eyes as you spoke and then you raised your right shoulder slightly, not both of them, just one. Both of those indicate that you're lying."

His face contorted in exaggerated indignation. "I'm not. What are you saying? How dare you?"

Jess held up her hand. "Stop. I don't want to hear your excuses. Just fix the problem without blaming anyone else."

He said something under his breath and then walked away, toward the apartment. The keys jingled with each step.

"You get Nettie settled, and I'll check out the scene with Milligan. He can give me a ride home."

Jamison nodded. "You sure? We can wait in the car for you."

More than anything she wanted to ask him to stay; that's why she shouldn't. They felt good together, normal. It would be far too easy to start believing this was real and they were okay. He had made his feelings clear. He was just too professional to allow his personal life to impact any aspect of a case. She needed to remember that. "No, I'm good."

Jess and the four officers followed Mr. Spiro up the stairs to where Milligan was waiting for them. With every step, the stench intensified. She wished she had VapoRub to put under her nose but it probably wouldn't help that much anyway; it was hard to mask the smell of advanced decomposition.

"Oh my God, that's awful," Mr. Spiro said.

"I know. Now imagine your tenants living here and never being able to get away from the smell," Jess said.

Mr. Spiro ignored her. Keys jingled on the ring as he looked for the right one and slid it into the lock.

Jess held a flashlight in one hand and used the other to clamp over her nose and mouth, leaving only the smallest space between her fingers to breathe. She moved her hand just enough to speak. "Does this apartment have the same layout as downstairs?"

Mr. Spiro nodded.

"There's no electricity in here," the red-haired officer said when he tried the switch. She hadn't even bothered to get any of their names because she thought she would be going home for dinner. The last thing she wanted to do now was eat.

"Fuck, that stinks. I can't." One of the police officers dry-heaved.

Jess turned to him. His eyes watered from the strain of trying not to throw up. "If you can't handle the smell, get out now. You'll just vomit and contaminate a possible crime scene."

He ran out of the apartment without a second thought.

Mr. Spiro turned to follow him.

"Nope, not you. You stay," Jess said. "This is your apartment building, your responsibility."

Jess walked through to the bedroom. Milligan was behind her with the police officers and Mr. Spiro. The only light was from their flashlights.

She looked over at the bed and gasped. "Oh shit," she whispered. "Get Jamison. This is our guy."

On top of a bare mattress was the decomposing body of a little girl. Her head was propped on a pillow. Her skin was like leather stretched over her skull. Sunken valleys replaced what should have been full cheeks. The fabric around her corpse was soaked in brown liquid. Like the others, she had been dressed in satin. The layers of her petticoat were stained orange and brown from the fluids that had been released from her small body. All of her nails had fallen out. Later, when the medical examiner opened her mouth, they would likely discover her teeth had fallen out too. Her exposed skin was a dark reddish-brown. Decomposition made it impossible to tell what color it had been when she was alive but the dark hair hinted at Asian or Latin heritage.

"I'll call Jeanie now," Milligan said, masking his nose.

"Yeah. We need our Forensics team down here," she told him before he left the small room.

"I'm going to throw up," Mr. Spiro said.

"Go outside." She couldn't risk him contaminating her crime scene. "But don't leave. I want to speak to you."

She took out her phone. "I need more light. Can you shine your flashlights more on her hands?"

"Ma'am, I can't. I can't. I can't take this smell anymore."

"Fine, go. Anyone who is going to vomit can leave. But leave your evidence bags and give me some gloves," Jess said.

Two more of the other officers left, leaving her alone with the skinny blond kid. He was young. His cheeks still had the fullness of youth and there wasn't even a shadow of stubble along his jaw. He looked like he had been plucked from a farm somewhere in the Midwest and transplanted into her crime scene. "You going to be okay? I can wait on my colleague to come back if you need to leave."

"No, ma'am, that won't be necessary. But thank you." His voice cracked. His wide eyes remained fixed on the body like he couldn't look away. His lips trembled.

Looking at him now she realized he hadn't stayed because he was brave; he was frozen in place because he was too scared to leave.

"What's your name?"

"Cody. Cody Cooper." The tremble in his lip spread to his jaw. The only sound in the room was the chattering of his teeth.

"Is this your first dead body, Cody?" Jess asked.

"Yes, ma'am."

"You're doing great. All I need you to do is watch me. When this goes to trial, some hotshot lawyer will try to say that we messed up or we planted evidence. I just need you here to document that we did everything by the book. Okay? Just hold up the flashlight, just like that, so I can see."

"Yes, ma'am."

"Good. I'm going to open your case and take some gloves."

He nodded.

"Okay, Cody, before we touch anything, I need you to take some pictures."

"Yes, ma'am." He pulled out his phone.

She squinted when the flash went off. "No, not of me. Just pictures of the body, how we found her, so we can prove we didn't interfere with anything." She snapped on one glove and then the other.

"I'm sorry." His teeth chattered as he bobbed his head up and down in a quick nod. The jerky movement looked like a bobblehead character stuck on a dashboard in stop-start traffic.

"That's okay, you don't need to apologize. You're doing great."

"Hey, Jessie. You okay?" Jamison's deep voice sounded from the door.

"Yeah, where's Nettie?"

"I asked Milligan to take her to the motel and get her settled in. I'll swing by and check on her when we're done. The police are escorting Mr. Spiro to headquarters. Jeanie will want to speak to him before he lawyers up."

"Good." Jess nodded. Two less things for her to worry about. She pointed to the bed. "This is our guy. Look at her. Those are even the same shoes that we found on Ava Marsden, and look at the ribbon in her hair. This is the same killer."

"Yeah," he agreed. "Jeanie said she can't get a Forensics team out probably until the morning. She said to take pictures and bag anything we find and then the police can secure the scene."

Jess glanced around the room. There wasn't much to log into evidence. The room was bare except the wrought-iron bed and a side table with a children's picture book and a glass with brown residue at the bottom.

"Do you think he poisoned her drink?" Jamison asked, reading her mind.

"He could have." Jess squinted as she walked closer. She shined her flashlight at the delicate crystal glass. "Look at that. There's a print. Looks like a thumb, I think." Exhilaration shot through her. This could be the piece they needed to nail Peter Reid. A good lawyer could easily explain away the hairs that were found on Ava's bed. He worked at the hospital; it would only be normal to find stray hairs at Peter Reid's place of work because the average person sheds between fifty and a hundred hairs a day. In this case prints might be more difficult to explain.

And there would be no need to get a warrant because his prints would be on file with the FBI. Anyone who worked with children had to have an FBI clearance. This could prove definitively if he had something to do with the murders. "This is it. This is the break we need."

"Bag it and we'll drop it off at the lab tonight," Jamison said.

Jess reached for the glass to pick it up. Pain tore at the tender flesh of her hand. The muscles contracted in a painful spasm. The glass slipped. She squeezed harder, fighting to keep the crystal in her precarious grip, but it fell to the hard floor and shattered.

Someone gasped. Jess couldn't move or speak. All she could do was look down at the shattered pieces and then at her hand. For a second she couldn't understand what had happened; her mind wouldn't compute the shards of glass and what it meant, that she had done it, that her body had failed her. And more importantly, that she'd just ruined the evidence that could have caught the killer.

CHAPTER TWENTY-EIGHT

No! A scream formed in the back of her throat. Slivers of glass glistened in the pale light. Their lead, their evidence, destroyed completely by her. There was nothing left, no way they could piece it back together and get a print. They had found valuable evidence and she had destroyed it.

Someone touched her arm.

"Jessie, it's—"

"Don't." She shook her head.

"It's okay. We'll still get him. We have his hair."

"Don't. Don't try to make me feel better. I fucked up." She was going to be sick. She ran outside. She grabbed the handrail to keep from falling as she ran down the stairs.

The frosty air was like a slap across her cheeks, stinging and burning through the chill.

She looked down at her scar. Her mind went back to the night in the basement. He had done this to her; she wasn't whole anymore because of that asshole.

Or had she done it to herself? With her stupidity.

Was this all her fault for everything she had done? All her mistakes, her lack of trust, and bad judgement—did she do this to herself? The answer screamed at her from every direction, every hidden crevice of her psyche where she had pushed something down until she could numb it away.

She shook her head. She couldn't think about this right now, she would drive herself crazy. She was fine, she just needed to get away and stop the voices. She just needed a few minutes of calm, without thinking or feeling, and then she would be okay. She pulled out her phone and summoned an Uber.

She heard heavy steps behind her. She didn't have to look up to know it was Jamison.

"Please don't tell me it's okay. Don't try to make me feel better." She would only feel worse if he were nice to her now, after everything she had done, what he had lost because of her. He was once the one she turned to but she had pissed that away. She didn't want to pretend that he would ever be that person for her again. Too much had happened. "You don't need me here. Can you stay with the police and make sure they secure the apartment?"

He reached out to touch her. Even through the glove she could feel the warmth of his hand on hers. She pulled away.

"Jessie, just go home. Don't…" His deep voice trailed off. There was obviously a lot he wanted to say but he stopped himself because he was too kind and noble to hit her with the truth of what he was thinking.

"Don't what? Say it."

He shook his head and frowned. They both knew where she was going, what she needed to do to cope. It wasn't even going to be about feeling good; it was about getting by and maybe escaping for a few minutes. She just needed to quiet the voices and get some distance so she could give herself back to her work.

"Just go home. That's all I'm saying. Go home. By yourself."

Before she could stop, she asked, "Why? Why do you care what I do?"

Jamison scrubbed at his face with his hands. He looked around but there was no one within earshot. "Let's not do this here. Not now. Not like this."

"When should we do it? When can I tell you I'm sorry for what I did… and for who I am? I am so sorry for all of it. I just want us to be the way we were. I want to go back to before I shot you, before you left. All of it. I just want a redo."

"Jessie, don't."

"Is it because…" A question burned in her mind. The answer terrified her but she was more scared of never knowing. "Did I fuck it up?"

"No, we have other evidence. We'll get him. It's okay."

She shook her head. She couldn't think about shattered glass right now. She would fix that mistake later. This one, though, had been preying on her mind for far too long and nothing she did would fully make it stop. "No, I mean us. Was there a chance of us… being us again, and I screwed it up?"

"Jessie, come on." His hot breath was a billowy cloud in the frigid air.

"Just answer me. That night when you came to my apartment you said we were both too messed up to be together. Is that true or did I fuck it up with what I did to you?"

He took a deep breath. "I don't know what you want from me."

"Just tell me the truth. That's all I want." She had never wanted a relationship. She actively fought to keep people out, but she wanted Jamison in her life, in some capacity. She hadn't even realized that she wanted him, that she loved him, until it was too late.

"I don't deal in hypotheticals."

"Please just tell me. If I hadn't screwed everything up by believing him, would we have had a chance to be… I don't know… something?" She didn't even know the word because she didn't know what she meant. She just wanted him back in her life. "Or was it what you said that night, that we are both too messed up to be together? Which is it?"

He shrugged. "Does it matter anymore? The result's the same."

She let go of the breath she was holding. All of the air left her body as well as any hope. She wasn't even sure what answer she was hoping for but that was not it.

She squinted at the glare of headlights as her Uber pulled into the parking lot.

"Please just go home," Jamison said.

Why? She left the question unasked. There was nothing waiting for her at home, no one that could make her feel good, or even less bad. She knew what she did was sometimes destructive. She had just enough self-awareness to know her coping didn't always help—it was just a Band-Aid—but she was okay with that because it was all she had.

She got in the car and shut the door.

Tomorrow she would deal with the mess; tonight she needed to get numb.

CHAPTER TWENTY-NINE

Slush seeps through the laces of my boots and soaks my socks as it melts. It's snowing again and she isn't even wearing a coat.

Someone screams, a reach-into-your-chest-and-rip-your-heart-out kind of screech, but no one stops to see what is happening. Parents mill at the gate of the school, laughing and gossiping, jerking strollers back and forth to offer some sort of stimulation to shut up whining toddlers desperate for attention. More than one mom is still wearing pajamas. It is three o'clock in the afternoon and they couldn't even get their shit together to put on real clothes to pick up their kids.

No one ever picks her up. Or drops her off. A crossing guard is there to make sure none of the kids go play on the tracks but once he escorts them past the platform, they're on their own, free for the picking.

She slings her backpack over her shoulder and then reaches for her little sister's hand. Her sister doesn't want to go so she gives her arm a slight pull.

They cross the street. The guard isn't even watching them because he is too busy on his phone. I could take her now and he wouldn't even notice.

She says something to her sister and they both laugh. They reach the corner and she looks up at me. And she smiles. My heart explodes into a thunder of frantic beats.

She quickly looks away because she doesn't know me, but I know her. And it was there, a smile, a recognition that she is meant to be with me. I'm supposed to have her. She knows it. She must feel it too.

I shove my hands deep into my pockets to keep from reaching for her and stroking her hair. There are too many people around now, but soon. I know her schedule. I know when to strike.

I glance over at her, willing her to turn around and smile again, just one more smile for me, but she doesn't. But that's okay because soon she is going to be mine.

CHAPTER THIRTY

Jess tried to stifle a yawn before she took a sip of coffee. The coffee kiosk wasn't open yet so she had to make do with the staffroom coffee which always tasted burnt no matter who made it or how fresh it was.

She looked up when someone knocked on her office door. It wasn't even seven yet; even Jeanie hadn't arrived for the day. Jess hadn't been able to sleep so at five she strapped on her gun and laced up her running shoes and ran to work because the Metro didn't open until six. She could use a shower but if she stopped working, she would lose the time she had gained.

The door opened and Lindsay came in. A flash of a purple shirt peeked out from under her buttoned suit. She always wore purple, even if it was just her socks or her earrings. She said it reminded her to be happy every time she looked in the mirror and saw the bright color reflecting back at her.

If only happiness was as simple as a wearing a certain color.

"I called you four times last night, where were you?" Lindsay said.

"Sorry, I was busy."

"All night? I'm usually only *busy* for like twenty minutes max these days. Back in college there was a guy in my dorm who could keep me busy for well over an hour. I thought he was some sort of tantric sex god but turns out he was just on antidepressants. Shout out to Eli Lilly for that side effect, am I right?" She sighed and sat down on the chair across from Jess.

Jess cleared her throat. She had never discussed the specifics of her sex life with Lindsay but she knew what she did and didn't judge her. "Sorry, I didn't call back yet. What's up?"

"A few things, well two really. First, did you make it to your session with Dr. Cameron this week?"

She was glad for the wall of monitors on her desk that kept Lindsay from seeing her completely. Lindsay was even more skilled than she was at reading body language and facial expressions. "I had an interview with a suspect yesterday so I had to cancel."

"Hmm," was all she said. She was hoping Jess would offer more information but she didn't; she just let the silence hang between them. "Hmm," she said again after about thirty seconds. She crossed and then uncrossed her legs. "Okay, I'm going to say it. You will always have an important meeting or interview, or you will be *unexpectedly* called out of town on a case every time you have a session scheduled. I know you. You don't want to go to therapy so you will find ways not to, and you'll get away with it because you're good at your job and you're pretty damn sneaky."

Jess didn't insult her by denying it. She had no intention of seeing Dr. Cameron again. It was a waste of both of their time.

Lindsay tilted her head so she could look at her around the monitors. "I think you should go to your appointments with Dr. Cameron. Obviously, it's your choice and you didn't ask me, but if you're taking a poll, my vote is go."

This time Jess didn't speak because she couldn't. She had nothing to say. She was fine, or at least no less fine than she had been two months ago. This was as good as she got.

"You want some more of my unsolicited opinions? Remember, people pay money to hear what I think."

"I'd pay you not to say anything right now." She was only half-joking. The top drawer of her desk rattled as she opened it and took out her supply of ibuprofen. There were only two left in the bottle. She swallowed them with coffee and then tossed the empty bottle in the trash. Luckily, she had more in her purse because she wouldn't be able to cope without her regular doses. Even with the medication, her hand still hurt but the pills kept it manageable.

"What are you scared of, Jess? You've been cleared. He's not going to take you off your team or give away your caseload. There is no downside to this."

Jess didn't say anything. She hoped by staying silent Lindsay would know to move on with the conversation without her having to be rude.

"You're not going to find anything horrible, I promise. That's what you're worried about, that if you peel back the layers and take a good hard look, you won't like what you find. But that won't happen."

Jess sighed. She couldn't have this conversation, not now. She wasn't sure when she could but she knew it wasn't before at least two more cups of coffee and maybe a Valium. "What was the second thing you wanted to talk to me about?"

"Jamison asked me to call you last night. He was worried about you."

"I changed my mind. Can we talk about my need for extensive psychotherapy instead, or maybe book me in for waterboarding?" Jess had to look away. She looked out the window at the bare branches of the oak tree.

Lindsay gave a heavy sigh. "You're a good person and you're worthy of love and joy and happiness. More than anything, I wish you knew that. I really want to give you a hug right now but I won't. But if you were a hugger, this would be a point where I would give you a really big one."

Pain radiated through her hand. She reached into her purse and took out a fresh bottle of painkillers.

"You've just taken two," Lindsay reminded her. "Is it for your head or your hand?"

Jess's back straightened. "I'm fine."

"If I had a dollar for every time I've heard you say that since your surgery. It's okay not to be fine sometimes too. You know that sometimes emotional pain manifests like physical pain. I'm not saying that's what's happening with you, I'm just reminding you it's a well-documented phenomenon."

Jess opened her mouth to tell her she really was fine but she stopped herself. "I know. I just have a lot going on with this case. I was going over something this morning and it got me thinking... I don't know, it just made me a little sad, I guess." She was being stupid. She dealt with murder day in and day out. She didn't have the right to be sad. That was reserved for the victims and their families.

"Do you want to talk about it?"

"Okay, well, all of the girls were found outside, where they would be discovered almost immediately so there was no time for decomposition except for the first girl."

"I meant do you want to talk about your feelings. But sure, we can talk about decomposition. I'm nothing if not a versatile conversationalist."

Jess kept talking. She just needed someone to spitball ideas off and Chan probably wouldn't be in the office until close to nine because doing his best to look like a GQ model was more important than punctuality. "He learned from the first girl. I think he wanted her to be found. He staged it. But when she wasn't, he knew he had to place the victims in public locations. He might be taunting us but I think it's really because he wants the victims discovered the way he left them. He took so much care in the way the bodies were presented."

"This is what's making you sad?" Lindsay asked.

Jess shook her head. "No, that was just a minor point I was thinking about when I was running this morning. What made me sad is that all of the victims had a horrible life before they were killed. Like really shitty. Every single girl had a life of abuse and neglect except for Ava Marsden. But in some ways her life was even worse. She was diagnosed with bone cancer as a toddler. She spent her entire childhood in the hospital in excruciating pain. All of them had shitty lives and then they were murdered. We are fed this lie that good people can eventually catch a break. Well these were innocent children and they never got a break and it just sucks."

"I'm sorry. That makes me sad too. But it makes me happy that you catch the assholes that do these things. Where are you at on this case?"

Jess tapped her fingers on the desk. "Hopefully we'll get a warrant for Peter Reid's DNA today. He has a connection with Shaniqua Jackson and Ava Marsden. I'm trying to find out where his path crosses with Jade and Amber. I want to be able to spell it out for a jury. There's no point in finding a killer if we can't convict. It's all about building the case."

Lindsay raised an eyebrow. "Dr. Peter Reid, Pamela's father?"

"Yeah, do you know him too?"

"Only… um… professionally." Lindsay closed her eyes a fraction longer than she normally would have but Jess clocked it. "I never met him when I was friends with Pamela, if that is what you're thinking."

That wasn't what she was thinking but Lindsay's reaction told her there was something more she wanted to say. Jess rolled her chair to the side so her computer monitor wasn't blocking her view. "What do you know about him?"

Lindsay pulled at her collar. Red crept up her neck and settled on her cheeks. "Um, not a lot, I mean nothing really."

If Jess were interrogating her, she would have asked that she specify which it was—not really or nothing—but Lindsay was her friend not a suspect. "He's an odd one, isn't he?" she asked instead.

Lindsay pursed her lips together, a subconscious sign she didn't want to say anything else on the matter.

"What about his partner, Martin Schofield? Have you heard of him? He's also a psychiatrist. They have been in practice together for more than thirty years. His car was found at our crime scene last night. He says he was on a cross-country trip in his RV when the last two murders took place. According to him his car was stolen and he didn't know about it until he got back."

The color drained from Lindsay's cheeks. She opened her mouth like she was going to speak but she closed it again.

"What is it? What are you thinking? Do you know Martin Schofield? Should I be looking harder into him?"

"I... um. This is the case with the blue cotton candy, right. And Ocean City, Maryland?"

Jess's skin prickled. "I didn't tell you it was connected to Ocean City."

"I know. Please just answer me." A bead of sweat rolled down Lindsay's temple.

"Yes, there was evidence that our victims were taken to the beach and given cotton candy."

Lindsay grimaced as she scrunched her eyes together.

"What? What is it?" Jess pressed "What do you know? Who should I be looking at? Martin Schofield? Peter Reid? Both of them? Do you think they acted together?" She threw ideas out, watching for a reaction.

"I don't know." Lindsay glanced down at the report on Jess's desk. "Can I read this?"

The hairs on Jess's arm stood taut. Something wasn't right. "Is there something you need to tell me?"

"I don't know. I just need to read this."

"Lindsay, what's wrong?"

Jess's phone vibrated on her desk. She picked it up and saw a message from Jeanie, asking everyone to go to the conference room early for a team meeting. "I need to go, but first tell me what's wrong."

Lindsay shook her head. "It's probably nothing. But just let me read this and I'll get back to you this afternoon, okay?"

CHAPTER THIRTY-ONE

Jamison and Tina were the only ones in the conference room when Jess arrived. Tina was typing away on her laptop and Jamison was drinking coffee and reading the paper.

"Good morning," Jess said as she entered the room.

"Morning." Jamison nodded but he did not look up.

Chan walked in wearing a new leather jacket. His movements looked stiff like he hadn't had time to break in the material. He handed Jess a cup of coffee and then sat down beside her.

"Thank you," she said. "I can't believe they've brought out their Christmas cups already. It seems too early."

"You say that every year, Scrooge," he reminded her. "Why does Jeanie want us in early?"

Jess shrugged. She took the lid off the coffee to let it cool down. "I don't know. Maybe they have made an ID on the dead body from last night."

"Good morning, everyone," Jeanie said from the doorway. Milligan was two steps behind her, his hair still wet from his morning shower and his cheeks flushed like he had run in from the Metro station.

Jeanie allowed everyone to get settled before she pulled down her bifocals from the top of her head and held up a piece of paper. "First some housekeeping before we get down to work. I've been made aware of a complaint from Peter Reid. His lawyer sent it to the director last night."

"What?" Chan's face contorted in confusion. "Wow, that was fast. We were there less than twenty-four hours ago."

Jeanie gazed up over tortoiseshell frames. "Well, it appears the two of you made quite the impression. Well, one of you did. Alan Chen not as much."

"Alan Chen? Honestly, he didn't get my name right? Is that racist? It feels racist. Just pick any Chinese-sounding name? That's not cool." Chan shook his head.

"I'm not sure it rises to the standard of racism but I would say it is incompetent. His lawyer, Mr. Berkowitz, charges $1,000 an hour. I would have thought that would include fact-checking." Jeanie put the paper down and looked over at Jess. "I won't insult either of you by asking if your conduct was unbecoming of a federal agent because I have no doubt that all of my agents act in a professional manner. I will say that his complaints are baseless. It reads like a preemptive strike. I believe he is trying to establish a case for victimization and malicious prosecution; however, following a line of inquiry is not harassment, it's good practice. He has every right to make a complaint but if he thinks this will dissuade us in any way then he is woefully mistaken. If anything, I feel compelled to look into him further."

Jess gave a faint smile. Privately Jeanie may have misgivings about Jess returning to work but she would never let anyone else question her competence.

"Next time we should send Jamison." Tina's bright eyes lit up when she smiled.

Jess had interviewed hundreds of people over the years, and by all standards her interaction with Peter Reid had been tame. He was hiding something. "We should also be looking at his partner, Martin Schofield. His car was used and his alibi is he was on a cross-country trip across America at the time. But we haven't confirmed that. His credit card statements seem to support his claim but I've not seen any visual confirmation. I need a picture of him in another state at the time of a murder if I'm going to rule him out."

"Have you checked ATM surveillance?" Jamison asked.

"This morning I put in requests for Wells Fargo branches in Texas, Arizona, and California. The West Coast is just waking up so it will be lunch time before I hear back."

"Okay, where are we on the ID of last night's victim?" Jeanie asked.

The keys on the computer clicked as Tina typed. "Forensics just got her back to the morgue half an hour ago. Based on her dental records, she had eight fillings and two silver caps. The medical examiner thinks it is Ximena Gonzales but she is waiting for a DNA test before she confirms."

"I don't know who that is. Was this CARD's case?" Jess looked around the room for some sort of recognition at the name. She got AMBER Alerts texted directly to her phone and that name didn't ring any bells. Even Jeanie looked puzzled.

"Until this morning no one knew she was dead. Her social worker assumed one of her extended family members had taken her back to Nicaragua. Her mom's in Fluvanna Women's Correctional Center. She hasn't been told yet her daughter is dead."

"She would know if she's the one who killed her. What is she in for?" Milligan asked.

"True," Tina admitted. "She's got a long rap sheet, mostly drugs and prostitution. She had a live-in boyfriend who is really not a great guy. He should not have been around her child, any child really. In fact, legally he is required to be at least 1,000 feet away from any school, day care center, and/or community safety zone. He is human trash but he is also not a viable suspect because he is serving eighteen years at Red Onion State Prison for the rape and attempted murder of a prostitute in Virginia. He was incarcerated before the murders began."

Jess shook her head. "Seriously, what is wrong with these women? On what planet is allowing a registered sex offender anywhere near your child an acceptable thing to do? You wouldn't put your kid in a lion's den and then just hope for the best. It's like Shaniqua's story all over again, or Jade's, or Amber's. All of these girls had horrible lives. The people who were supposed to be looking out for them were either asleep at the wheel or didn't give a damn." If she had ever been under the illusion that life was fair, this case would dispel that infantile notion.

"That's not surprising though, is it? Abuse victims are more likely to be abused again than someone who has never been assaulted," Jamison said.

Tina's head shot up. "Is that true?"

"Yeah. One study found that if a woman had been raped once she was thirty-five times more likely to be raped again in her life," Jess chipped in. "Revictimization is a well-known phenomenon in sociology. Some people believe there is a subconscious compulsion to recreate trauma but that only explains part of it because people whose houses are broken into once are more likely to be broken into again too, and no one is suggesting they are trying to recreate that experience. Like most things, there are a lot of factors at work. It could be what allowed our killer to get close to his victims was that their boundaries had been annihilated through years of abuse."

Jeanie tapped her pen on the conference table as she thought. "But that's not what you think happened?"

Jess looked at the pictures of the victims taped to the whiteboard. "Ava Marsden doesn't fit. There were no signs of abuse of any kind. She had a loving, stable family."

"Victim of opportunity?" Milligan suggested.

Jess shook her head. "Her abduction was planned. Our killer put in a lot of effort to get her. And the way the bodies were staged—he is organized and methodical. This guy knows what he's doing. This is not his first rodeo."

"That reminds me." Tina pushed back from the table, walked over to the whiteboard, and taped two pictures to it. "We may have dismissed John O'Reilly, the park ranger, too soon. He doesn't have a criminal record but I found something else. A couple of years ago his ex-girlfriend made a complaint to the Virginia Department of Conservation and Recreation. She said he was too attentive to her then ten-year-old daughter. The complaint didn't outline any specific allegations but the state stopped him working with the primary school environmental education program."

"She reported him to his work but not to the police?" Milligan asked.

"Yep."

"That's weird. That sounds like she had an axe to grind. If she were really concerned she would file a report, not try to jam him up at work," Milligan said.

"I agree. And the fact that she didn't make an outright allegation makes me think she was trying to avoid a libel charge. Calling him a pedophile would be defamation but saying he is over-attentive gets the point across without leaving her open to a lawsuit. Sounds well-thought-out."

Tina nodded. "True but he does like to frequent dating websites for single parents. And ninety-eight percent of the women he messages are moms of daughters between six and twelve."

Jess groaned. "Yep, that's not a great sign. Those websites are like a catalog for sex offenders. Child molesters target single moms. Why would these women advertise the fact they have children? Are they really that naïve?"

"I know," Tina agreed as she tapped the second picture she had taped on the board. "Also, your new friend Costas Spiro has a few skeletons of his own. He is quite the entrepreneur. In addition to his rentals he also owns Amateur Hour Entertainment."

"Seriously?" Chan said.

Tina made a disgusted face. "Of course you know who they are. Why am I not surprised?"

"What? What did I miss?" Milligan asked.

"Amateur Hour is an online porn streaming service. Lots of barely legal and fetish stuff; some of it is extreme."

Jess rolled her eyes at Chan. If he were closer she would be tempted to smack him upside the head.

"It's all legal," Chan said, clearly defensive.

"Except the stuff that isn't. He's currently under investigation because some of the barely legals aren't legal at all," Tina said.

"Are there any decent people left in the world?" Milligan shook his head.

Someone's phone chimed as a text message came through. "Sorry," Tina said as she glanced down at her phone. Her brows knitted together as she read the message. "Oh no, it's a message from Claire Ayres. CARD has responded to a possible abduction at Woodhall Elementary."

A shocked silence descended on the room. For a few seconds, all anyone could do was blink. Milligan was the first to speak. "This can't be our killer. The time interval is too short. Ava Marsden hasn't even been buried yet. Where is the cooling-off period?"

"There wasn't one. He's escalating," Jamison said.

CHAPTER THIRTY-TWO

Woodhall Elementary was located in the Brentwood area of DC. The neighborhood was crime-ridden. Litter filled the streets on both sides. Every building had at least one boarded-up window and the elementary school was no exception.

The school was dilapidated with chipped paint, missing roof tiles, and crumbling brickwork. If it weren't for the flyers taped on the gate, advertising the upcoming Christmas book fair, she would have assumed it was an abandoned building.

The street signs shook as a train thundered by. Jess looked over at the blinking neon light above the metal shuttered window of Al's Liquor Emporium. "A liquor store across the street from an elementary school. That's always a mark of class."

"The teachers probably keep him in business. If I worked here I'd need a drink to get through the day too," Chan said.

Jamison and Milligan pulled up beside them. Jess waited for them to get out before she said. "Claire's inside with the principal. The missing girl's name is Eve Fong. She's eight years old."

A carved wooden sign with a bald eagle marked the entrance of the school. Most of the paint had chipped off and someone had vandalized the final letters in Woodhall, turning the Ls into a giant ejaculating penis.

"What else do we know?" Jamison held the door open for her.

"That's all we have so far. Details are sketchy."

"Agent Ayres," Milligan called when he saw her come out of the office.

Claire walked toward them. She gave a faint smile. "No offense but I was really hoping not to see you guys again anytime soon, but I think this is your killer. The victim's younger sister, Liag, ran into the office this morning screaming and crying. She was holding this." Claire held up an evidence bag, and inside was another bag with a Blueberry Surprise label.

"Yeah, that's our guy," Jess said sadly.

Claire winced when she looked at Jess's face. "Wow, I heard you took a whack but I didn't realize it was this bad." When she shook her head her short purple hair fell from behind her ear. "All in a day's work, right? They always fail to tell new recruits about that perk of the job."

"It's fine," Jess said. Subconsciously she brought her hand to her face but she winced and pulled it away when she made contact with the tender flesh. "Where's Liag now?"

"She is in with the principal, Mr. Fields. She hasn't stopped crying since she came in. But at least she's stopped screaming."

"You need to get your team to Ocean City. He always takes the victims there," Jess said.

"We sent out an AMBER Alert, and the Ocean City Police Department and the Worcester County Sherriff's Office have been contacted. They're on high alert."

"Good." Jess nodded. "We also need to track our suspects. We need tails on Reid, O'Reilly, Schofield, and Spiro. I would add Schwartz to that list but he hasn't made bail."

"Already done. Tina's on it," Claire said. "And we're setting up roadblocks on all the major roads into Ocean City."

Jess nodded. "Good. Have you spoken to Liag? Did she give you a description of the man who took her sister?"

"No. She is too upset to speak. According to Mr. Fields, her English is broken at best. We're talking she knows her colors and maybe half the days of the week. I don't think she is going to be a lot of help."

"Is there a translator in the school?" Milligan asked.

"I just had this conversation with him. There are nineteen different languages spoken in Liag's kindergarten class, and no, there is not a single translator. It's full immersion: sink or swim."

Based on the run-down apartment blocks that flanked the school, it looked like most of the people in Brentwood were sinking.

"What language does she speak?" Chan asked.

"She's Hmong."

Jess's phone vibrated in her pocket as a message came in. She unzipped her coat enough to reach into her suit pocket and pull out her phone. "That's the AMBER Alert just going live now. God, she's so young. She looks like a baby." Eve Fong's two front teeth were missing. She had black hair and high cheekbones that looked even higher because her broad smile pushed them up until they almost engulfed her broadly spaced brown eyes.

Jess studied the picture, taking in every feature. She couldn't fail again and let another child die. She had to save her. *You're going to be okay, little girl. I'm going to find you.*

She glanced up. "If he sticks to his MO, he will kill her within thirty-six hours. We don't have any time to waste. Where do you need us?"

Claire nodded. "I'm going to stay here and wait on a translator for Liag. We need to find out what she saw. My team is already out canvassing. The Baltimore office has agents in place now in Ocean City. You can stay here and help my guys or you can go—"

"We'll go to Maryland," Jess interrupted.

"I thought you might say that." Claire smiled.

Jess grabbed the keys from Chan and headed for the car.

"Hey, it's my turn to drive," Chan called from behind her. He said something else but she was too far in front of him to hear what it was.

"Come on, let's go," she shouted over her shoulder, heading toward the driver's side. The clock was ticking. She got into the car and slid the keys into the ignition. Rap music blared when the radio came on. "We're not listening to this station all the way to Maryland."

"We could always talk," Chan suggested.

"Fine we'll listen to this." She turned it down until she could not feel the bassline pulse in her ears. "Should we take Route 50 from the Beltway to Annapolis?" She tried to get in the mindset of the killer. Which route would he take?

"That will be bumper to bumper right now. We should take the 404."

"Yeah, and that's scenic." She tapped her fingers on the steering wheel as she thought. "No, it's a longer route. He wants to get there as fast as he can. He only has thirty-six hours max. He is going to make the most of them."

"It's scary the way you think like a killer. I'm just saying, it's kind of weird."

"Says the man who admitted in front of the entire office he accesses illegal porn. That's weird. No 'kind of' about it." Jess turned up the radio to drown out his response.

They drove without speaking until they reached the Bay Bridge Toll Station. "Do you have any cash?" she asked as she maneuvered into the correct lane behind a rusted Volvo with a "Dole Is a Pineapple Not a President" bumper sticker. As always, the cars were at a standstill with heavy traffic. She would have avoided the bridge if she could but there was no way to get to Ocean City from DC without going over it.

Chan handed her the dollar bills required for the toll. Jess looked at the woman taking the money. Rather than the usual vacuous stare and monosyllabic speech of toll booth operators, she was staring intently at every car, taking in each passenger, studying everything, clearly looking for something or someone in particular. She was a federal agent. Claire had not specifically mentioned putting agents at the bridge but it made sense.

Jess turned off the music and rolled down her window. "Have you seen anything suspicious? Anything I need to know about?" she asked as she held up her badge to be inspected.

"Just commuters. I thought I had seen Eve Fong an hour ago but it was just a little girl with her mom."

"He might be transporting her in the trunk. Any suspicious single men?"

"Ma'am, I've been in this game a long time: All men look suspicious to me."

The car behind them beeped their horn. Jess looked in her rearview mirror to see a bald man in a black SUV, wildly gesticulating, clearly annoyed that Jess was taking too long at the toll.

"See what I mean?"

"Yes, I do," Jess agreed. She paid her toll and then drove away.

Her phone vibrated in her pocket as a call came through. She took it out and handed it to Chan. "Can you see who is calling?"

"It's Lindsay, you want me to answer?"

"No, it's okay. I'll call her back later."

"Really? Because I'm happy to talk to her." Chan winked.

If she didn't need both hands to drive she would have been tempted to slap him. "Seriously? Lindsay? Yeah that's never going to happen. You have as much of a chance with her as you do with Tina, which is none, by the way. Ever heard the saying, don't shit where you eat?"

"Ever heard the saying, the heart wants what the heart wants?"

"Boy, it's not your heart that is the issue." She put on the turn signal and merged into the fast lane.

It took just over three hours to drive the 100 miles from the bridge to Ocean City. The Maryland State Police had staged an accident which slowed traffic and forced everyone to drive single-file, effectively creating a covert checkpoint. It was a good idea but obviously it had not been successful because someone would have called to say they had found Eve Fong, and the only call she got was another one from Lindsay, which she sent to voicemail rather than let Chan answer it and hit on her. She would call her back when she got a chance.

Jess drove around the parking lot twice before she found a space. Cars were parked everywhere, including on the sidewalk.

"Who goes to the beach in the winter?" Chan asked.

"Half of Maryland, apparently. The chamber of commerce has an entire page dedicated to things to do in Ocean City in the winter. I emailed the link to everyone on the team after the ME said she found diatoms from here in Ava Marsden's hair. Do you ever open any of the attachments I send?"

"I'm not going to lie, I don't read most of your emails. A squirrel farts, and we get an update. We get it, you're methodical." Chan sighed in exasperation.

Jess ignored him, pulled out a bottle of ibuprofen, and swallowed two without any water before she got out of the car. In the future if she ever wanted Chan to read an important email, she would include the words naked and barely legal in the subject line.

"I'm starving. We should stop for lunch soon." Chan zipped up his coat.

"Yeah sure, once we speak to the cashiers of all the shops on the boardwalk, we'll get something."

"Cool."

Jess smiled to herself. If he had opened the email, he would know that was going to take all day. They walked up toward the boardwalk. Jess had a good hard look at everyone she passed, searching the crowd for Eve. There were lots of children running down the worn wooden planks but they were mostly all babies and preschoolers because older children would be in school.

Jess's phone vibrated in her pocket. She pulled it out and read the message. "That's Jamison. They're twenty minutes away. They got stuck in a checkpoint."

Chan snorted. "That doesn't surprise me. Jamison looks shady."

"Says you."

"What? I don't look shady."

"No, you look like a GQ model but you're definitely shady. Now come on."

"Stop, you're making me tear up. That's the nicest thing you've ever said to me." Chan pretended to wipe his eyes.

"They're going to take the beach; we'll take the stores."

"Let's start here." Chan pointed to a café. A group of mom and toddlers sat by the window. "You talk to the barista, I'll speak to the ladies."

Jess shook her head at his transparency. He just wanted a chance to hit on women. Half of them were breastfeeding and the other half were wiping snot from their toddlers' noses but that wouldn't stop him from trying to score. He had literally no chance but trying to stop him would be as effective as keeping a dog from pissing on a fire hydrant.

"Fine." Jess opened the door and held it for Chan. She closed her eyes and took a deep breath. She hated this part, interacting with the public, searching their body language for a spark of recognition that would tell her that they knew who she was, who her father was. She silently practiced her well-rehearsed response for when anyone recognized her until she relaxed. "Okay, let's do this."

There was no line so she walked straight to the counter. A middle-aged woman with curly salt-and-pepper hair stood behind a pastry cabinet. Agnes was embroidered on her red apron just above a coffee cup with hearts coming out of it like steam.

"Hello, what can I get you?"

"Hi, good morning. Can I please get two coffees, one black, one with cream and four sugars and a—" She glanced behind her where Chan was working the mom and tots crowd. If he was hungry now,

he would be starving by the time they finished. "And... um..."
She looked down at the pastries trying to pick which Chan would
like best. "And a raspberry strudel muffin to go."

Jess took out a twenty-dollar bill to pay along with her phone.
She opened up the picture of Eve Fong and held it up to be
inspected. "Have you seen this little girl? She was abducted on
the way to school this morning and we have reason to believe
she may be in Ocean City."

"Oh, that is horrible. Her poor parents." The woman brought
her glasses down off her head to examine the photo. "She's beautiful, that's such a shame. Do you know who took her?"

"No. Have you seen her?"

She pursed her lips as she considered. "No, I can't say I have.
I'm sorry."

"That's okay." Jess scrolled through her photos until she found
a picture of Peter Reid. "What about this man? Do you recognize
him? Have you ever seen him around here?"

"Is that who took her?" Deep lines formed on the sides of her
mouth as the muscles pulled down into a frown.

"He is a person of interest in the investigation. Have you
seen him?"

"Maybe, I don't know."

Jess scrolled through to a picture of Martin Schofield. "What
about this guy?"

"Hmm, I don't know. Um..." She looked up at Jess for a clue
as to how she was expected to respond. "Maybe."

"It's okay," Jess assured her. People often felt pressure to be
helpful, even when they had no information to offer. This pressure
could sometimes lead to unintentionally false statements.

She showed her pictures of O'Reilly and Spiro but was met
with the same unsure response. "Thanks for your help. If you see
this little girl," she showed her Eve's picture again so it was fresh
in her mind, "call 911 immediately."

She picked up the muffins and coffee and went to see how Chan was faring. He clocked her walking toward him and came to meet her halfway. "How did you do with the hot moms?" she asked.

"The term is MILF."

"Yeah, I'm not going to say that. Have they seen anything?"

"Nope. What about the barista?"

"Nothing. Here," she handed him the bag with the raspberry muffin, "this is for you."

Chan groaned. "This means we don't get to stop for lunch, doesn't it?"

"We'll stop for dinner. I promise."

"Don't lie to me." A piece of strudel topping dropped onto his jacket. He said something else but his mouth was too full for her to make it out.

The rest of the afternoon was spent going to every store, coffee shop, and restaurant within a mile of the beach. The reaction she got when she showed Eve's picture was always the same: It was sad because she was such a pretty little girl. Jess never said anything, but it wasn't sad because Eve was pretty; it was sad because she was an innocent child. It would be just as tragic if she were ugly—people should have the same amount of compassion for all children.

"Okay, let's go in here." She pointed to the Smokey Joe's BBQ sign. "I'll take the left side, you take the right. We'll meet in the middle."

"Or we can have dinner and then worry about it. It's almost eight and I'm starving."

Jess thought for a second. "Yeah, sure."

He blinked in surprise. He expected her to fight him on it but she was hungry too and she wouldn't mind sitting down for half an hour. Her boots had rubbed the back of her heels raw. She was going to need to put on a couple of Band-Aids and take an extra dose of ibuprofen before she walked another step. She would pound the pavement until her feet fell off if she needed to, but they weren't getting anywhere. Not a single person they had spoken to had seen anyone who looked like Eve, and even more surprisingly, none of them could definitely say they had seen O'Reilly, Spiro, Reid, or Schofield. Hopefully Jamison and Milligan were having better luck. She needed to call and check on their progress, which reminded her she needed to call Lindsay back. She would do that as soon as they ordered.

Jess held open the door for Chan. A hostess greeted them with a smile and two menus featuring a picture of a pig with all the parts outlined to show where every cut of meat came from. "Table for two?" she asked.

"Please." Jess nodded.

"Are you celebrating anything special tonight?" She waited for Jess to sit down in the mustard-yellow booth before she handed her the menu. Wooden blades of a fan swirled slowly above them like an airplane propeller.

"Oh, you think we're a couple?" Chan shook his head. He made a face like he had just smelled a dirty gym sock he had found buried in his locker. "No, definitely not a couple. God no." He looked over at Jess, suddenly realizing what he had said. "I mean, no offence. Normally I wouldn't mind but you're not looking your best and—"

Jess held her hand up to cut him off. "Stop talking, Chan. I'm hungry."

"Oh okay," the waitress said and smiled awkwardly. "Well, um, anyway would you like to hear our specials?"

Jess's phone vibrated in her pocket. Claire's number flashed on the screen. Her heart picked up speed when she read the message. She glanced up at Chan and read it out loud. "There have been sightings of Eve Fong at Trimper's Rides. Three people have separately called it in. She is with a white man. Jamison and Milligan are en route but we're closer."

"Seriously, we just sat down."

"Sorry, we have to go," she apologized to the waitress as she ran for the door. Trimper's was just at the bottom of the boardwalk. They had been there less than two hours ago.

The wooden planks creaked as she ran as fast as the crowd would let her. People were everywhere, standing and talking in front of the storefronts instead of actually going inside. "Sorry," she called behind her as her shoulder slammed against someone.

She sprinted up to entrance to the amusement park. Three security officers stood at the ticket booth. She glanced behind her to see how far back Chan was.

She held up her badge. "I'm Special Agent Jessica Bishop. Have you closed all of the exits?"

"Yes, ma'am, Code Adam. No one is going in or out until she is found."

"Good. Can you give me a description of the man Eve's with?"

"White man, middle-aged, average height, medium-build."

"So, he looks like pretty much every other man in America. Any scars or tattoos?"

The security guard shook his head. "Not that I know of, but he's wearing a Nationals hat."

"Like the baseball team?"

"Yes, ma'am."

Chan finally reached them. He coughed to cover up the fact he was breathing heavily from the exertion of sprinting up the boardwalk.

"This is my partner, Alex Chan." She introduced him to the security guards with a nod. "What about the little girl? What is she wearing?"

"Blue jeans, purple jacket, and white sneakers."

"Good. Okay. All the bathrooms need to be checked. If he thinks we're on to him he might try to change her appearance. I've seen assailants cut and dye victims' hair to disguise them. He could try to pass her off as a boy because we're all looking for a girl. He might create a medical emergency to get through our checkpoints. If we let anyone out we have to be absolutely certain it's not Eve Fong. If we lose her now, she's dead."

"Yes, ma'am."

"Thank you. Here is my number if you need to get in contact with me directly. You can also call Claire Ayres at CARD directly and it will be filtered through to everyone." Jess pushed through the turnstile to go into the amusement park.

Families with children of all ages milled around, holding hands to keep from losing someone in the chaos. People stood shoulder to shoulder at the exit, unaware of the reason for their forced captivity. She hoped Jamison arrived soon. He was the best at crowd control.

She pulled out her phone and called Claire. She answered on the first ring. "Talk to me."

"Chan and I are at the amusement park now."

"Good. Briggs and Milligan are about ten minutes away. There are eight field agents from the Baltimore office in the area. Two of them should be arriving any minute. We're holding off on sending uniformed officers in because we don't want to scare him, so they will guard all the exits. All of the employees have walkie-talkies. They're all on the lookout too."

"We're going to find her." Jess's heart slammed against her chest in violent beats. They had to. Another little girl couldn't die.

She cut the call and then pulled up Eve's picture. *We're going to find you. You're going to be okay.*

She glanced over at Chan. "Okay, let's start with the bathrooms. Shit, I don't know where the bathrooms are. I forgot to pick up a map."

Chan held up a pamphlet. "Well, it's a good thing I'm not just a pretty face."

"That's right, you're also shady." Jess smiled as she swiped the map from him.

"I think you meant to say, 'You're awesome, Alex, what would I do without you?'"

Jess pursed her lips together like she was thinking. "Nope that wasn't it. But thank you." She opened up the map. "Okay, here we go." She pointed to the bottom center of the page.

"Do you want me to read the map? I know women struggle with spatial awareness."

Jess help up her hand, her thumb and forefinger about an inch apart. "This close. You were this close to being a decent human and then you fell at the final hurdle."

They walked past a raised plant bed filled with red and white poinsettias to the restrooms. At the entrance, a trash can overflowed with corndog sticks, cardboard trays with congealed nacho cheese sauce and broken tortilla chips, and tubes with the remnants of blue cotton candy.

"I'll check the disabled toilet," Jess said.

A woman in a wheelchair shouted in surprise at being walked in on.

Jess looked down so she wasn't staring directly at her. "I'm sorry, ma'am, my apologies. We're looking for a missing girl," she explained quickly before she closed the door firmly behind her.

The line for the women's bathroom snaked out the door. She held up her badge as she pushed her way to the front.

"Hey, don't cut. I don't care if you're a police officer. You have to wait like the rest of us," a woman toward the front of the line complained. Her hair was permed into tight rings. Product made the curls look crunchy to the touch. On each side of her she had a little girl, each of them wearing hot-pink sweats to match their mom's.

"I'm searching for a kidnapped child," Jess said.

"In the bathroom?" she asked, her lip curled in disdain.

Jess didn't answer. She squeezed past another woman to get into the bathroom. She held up her phone. "Excuse me. I'm looking for this girl. If you see her, please call 911 immediately. Please also note exactly where you saw her and who she is with."

Only a few people looked at the picture; most pretended not to hear her. It was unlikely the killer would take Eve to the ladies' restroom but she had to check. Jess waited for every stall to open to make sure Eve was not in any of them.

Her phone vibrated in her hand as it rang. Claire Ayres's number flashed on the screen. "Have you found her?" Jess asked when she answered the phone.

"No, but there has been another spotting. She is in the Mirror Maze."

She pulled out the map of the amusement park. "That's 200 yards from where I'm at."

"Excellent. Go get her. And be careful. I don't want any more injuries on my watch."

Jess hung up before she pushed her way back through the crowd. As usual there was no line to the men's toilets. Chan was standing outside monitoring who went in.

"Come on. Someone spotted Eve at the Mirror Maze." Jess started running. "Please keep up this time," she shouted over her shoulder.

She ran through the crowds. She swerved to miss a double stroller with twins that looked old enough to walk on their own and kept running past the Ferris Wheel and Wild West Train to the Mirror Maze. The doorway was painted yellow with three smiling clowns peering down at them from above. A teenage employee with an orange Trimper's shirt stood blocking the entrance to the maze.

"Did you see Eve Fong go in there?" Jess asked, Chan two steps behind her.

"Yes, ma'am. She is with a creepy white guy with a red, white, and blue Nationals hat, you know the ones that look like the American flag?" He gestured to his own head. "I didn't say anything to him. I just called it in and I didn't let anyone in after them." He shook when he spoke, his voice just a whisper.

"Good job. You did great," she reassured him. "Just keep doing what you're doing, don't let anyone else in. I'm going to go in and my partner is going to wait at the end. Is there an emergency exit we need to know about?"

He shook his head.

Chan ran around to the back of the ride. Jess grabbed the metal banister to keep from falling when her shoe caught on the jagged edge of the ramp that led to the entrance of the maze. A dog with a bandaged head was painted on a wooden sign with a warning for people to use their hands to guide them around so they wouldn't fall.

Jess patted her gun to reassure herself it was there before she went in. The eerie whine of carnival music surrounded her. She was greeted with eight reflections of herself. Even with heavy concealer, the blue hues of bruises shaded her cheek. A single tight black curl had escaped her ever-present ponytail. When she tucked it back in place, eight versions of her did the same thing, each with a disfigured hand in case she needed reminding that her body was broken.

She stepped around the corner into a tunnel of mirrors. Miniature versions of herself stretched into infinity, getting smaller and smaller until they merged on themselves on the horizon. She held out her hands to guide her to the end. Even holding the wall, she felt dizzy from the optical illusion.

A child cried.

"Eve," Jess whispered.

A flash of purple streaked across the mirrors as the little girl ran, her hand outstretched as her captor pulled her forward.

Jess's skin burned as each painful beat of her heart pushed blood to the surface. She couldn't hear the music anymore past the whoosh of blood in her ears. She lunged forward to follow Eve.

"Ah." Her body collided hard with a mirror. She held her hands out to guide her.

Eve cried in the distance. She looked like she was a mile away but when Jess closed her eyes she could hear that it was really only a few feet. *You're okay. You're going to be okay.*

Jess ran her hand along the mirror so she would not run into it again as she followed it around the corner. Her vision filled with Eve in her purple jacket and blue jeans. She just was two steps ahead. Jess reached out to grab her hand but it was just her reflection.

"Eve," she called again. "I'm here to help you. You're going to be okay."

Jess held her hand out in front of her and walked around the corner, following Eve's reflection. "I'm almost there." She reached out and grabbed Eve's hand just as her captor pushed open the exit.

Jess pulled Eve toward her and scooped her up. "I got you. You're okay. I'm a police officer," she explained because Eve was too young to know what the FBI was. Eve's tears wet Jess's cheeks as she held her. "You're okay, Eve. No one is going to hurt you." Her heart hammered against her chest, refusing to slow.

Chan drew his gun and pointed it at the assailant. "FBI! Get down on the ground. Now! I said get on the ground."

He was turned away so Jess could not see his face.

"Get down!" Chan screamed again.

The man complied and dropped to his knees. Chan helped him reach the ground faster with a swift kick to his back before he handcuffed him. "Stay down, asshole."

Jamison and Milligan ran up, guns drawn and pointed at the man.

Jess winced as Eve's screech pierced her eardrum. She kicked and fought against Jess, screaming to let her go. "You're okay now," Jess assured her but Eve would not stop fighting.

The man's baseball cap fell off when he turned and looked over his shoulder. "It's okay, honey. Daddy's okay."

Jess's heart sank when she realized it wasn't Peter Reid. She had been so certain he was involved but it wasn't him or Schofield or O'Reilly or Spiro. She scrutinized the man's features, trying to discern if she had ever seen him or his picture in the investigation, but she hadn't.

Eve whimpered something in Jess's ear but she could not make it out. Jess looked up when an Asian woman with an infant ran toward them screaming. "Put my daughter down," she screeched.

Eve turned with her hands outstretched. "Mommy!" she cried. "Mommy!"

Jess's heart stopped with a painful thud. Her skin went cold as her blood stagnated in her veins. The little girl struggled against her until Jess sat her down. She ran to the woman, threw her arms around her leg, and wept.

"What the hell are you doing?" the woman screamed. "Why did you handcuff my husband?"

Jess shook so hard her teeth chattered. Her gaze darted around, taking in the pieces, trying to understand what had happened. Four people had independently called in the sighting of Eve Fong. *Caucasian man. Average height. Average build. Nationals hat. Little girl. Purple jacket. Blue Jeans. White sneakers.*

They had the little girl that the people had described but they had gotten it wrong. They all had. This wasn't Eve Fong.

"Oh shit," Jess whispered. "Eve's still out there. This isn't her." She looked to Jamison, willing him to say something, to tell her it was going to be okay, but he couldn't.

"Where's your wallet?" Jamison asked the man on the ground. "I need to see some ID. Is there anything in your pockets I could cut myself on?"

"There's nothing in my pocket except my wallet. My name's Michael Brewster. That's my daughter Kerris."

'Why was she crying?" Jess demanded.

"She hit her head on the mirror and she wanted her mom."

Jamison reached into the man's pocket and pulled out his wallet. "He's who he says he is." He held up Michael's driver's license for Jess to examine. Beside it in a plastic photo leaf was a picture of him with his wife and daughter building a snowman. The little girl was wearing the same purple coat. The inscription on the back said it was taken in Aspen the previous year.

"Where's Eve?" Jess mumbled to herself. A frantic energy roiled through her, the intensity crushing her from the inside. It felt like someone had reached down her throat and squeezed until all the air was forced out of her body. "We're running out of time. Where is she?" Her head clouded with uncertainty and fear. She couldn't think.

"Jessie…" Jamison stepped toward her.

"We're almost out of time!" The need to run overpowered her, to tear the world apart and search until she found her. But where? Where could they look? Where was he hiding her? "I promised her."

"Who?"

Jess blinked, unaware that she had spoken. She couldn't admit aloud that she had promised Eve. Everyone already thought her grasp on reality was tenuous. She didn't need anyone to question her sanity further.

Jamison turned to Milligan. "Can you deal with this and take Chan back to DC?" He gestured to Michael Brewster, who was still lying prostrate in a murky puddle. He wasn't asking. He was telling Milligan to clean up the mess because he had a bigger mess to deal with.

"Come on, Jessie. I'm taking you home."

"No." She shook her head. He wanted to make sure she went home and not out to pick up a stranger but she needed to stay and search for Eve. Her time was running out.

"Every law enforcement agent on the Eastern Seaboard is looking for her. You don't need to be here. You need to go home and get some sleep."

Jess wanted to scream and shout and tell him not to give up on Eve, but he was right. There was nothing more she could do for her tonight. CARD and the Maryland State Police had the manpower to work the case around the clock. She wasn't needed right now. A boulder settled in the pit of her stomach as she realized there was nothing more she could do.

CHAPTER THIRTY-THREE

Jess jumped awake with a start. Drool dripped from the corner of her mouth and pooled on her pillowcase. Her phone vibrated on the bedside table as the alarm chirped its high-pitched whine. It was only set as a precaution; she was usually up long before it went off.

Faint beams of light filtered through the slats in the venetian blinds, creating long pillars across the hardwood floor. A panic squeezed her heart when she realized it was dawn and now almost twenty-four hours since Eve was abducted. If the killer adhered to his MO, she would be dead soon and Jess had chosen now to succumb to exhaustion.

Every other morning when she woke up the sheet had popped off the corner of the mattress because she thrashed around all night fighting for sleep, but not last night. She had fallen into a coma-like sleep. Her body had desperately needed it but she felt shitty just the same for sleeping through what could be Eve Fong's final hours.

Guilt smacked against her like a tidal wave. Sinister voices told her that she had given up on Eve. No matter what she told herself to justify coming back to DC, she could not escape the drowning waves of culpability.

She reached for her phone but it dropped to the floor when she tried to pick it up. "Shit," she mumbled as she pushed herself up from the bed and bent over and grabbed it, ignoring the stabbing pain in her hand.

The screen lit up, alerting her to four earlier missed calls and a text message from Lindsay asking Jess to call when she was free. She had wanted to call her last night when she got home, because she knew she was the only one who could help her untangle the twisted mess of her thoughts when things got really bad, but it had been too late. It was bad enough Jess burdened her during business hours, she didn't deserve to be woken up just to be told things had gone to shit with the investigation.

Jess hit the link to listen to the messages.

"Hey, Jess. I… um… I've been thinking. It might be nothing but something you said reminded me of something I heard years ago in a fishbowl—again might be nothing. I could be being really stupid but the more I'm thinking about it, the more I think I should run it by you. So yeah, call me," Lindsay's voice said down the line.

"Fishbowl?" Jess wondered aloud as she deleted the message.

Jess dialed Lindsay's number but after four rings it went to voicemail. "Hey Lindsay, it's me. Sorry I didn't call you back yesterday. Things got hectic and then it was too late. Call me back when you get this or I'll see you in the office in about an hour. I have no idea what fishbowl you're talking about but that reminds me I need to feed my fish, so thank you. Call me back."

Jess cut the call and then went for a shower to help her wake up. She sighed when the hot water hit the tight knot between her shoulder blades. If she wanted to work the knot out, she would have to stand in the jet for at least fifteen minutes, but that was time she didn't have so she washed off and got dressed.

She shoved a clean shirt into her bag so she could change into her suit when she got to the office and then strapped on her gun and put on her running shoes.

*

For the first ten minutes of her run, her body was sore and stiff from the awkward position she had slept in. Every time her foot hit the ground, the impact radiated up her leg and into her hip but eventually the dull ache was swamped out by the rush of endorphins. She felt like she was flying; all the aches and pains were gone and she could think about the case completely analytically, just facts and numbers and probabilities, jigsaw pieces in a puzzle she would solve.

By the time she had turned down 10th Street and the American flags of the J. Edgar Hoover building came into sight, she had shaken off the disappointment from the day before. They still had time to find Eve and she would not stop looking until she did.

She went through security and then ran up the stairs, taking two at a time. She found Tina in the breakroom cleaning out yesterday's coffee grounds from the machine.

"Morning," Jess said.

"Good morning." Tina turned to her and smiled. "It's Chan's turn to clean the coffee maker, but what are the odds of him actually doing it? I bet he wouldn't forget if I put all the old filters on his desk." She pressed the pedal on the can and dusted grounds straight into the trash.

"That would work. You've seen how anal he is about having everything in just the right place. Put some coffee grounds in his top drawer, spread over his ballpoint pens. He wouldn't forget again."

"Yeah but he might also go full postal and murder me. The man is wound tight. But at least I could die knowing he finally cleaned out the coffee maker. Plus, I know you would avenge my death so it's all good."

Jess smiled. "Hey, did they find a translator for Liag Fong?" She needed to get back into case. They had an eyewitness. Instead of worrying about mistakes and near misses, she needed to focus on what they had. She could write off yesterday once she made things right and found Eve.

"Yes, now we're waiting on a psychologist to interview her. She won't talk to anyone. She's really scared."

"Poor kid. She must have been terrified. Have you asked Lindsay? She could do it. She's great with kids. She'll get her talking."

Tina shook her head. "That's what Jeanie said too but no one has seen her since yesterday. Did she take vacation time and forget to tell anyone?"

Jess shook her head. "No. She's not going anywhere until Christmas. Have you called her?"

"Yeah, there's no answer. Maybe she had a family emergency or something and needed to go out of town." Tina shrugged.

Jess pulled out her phone and checked the time Lindsay had last called. "She called lunchtime yesterday. She didn't say anything and she wouldn't just take time off work. That's not like her."

Jess glanced up when Chan walked into the room. "That's not like who?" he asked. His leather jacket was gone, replaced by yet another winter coat. This one a black wool with velvet at the cuffs and collar.

"Lindsay. No one has seen her since yesterday."

"She probably just forgot to log in her vacation time."

Tina nodded. "That's what I said."

Unease crept along Jess's skin. Lindsay wouldn't forget. That just wasn't like her. "Maybe something happened with her dad," she thought out loud. "No— even then she would have called us. She wouldn't have gone to New Jersey without telling me. She always leaves Stan with me." Jess dialed Lindsay's number but again it went to voicemail. "What time is Claire coming in?"

"She decided to do the press conference at Woodhall Elementary. Jeanie's going to be there too. It starts at ten. She's hoping the attention might bring out some potential witnesses. She wants you guys to meet her there for that to watch the crowd."

Jess glanced at the clock as she considered what to do. She wanted to go meet Claire before the press conference but she knew she would be useless to anyone until she had checked on Lindsay. She had probably just gotten sick or overslept. No doubt there was a logical explanation for everything but Jess was not going to be able to concentrate on anything else until she knew what it was. "I'm going to go check on Lindsay. Chan, do you want to come with me and we can go directly to Brentwood from there?"

He glanced at Tina and then back at Jess. "No, I'll just meet you there."

Jess had to roll her eyes at his transparency. He wanted to stay so he could speak to Tina on his own. He still thought he had a chance with her. His confidence had reached the heights of delusion but on some perverted level she had to admire his tenacity. He was like the marathon runners at the back of the pack who couldn't even bring their arms up so they dangled at their sides like limp, overcooked pasta. Their legs heavy and aching, but they carried on, even after the crowds had gone home because they had a goal and nothing was going to keep them from it. "Okay fine, see you there at quarter to ten. Text me if anything changes."

Jess caught Tina's gaze and gave her a knowing smile before she went downstairs and jumped in a cab.

It took twenty minutes to get to Lindsay's townhouse in Columbia Heights. Jess ran up the steps and rang the doorbell. She could hear Stan barking behind the door. She pulled out her phone and called Lindsay again, this time leaving a message. "Hey, it's me. I'm outside right now. It's eight thirty. I'm a little worried because you have not called in to say you weren't coming in. I just want to make sure you're okay and I need to talk to you. Why aren't you picking up? Just call me, please." Jess cut the call. She tapped her foot on the brick landing as she thought about what she should do, suddenly remembering where Lindsay kept her spare key.

She found it in the belly of an ugly ceramic turtle at the side of the house and then let herself in. Stan was in his crate beside the fireplace. He whimpered when he saw her, his golden tail waving frantically, rattling the cage as it banged off the bars.

"Hey, buddy. Where's your mom?" When she opened his crate, he bounded for the front door desperate to get outside. A pool of urine had puddled under his soaked blanket where he had wet himself. He scratched at the door and gave a high-pitched whine.

"Okay, Stan. Poor guy, you must have been desperate if you wet yourself. How long have you been in there, buddy?" Jess spoke to the dog as she opened the front door. It didn't escape her that she was far better at small talk with dogs than humans. In her defense, dogs were nicer than most humans.

He pushed past her and ran outside and down the stairs. He didn't even make it to the street before he cocked his leg and peed on a gatepost.

It wasn't like Lindsay to leave Stan crated for hours on end. She only put him in there at night to keep him from going through the trash. Every morning she dropped him at Doggy Daycare so he wouldn't be alone during the day.

Unease crept along Jess's skin. Lindsay would never leave Stan alone in a cage long enough for him to pee on himself.

"Come on, Stan. Let's hurry this up. We don't have time for you to read the paper and have your morning coffee. Come on, buddy, I've seen you poop lots of times, don't get shy on me now." She looked away so he felt comfortable enough to crouch on the sidewalk.

She didn't have a bag but she had a wadded-up glove from a crime scene so she snapped that on, picked up after Stan, and tossed it all in the metal trash can outside Lindsay's building because there was a special place in hell for people who don't pick up after their dogs.

"Come on, big guy, let's go find your mom." Stan rubbed up against Jess's legs, desperate for some attention. Jess happily complied and reached out and scratched him behind the ears. "You're a good boy, aren't you? Yes, you are."

Jess walked back up the steps and into the house. She didn't have to ask Stan to come in, he was right beside her every step.

"Lindsay," Jess shouted from the bottom of the stairs in case she was upstairs sleeping or with someone. "Lindsay, it's Jess. I'm coming upstairs." Jess bent down to take off her shoes. When she turned to put them beside Lindsay's at the door, she saw the lamp on the side table had been knocked over and the mail had been scattered. On the corner of the latest issue of *People* magazine, there were small droplets of what looked like blood.

Jess's pulse spiked. All the warning bells she had tried to silence rang in a deafening cacophony. Jess pulled out her phone and called Chan. "I need you to come to Lindsay's house right now. We might need backup," she said when he answered. She didn't wait for him to respond before she hung up and put her phone back in her pocket.

She drew her Glock and then pressed her back to the wall. When she looked down at the first step she noticed the splattering of blood. With each step up, the spray was heavier. *Oh shit.* Her heart stopped. She closed her eyes for a fraction of a second to give herself enough distance to push down the emotion that was fighting to break free. She had to keep it together. This was like any other crime scene. She knew what to do.

Jess checked Lindsay's bedroom. The bed had not been made but there were no obvious signs of struggle. With her back pressed against the wall, she turned the corner to the master bathroom. The door was open and the shower curtain had been pulled down. Only three brass hooks partially held up the paisley-patterned material.

Her heart skipped several beats when she saw the closed lid of the toilet seat. A massive scarlet pool of blood had congealed on the edge of the white plastic, streaking down the side and puddling on the marble tiles. She gasped. "Oh my God." Her legs went slack but she righted herself before she fell.

A million possibilities played in her mind at once as she tried to make sense of the incongruity of what looked like a crime scene in her best friend's bathroom. It didn't make sense. No one would hurt Lindsay. She didn't have any enemies. She must have hurt herself. Yeah that was what happened. She fell and maybe hit her head and then called an ambulance to take her to the hospital.

Jess needed to check local hospitals. She pulled out her phone. When she looked down to dial she saw streaks of blood across the tiles. At the threshold, below the door, the blood splatter stopped looking random. The smears looked like the intentional strokes of letters.

Lindsay was trying to tell her something. The letters P and R were scrawled in her own blood.

Peter Reid. A sudden sinking feeling invaded her chest. Lindsay wouldn't have known anything about the case if Jess hadn't told her.

This was Jess's fault. Why? Why did she tell her anything? She hadn't needed to involve her in any capacity. Why did she always depend on her for everything? If she had just dealt with things by herself…

Why hadn't she just taken Lindsay's calls yesterday or forced the issue when it became clear Lindsay knew more than she was letting on? She could have pressed her further. Lindsay had wanted to tell her.

"Oh God." If something she had done had unintentionally hurt Lindsay… No, she could not think about that now; she could feel guilty and scared later. Right now she had to stay focused. She closed her eyes and sucked in a ragged breath, forcing her lungs to fill to capacity. She held the breath as long as she could and then slowly let it out before she opened her eyes.

She needed to go downstairs and wait for her team.

"Forensics," she said aloud. She needed to get a Forensics team down here too. She hit redial on her phone.

A burning pain stabbed at her neck, like a nail being driven deep into her jugular. She raised her arm to rub the tender spot but she could not lift her fingers more than a few inches from her sides. The edges of her vision went black and the remaining center swirled in color as the shapes of objects morphed and bled into each other. She tried to scream but her mouth would not open so only a garbled sound escaped. Her knees went slack. They could not hold her up any longer. She was going to fall. The hard tiles were getting closer.

But everything went black before she hit the floor.

CHAPTER THIRTY-FOUR

Pain pulsed through her with every beat of her heart, and her mouth tasted like someone had cut out her tongue and shoved a moldy dishcloth in its place.

Her knees were folded hard against her chest and her arms stretched behind her. Her cheek was pressed to the ground, slick from sweat or drool.

The room was completely black. She blinked a few times to clear her vision but it didn't work so she tried to rub her eyes, but metal bit into her wrists when she tried to move her hands.

"What the hell?" she croaked. Even speaking hurt.

She pulled again but her arms wouldn't move more than an inch. She was handcuffed. Her wrists burned as she pulled against the restraints, cutting into her. Panic shot through her; it squeezed her lungs in a vise grip and made her heart hammer painfully against her chest. She pulled fruitlessly against the handcuffs. She winced at the sharp pain but kept pulling until she screamed out in agony.

"Stop," she commanded. Her instinct was to fight against the restraints but that would only injure her and waste energy. She needed to calm down and think, remember where she was and how she got there and figure out how to get out.

She closed her eyes and took in a deep breath, pushing oxygen down even after her lungs burned, and then slowly exhaled. She had to stay calm. Fear would not serve her now. The first thing she needed to do was get her hands in front of her.

She tried to sit up but her head hit something hard. She tried to shuffle to the side so she could try again but a wall confined her. She moved in the other direction but another wall kept her firmly in place.

"Fuck!" she screamed until her throat was on fire. She was in a box. She was folded over, huddled in a fetal position because that was the only way she would fit.

"Oh God." The walls were hard against her skin, crushing her. Every second they edged in closer. She shook her head. "No." The walls weren't really moving, that was her mind playing tricks on her. She tried to breathe but her body would only take small, shallow pants. Her mind started to spin because not enough oxygen was reaching her brain.

"Stop," she commanded herself again. If she panicked she would hyperventilate and pass out. She needed to be calm. She searched her mind for what she would say to someone in this situation.

It's okay. You're okay. Breathe.

Jess took the deepest breath her current position would allow. She kept forcing in air until her lungs burned, and then she held it while she slowly counted to four and then exhaled to the count of eight, her mind focused only on reciting the numbers. There was nothing else in the world except the steady cadence of integers. She watched them play in her mind, their shapes curling and changing. *It's okay. I'm okay.*

She pulled again on the handcuffs; this time her actions were slow and deliberate as she tested her mobility. If she could get her hands in front of her she would be in a better position. The manacles were connected with a chain. *Good.* That was a good start. It meant they were an older model and relied on a simple spring mechanism, one tiny lever. They were easily picked. No key required.

She flopped onto her side to free her knees from under her. The wall kept her from fully turning over but there was still enough room to try to get her hands under her butt and in front of her. She held her breath as she tried to force her hands to go under. "Come on," she grunted, pulling her hands as far apart as they would go but she could not get them past her hips. Her arms were too short and the puffy winter coat she was wearing didn't help things either.

"It's okay. I'm okay." This time she said the mantra aloud. She would repeat it until she believed it.

She couldn't get her hands in front of her but it was okay. She could still make this work. She was fine. She just needed something to pick the lock. Anything small and hard with a slight bend would do. *A twig, a hair pin, a paperclip.*

Think.

Her bra had underwire. That would work. But how could she get to it? Maybe she could use her zipper. That could work. If she could tear it off with her teeth, her dentist could deal with the damage later. She pressed her chin to her chest, bit into the material of her jacket, and pulled up. She craned her neck back as far as it would go but her coat barely moved. There was no way she could get it off.

"Fuck," she swore again. There was nothing to use. Her lip started to tremble. She bit hard into it until she tasted blood. She would not let herself panic again.

Her phone.

If she had her phone she could call for help, but even if she couldn't her team could track her. They would find her.

She pressed her arms to her sides, checking for the hard outline of a phone or her gun but she couldn't find either. He must have taken them off her after he knocked her out. Why? Why move her?

She knew the answer and it left her cold. Abductors move victims to kill them. Peter Reid was going to kill her. And he wanted time to do it undisturbed.

She bit harder into her lip. She had to focus on finding a solution. She closed her eyes and took a few steadying breaths. She was alive, which meant Lindsay was probably alive too, and Jess would find her and Eve Fong. She just needed to get out of here.

She had heard stories about people dislocating their thumbs to get out of handcuffs but as far as she knew that was an urban legend. She wasn't going to break her thumb unless she was absolutely sure it would work.

Several escaped convicts had been found with handcuffs dangling from one wrist; none that she knew of had broken any bones to get them off. In most cases improperly fitted handcuffs had allowed them to pull them off. Seasoned criminals knew to put the widest part of their wrists vertically when the handcuffs were being put on so when they turned them flat they would have room to wiggle out.

She could only pray that even in a drugged state, she would have remembered what to do.

Jess held the shackle with one hand as she tested to see how much room she had in each cuff. The metal bit into the side of her hand. She groaned at the slight movement. It wasn't going to just slip off but she could force it.

For a second she considered trying to free her good hand because there seemed to be ever so slightly more give in that cuff, but she quickly rejected the idea because whatever hand she picked was going to be rendered useless for the foreseeable future. She already had one hand that had failed her, she really didn't need another.

She took a deep breath, used her good hand to steady the cuff, and then gave a sharp tug. She froze, searing pain engulfing everywhere below the wrist. She told herself to keep pulling but her body refused to comply.

Millions of years of evolution had taught people to flee from pain. But reflexes could be overridden. Mind over matter. She could do this. She could fight through the pain.

The tendons had been decimated in that hand anyway. Even if she broke every small bone, she could not inflict any more damage than she already had. She already lived with constant nagging pain. This couldn't make it much worse.

Constant nagging pain. That was what she was fighting to return for. And failed relationships, and fear of being recognized, and guilt.

What else? What else did she have? Her mind screamed at her, telling her to find a reason to fight. She needed something to keep her focused but she could not think of a single thing. Where there should be motivation there was a dark, cavernous void.

Jess lay still, paralyzed by the realization that there was nothing. Years of shoving away anything that resembled an emotion had left that part of her atrophied and broken.

Was there really nothing?

Not long ago she had fought so hard to escape the basement but that seemed like a different life now.

Victims. That was who she had fought for. They had kept her going long after her body should have given in. She fought for them. And she fought for the people who had lives they wanted to live.

"Lindsay," she whispered. She had to fight for Lindsay and for Eve. That's who she was fighting for now. She could do this for them.

She took a deep breath. She used her good hand to steady the handcuff. She gave herself a few seconds to prepare for the onslaught of inevitable pain. Once she started to pull she was not going to let herself stop until the shackle was off, so she sat for several minutes and allowed herself to feel every sensation in her body, enjoy the calm before the storm.

She clamped her teeth together to keep from screaming. And then she pulled. Searing pokers jabbed at her tender palm. Every part of her cried out for her to stop but she ignored all reason and yanked harder. Her bones ground against each other, crushing the tendons between. Metal scraped over her skin, tearing the flesh, but she would not give up.

A guttural scream tore through her, propelling her to push farther, fight harder. She had to tell herself she was making progress because she could not feel progression past the blistering agony, but then something inside snapped, and with a final yank her hand slid free. Metal clinked against wood as her hand collapsed on the floor next to her.

Her head spun. Blood rushed to her newly liberated limbs, bringing an electric current of heat and pain. Her stomach clenched in a painful spasm as she vomited. Bile burned the back of her throat as over and over again she heaved until nothing was left in her body.

Without thinking she brought her injured hand to her lips, like a mother kissing away the hurt of a child, or like a fatally injured animal licking at a mortal wound. The metallic zing of blood filled her mouth. She wasn't sure if it was from her hand or biting the side of her mouth but she was grateful for the darkness so she could not see her injury.

She changed position so she could sit up. She winced when her hand took some of her weight as she shifted. She gasped in a frantic breath to quell the sharp pain but nothing helped. "Oh God," she moaned.

For a few seconds all she could do was breathe and try not to vomit on herself again. Slowly she moved again, careful not to put any weight on her hand. She had to duck slightly to move but she fit.

She ran her good hand along the walls, searching for an escape. Her fingertip ran along the broken surface. There was a pattern or markings on the sides but no latch or handle.

She turned and there was the faintest sliver of light at the bottom edge of the wall, just a hazy glimmer. She blinked several times to make sure she was not imagining the small variation in darkness. It was there, the tiniest fragments of light fighting against the dark. That was the door. That was her way out. She held her arm against her chest to protect it and slowly rotated, inching around bit by bit until she was facing the entrance.

She leaned against the back wall and brought her knees up hard against her chest to give her the maximum range. She kicked the door. For a second, the wood buckled and light peeked through the crack. She brought her legs up again and kicked out. The door whined as the wood bent but it didn't break.

Jess's heart thundered for the exertion and the adrenaline that flooded her body to deal with the trauma. She stopped to get her breath back and then kicked the door again. There was a crunch of wood splintering followed by a thud of a deadlock hitting the floor.

"Thank you," she whispered into the darkness. She wasn't sure who she was speaking to but she felt compelled to express gratitude for her liberation. Relief washed over her. Finally, she could breathe.

Dim light filtered into the small box, enough to see the faded crayon drawings on the walls. She squinted to make out the forms. Pictures of monsters filled every space. The same graphic scene played out in each drawing. A child on a bed, screaming as a monster towered above.

"Oh no," she whispered when she realized what she was looking at.

CHAPTER THIRTY-FIVE

Her stomach cramped. She squinted her eyes to make out each drawing. A child had cataloged her abuse here. The progression of intricacy in the drawing testified to the maturation of the little girl. Some of the drawings were merely stick figures but others were detailed. The same child had drawn all of them over several years.

Peter Reid had kept a child captive, and by the looks of it for years. How? How had he managed to abduct and keep a child without anyone knowing? Who was she? Where was she now?

Realization crept over her, igniting her skin as it went. She knew what had happened.

Fishbowl.

She heard Lindsay's message again in her mind. It all made sense, like jigsaw pieces slotting into place to show the entire picture. *The positioning, no sexual assault, poison.*

"Oh my God," she whispered again.

She had to tell her team. With her good hand, she reached for her phone, forgetting it wasn't there. She needed to get out and get help, tell her team what had happened, and why.

Jess looked around the room. A single filament bulb provided light. Jess flinched as she looked at the unfinished concrete floors and low ceilings. She was in a basement. Blood whooshed in her ears as her pulse spiked as her heartbeats merged into a continuous buzz. Not a basement, she couldn't deal with that again. Nothing ever good happened in basements. It's where she had learned her father's horrible secret, where she had made the fateful mistake to protect him and not to tell anyone the horror that she had witnessed. And it was where she had faced up to another serial killer. It was where she had almost died. Pain pounded at her temples as memories blindsided her. Visons of her own monsters played in her head, robbing her of breath. Her entire body vibrated as she shook.

Stop! her mind screamed. That was a long time ago. It wasn't her fault. Or was it? She couldn't breathe. This had nothing to do with her or her father or any mistake she had made. She had to get out.

But she couldn't go running from the basement like a lunatic. She had no idea who or what was waiting upstairs. She had to be slow and prudent. *It's okay. I'm okay.* The stair creaked under her weight as she started her slow ascent.

She held her breath as she waited for someone to hear her and come down. When he didn't, she took another tentative step. She startled when the metal cuff clanked against the banister but she forced herself to inch forward. Step by step she creeped up the stairs until she reached the top.

The doorknob was like ice against her palm. Slowly she turned the handle. She let go of the breath she was holding when the door creaked open. She glanced around. She was in the kitchen of an obviously expensive house. Everything was high spec, from the Sub-Zero refrigerator to the integrated coffee maker. The room was immaculate, not a single ornament or embellishment on the gray marble countertops. It looked cold and austere, unlivable but pristine.

Jess scanned the room for a weapon, anything she could use to defend herself. Most people had a knife block on their counter but Peter Reid wouldn't tolerate the clutter. Cutlery rattled as she opened drawers, frantically searching. She took out a paring knife, examined it, and put it in her coat pocket before she continued looking. It was small but better than nothing.

Where are the real knives? she wanted to scream. In the third drawer, she found a pair of silver scissors. The handles were ornately carved to look like ivy but the blades were long and sharp, tapering to a razor-sharp point. She put them in her pocket with the knife.

Phone. Where is my phone? Jess scanned the kitchen but there was nothing. She pressed her back hard against the wall so no one could come up behind her, and she turned the corner to the hall, sliding her feet along the polished walnut floorboards. She crept to the study. Just like his office, Peter Reid's home study was stark, just a black leather couch across from a modern teak desk.

Jess breathed a sigh of relief when she saw a small black phone sitting in its cradle on the desk. Her hand shook as she picked it up. She had to lay it on the desk to dial because she could not hold it in the other hand.

"911. What is your emergency?" a woman answered.

"This is Special Agent Jessica Bishop. I was kidnapped while investigating the disappearances of Eve Fong and Lindsay Dixon. I need police and an ambulance."

"Ma'am, what is your location?"

Jess looked out the window. At one point in time she knew Peter Reid's home address; she had seen it written down but it escaped her now. She couldn't think. "I don't know. It's residential. I see trees. The house across the street is brick. Looks like Georgetown. I think it's Dr. Peter Reid's house. Just trace it, please. And please patch the call through to Jeanie Gilbert at the FBI Headquarters. She's my team leader. I need backup."

Jess turned when she heard chimes in the distance, coming from upstairs. It sounded like a music box. A chill ran the length of her spine. "She's here. I think Eve Fong is here."

"Ma'am, I see where you're at. Can you get outside? The police are on their way."

Jess glanced at the door. She was inches from freedom. She could wait outside for the police. She would be safe. But Lindsay wasn't safe. Eve wasn't safe. They needed help and Jess was the only one here. She squeezed her lids together. "I think Eve Fong is upstairs," she said again. "Tell the paramedics they need naloxone. Lots of it. I think she has been given fentanyl. I'm going upstairs. I need my hand so I can't talk but I'll stay on the line. If the call ends, it wasn't me. I won't hang up until the police are here."

"Ma'am..." Her voice trailed off as Jess reached around her body and shoved the phone in her empty pocket because she needed her good hand. She hoped the dispatcher could hear everything through the thick fabric of her coat because later it could be used at trial no matter what happened to Jess.

Her hand trembled as she clenched the banister. She looked behind her once more to make sure no one was there before she took her first step.

Adrenaline surged through her. By the time she reached the top step her heart felt like it was going to shatter her sternum.

She stood perfectly still at the top of the stairs, listening for the soft chimes, but there was nothing, no sound except the methodical tick of a grandfather clock and then a tiny splat. Jess looked down at the drop of blood on the floor. She knew it came from her hand but she refused to look at the carnage now. She had ripped her skin off breaking free. She couldn't think about that now. If she made it out of here, the doctors could deal with the aftermath.

She had to hold the rail as she looked around the hall because the room refused to stop spinning. She blinked to clear her vision as it tunneled to a dark pinpoint and then fanned out again. Her pulse drummed in her ears and her stomach roiled. She felt like she was going to pass out. Her heart was beating too fast. She squeezed the banister until her hand shook.

She took a deep breath and told herself she could pass out later; right now Lindsay and Eve needed her.

She took a tentative step forward to check her balance. There were four doors, all closed except one which was open just an inch. Jess stroked the scissors in her pocket, tracing the ridged pattern of the cold metal. She pressed her back against the wall, as much for balance as security, and pushed the door open with the back of her foot. She held her breath as she waited until the count of five. When no one spoke or came out, she slid closer to the door. The frame pressed into her back as she rounded the corner.

The curtains were drawn and the lights were off but a bedside lamp partially lit the room. Like the rest of the house, the room was monochromatic, stark white walls with a black leather bed. Photos in black frames lined the walls.

On the bedside table was a bottle of Scotch, a crystal tumbler that matched the one Jess had shattered, and a handwritten note. She didn't dare risk contaminating evidence by touching it and bleeding on it. Someone on her team would have to collect it. She knew what it was anyway.

Jess checked that the bathroom and the closet were clear before she went to the bed. Peter Reid lay on his back, eyes closed, vomit dripping down his cheek onto the white sheets.

Jess crouched beside him. His pulse was faint and slow and his breathing labored. Jess pulled back the sheet. His body was large and hairy. How frightening it must have been for a child to see him towering above her bed, coming down on her with lust and malice in his eyes. He really was a monster.

He was completely naked except for the three fentanyl patches stuck to his hip.

Jess ripped the first one off, careful not to expose her own skin to the potent drug. She was already barely hanging on to consciousness; any amount of opiates and she knew she would collapse.

"You're not going to die today. I'm not going to let you. I know what you did and you're going to pay," she whispered in his ear as she pulled off the second patch.

She grunted as she rolled him over on his side so he wouldn't choke if he vomited on himself again.

His lids opened, and his eyes rolled back.

"Where are they?" Jess rubbed her knuckles against his sternum to rouse him. She pressed hard, putting all of her weight behind it. If he weren't drugged, the pain from it would be excruciating.

He mumbled something incoherent before his eyes rolled back again.

The chimes started again. Jess stood perfectly still as she listened. She turned to face the open door so she could make out where they were coming from. It was the farthest room down the hall.

The wooden floorboards creaked under her as she crept along the corridor. She stopped when she got to the bedroom. Silently she begged her heart to slow down enough for her to feel in control of her body again, but her pulse only edged higher as anticipation shot through her. The beats bled together to create a buzz in her chest.

She stroked the scissors in her pocket again, like a security blanket, before she opened the door.

It was a child's bedroom. The walls were painted a pale pink. In the center of the room was a white canopy bed draped in gauzy white curtains. It looked like it belonged in a fairy tale not a nightmare, but Jess had seen the drawings.

Eve Fong lay in the bed. Her eyes were closed and black hair fanned out around her like a mermaid. Her chest slowly rose and fell in shallow breaths. Joy and relief washed over her. She was still alive.

Her gaze darted around the room searching for Lindsay but she wasn't there. In a rocking chair beside the bed sat the killer reading a picture book.

CHAPTER THIRTY-SIX

Pamela Reid looked maternal and serene as she sat watching over Eve. She looked every bit the protective mother but the syringe and box of fentanyl patches on the table beside her told a far darker story.

She was a child psychologist. She had taken an oath to help the most vulnerable and desperate but she had murdered them instead.

"Pamela, step away from the bed. The police are on their way. They will be here any second. It's over." Jess held the wall as the room spun around her like the vortex of a black hole sucking her into the darkness.

Pamela looked up. There was no surprise on her face. She looked like she had always known she was going to be found, and Jess suspected that's why she had tried to kill her father first.

"I'm not done. She hasn't had her perfect day. You robbed her of that. I couldn't even take her to the beach because of the roadblocks you set up. I just wanted her to have one perfect day, that's it. She deserved that and you took it from her," Pamela said.

"She can have a perfect day, Pamela. She can have lots of perfect days." Jess eased closer to them, looking around the room for a gun or other weapons but there wasn't anything other than the opioids on the dresser.

Of course, Jess thought. The clues were there all along. Female killers often use poison to murder. Why had they not suspected the killer was a woman? Why had they not seen it?

Pamela shook her head. "There were never any good days for her. Her father and her uncle abused her. They broke her. No one could ever put her back together. I know I couldn't. There is some damage you can't fix. Just like the other girls. There was no hope. They could never get past the horrors that were inflicted upon them. It was part of them. It warped them. They could never live happy normal lives. Why should they have to suffer through a lifetime of pain? We don't even let animals suffer like that."

Jess edged closer. Where was the police? She had to keep Pamela talking, stall for time because she didn't have the strength to fight her. She was too weak and her body too battered. "Is that how you feel, Pamela?" She used her name again to reinforce familiarity and try to create the illusion of intimacy, and because when this call was played in court she wanted the jury to know exactly who she was speaking to. "Do you wish someone would have put you out of your misery? I know what you father did to you. I know how he hurt you. I saw the pictures you drew in the basement. Did he keep you in there very often?"

A surprised look flashed on Pamela's face as she shook her head. "You don't know anything."

"I know you wanted us to think it was your dad who murdered those girls. You planted evidence to implicate him. You dressed as a man. You wore his hat. You led us to him for a reason."

When she didn't immediately say anything, Jess kept talking, stalling for time. "Did you want us to know about O'Reilly and Spiro too?"

"They're bad men. People should know that."

"But what about your father's partner, Martin Schofield? He's doesn't have a record. We couldn't find anything on him. Why use his car and try to implicate him?"

Pamela twitched at the mention of his name.

"What?" Jess pushed "What is it? Why would you want us to think he had something to do with this?"

"He's not a good man," was all Pamela would say. She reached for the syringe. The patches weren't working fast enough so she was going to finish Eve off with an injection.

Jess wasn't quite close enough to reach her and even if she was, she didn't have the strength left to safely wrestle the needle away.

"Why did you take Ava Marsden? She wasn't being abused. You didn't need to save her from a life of pain. She was going to die anyway."

"Exactly, she was going to die anyway. Her parents should have been focused on controlling her pain and giving her a perfect day but instead her mother was torturing her just to get a few more days with her. She was in agony but her mother kept pushing for her own selfish needs."

"You keep talking about a perfect day. What is a perfect day, Pamela?"

"A perfect day for a child would always involve feeling safe and loved, knowing no one is going to hurt them. They can just be happy and at peace." When she sighed, she lowered the needle slightly. "And it would involve the beach. Every child should see the ocean at least once. Eve has never seen the ocean. I was going to take her but you ruined that." Her face contorted in anger. She raised up the syringe again.

"What else is in a perfect day? Cotton candy?" Jess's heart hammered in her chest. "I know you gave them cotton candy before they died." Jess was careful not to say murder because that would make Pamela shut down, and she had to keep her talking.

"Every child loves cotton candy. It's like a sweet cloud. There is something magical about it."

"You never got a perfect day, did you?"

Pamela shook her head. "No, I did." She sighed, almost whimsically. "I had the best day. We walked on the beach. She held my hand. I felt so loved and so safe. And I was so happy."

"Who?" Jess asked, unable to keep up with what Pamela was saying. She realized now she knew nothing about Pamela Reid because she hadn't been a viable suspect, and Jess only had time for suspects and victims; everything else in her life was just noise to be tuned out.

In the faint distance, sirens wailed.

"Who gave you your perfect day, Pamela?"

"It doesn't matter." She shrugged.

"It matters to me. I want to know who was kind to you. You were a child, you deserved kindness. Who was it? Who gave you your perfect day?"

Pamela gave a faint smile that didn't quite reach her eyes. "My mom did. She knew she was dying and she was going to have to send me to live with him, but before she did, she took me to Ocean City and we walked along the beach eating cotton candy. She held my hand and we looked for seashells. It was the best day. It should have ended there." She breathed a heavy sigh. "Then it would have been perfect."

Ended. Jess swallowed hard. Pamela wished her mom had killed her rather than sent her to her father to be abused. Her stomach clenched at the admission. How desperate she must have felt, how sad, and lonely, trapped in her own horrible world of shameful secrets.

Even now, with a syringe in her hand and a victim at her side, there was part of Jess that felt sorry her. She knew how she felt because Jess had felt all those things too. And they hurt. Sometimes they hurt in a way that nothing could numb. Pamela was killing children because in her warped mind it was the humane thing to do. It was the only way that was guaranteed to end their pain.

Pamela was a murderer but she was also a victim, a little girl who should have been protected. There was no separating the two halves to her broken whole.

A question cried out to Jess from the darkest depths of her mind. Did the boys her father tortured ever in their short lives get a perfect day? Did they ever get a moment of complete joy? She couldn't breathe. Her legs nearly buckled. She tried to push the thought away but it wrapped around her conscious like barbwire, piercing and tearing. It was so unfair, the way their lives were stolen, by her father, the man she had loved and protected. *Please let them have had joy in their lives before he brutalized them.*

Jess blinked to try to focus and push out the grief and shame she felt for the secrets she had kept. "Your father will be punished for what he did. I'll make sure of that. He will be tried. I will testify against him if you can't," her voice faltered.

Pamela's face contorted in a desperate plea. "No! He's dead. He killed himself."

Jess gave her head a single shake. "He's not dead. You forged a suicide note for him. I saw it beside his bed. You wanted us to find his dead body along with Eve's so we would think he killed all those girls. But he didn't kill them. You did, Pamela."

"No!" Vehemence raised her voice to a high shrill. "He has to be dead. No one will believe he killed the girls unless he dies. Then they will read his note and they'll see. They'll know how evil he was." She sounded like a terrified child desperately begging and pleading.

"You think no one will believe it because no one believed you, did they? Is that what happened? You tried to tell someone and they didn't believe you?" Grief pulled at Jess. She tried to shrug it off but there was no shaking the pain she felt for the child Pamela had been. She had suffered the way the boys her father had victimized had. What would have become of them, had they lived? Would they have moved on and found peace and happiness or would they have become the monsters Jess hunted? Would her father's evil have corrupted them so badly that they would never be the same? She tried to swallow but her mouth was too dry. She couldn't think about them now. She tried to push their faces away but they refused to leave her.

It must have been the drugs leaving her system but when she looked at Pamela she saw one of her father's victims, the one she had seen in the basement, lying naked on the ground, his body battered and broken. Jess rubbed her eyes to clear her vision but it didn't help.

"I'm sorry you weren't heard. I believe you, Pamela. I know what he did to you," Jess said.

Pamela wiped at her eyes with the back of her hand. "He explained everything away. He said I was delusional and a compulsive liar. They had me committed to a mental hospital."

"They?" Jess asked.

"He convinced his partner that I was insane. But he knew I wasn't. He knew he was hurting me."

"Martin Schofield," Jess whispered. The final piece of the puzzle slid into place. That was why Pamela had used his car and tried to implicate him. She wanted him to pay for what he had done to her.

The wail of sirens grew louder. They were on the street.

"The police are here, Pamela. It's over. Put the needle down, slowly get on your knees, and put your hands on your head."

"No." She shook her head. "I can't let you send her back to be abused. It's cruel. She deserves to be released from all this pain. No one should have to bear it."

A loud thump was followed by the splintering of wood and the split of a door as the police forced their way into the house.

Hurry. She silently begged the police to find them. Her head was spinning and she was almost too dizzy to stand. Something was wrong. Maybe it was the effects of the drug Pamela had given her or maybe she had injured herself more than she realized but she wasn't doing well. "They're here, Pamela. Don't make this hard."

"No!" she shrieked. She raised up the hypodermic needle.

"Put the needle down."

Footsteps thundered on the stairs. The police were almost here. They would shoot to kill. Jess needed her alive to find Lindsay.

Jess wrapped her hands around the scissors. "Where's Lindsay? She knew it was you. When you were in grad school together, you told her something in a fishbowl and that's how she figured it out. She pieced it together. Is that why you kidnapped her?"

Lindsay had been trying to tell Jess she knew who the killer was because of something she had heard Pamela say in in a therapy session in graduate school.

Tears welled over in Pamela's bloodshot eyes. "I just wanted to explain and make her see. I didn't mean to hurt her. I just needed time." Pamela lowered the needle to Eve's neck.

"Where is she?" Jess demanded.

"I didn't mean to hurt her." She pressed the needle against Eve's skin.

The blades of the scissors were cold. She wrapped her fingers around them and squeezed. She pulled them out of her pocket and lunged at Pamela's shoulder, aiming for the tender bit just below her clavicle. She plunged the blades deep into her flesh. The needle slipped through Pamela's fingers to the floor.

At first there was no blood, then slowly crimson dots appeared, growing and seeping, fanning out into an expanding scarlet ring.

Pamela's eyes widened in shock but the surprise soon turned to distressed sadness. "Why? Why didn't you kill me?"

Realization struck Jess. That's what Pamela had always wanted: to die. She wanted to be killed but she was too scared to do it herself so she wanted to force Jess's hand. "You have to pay for what you've done the way your father is going to pay for what he did. Now where is Lindsay?" she demanded.

Boots pounded on the stairs. Police stormed the room, guns drawn. There were uniformed officers everywhere. "Get down, get down, get down," one of them shouted.

Jess held her hands above her head, the handcuff dangled from one arm.

"Get down!" he screamed again, his gun trained on her.

She could not use her hand to help aid her descent so she crashed down hard on the floor. Pain radiated up through her knees as she collided with the walnut floorboards.

"I'm Special Agent Jessica Bishop. I'm the one who called it in. Where are the paramedics? We have two opioid overdoses here. They need naloxone. And we still have not located Lindsay Dixon. A federal agent is still missing," Jess screamed over the commotion but no one listened. The floor rumbled under her from the commotion as they searched the room.

Metal clamped over her wrist as an officer tried to handcuff her. Jess screamed as she pulled away, the claws of the cuff catching on her already torn flesh. "No!" She would not let herself be handcuffed again. He had no idea who she was. He was only following protocol. All he knew from the evidence at hand was that she had stabbed someone but there was no way in hell she would be cuffed again. She would rather be shot. "I will stay on the ground with my hands up but don't you dare put handcuffs on me," she seethed. Her nostrils flared and her teeth chattered in rage. Adrenaline flooded her as her fight or flight response surged. "I'm a federal agent. Call Jeanie Gilbert at FBI Headquarters if you want to verify my identity but don't you dare touch me again."

Blood dripped on the floor from her hand in tiny splats. He kept his gun pointed at her but he didn't try to handcuff her again. "Stay down!" he warned.

Two emergency medical technicians, a man with a short red beard and a woman with her hair scraped back into a severe bun, entered the room. They weren't wearing coats over their short sleeves even though it was freezing outside.

"That's Eve Fong, the girl the AMBER Alert was issued for. I think she has fentanyl patches on her."

One of the paramedics pulled back the pink polka dot duvet that covered Eve. He snapped on a pair of blue gloves and pulled up her nightgown. He pulled off the patch on her hip before he took a syringe out of a black case and injected her thigh. He rubbed her sternum with his knuckles to try to rouse her. "What did you say her name was?"

"Eve."

"Come on, Eve. I need you to open your eyes. Wake up, Eve. Come on." He continued rubbing her sternum. After a few seconds he looked up at his colleague. "She needs another dose." He pulled out another vial and sucked up a caramel-colored liquid into a fresh syringe.

"Just leave her," Pamela begged. "She's hurting. She has nothing to live for. Please," she cried. Her eyes pleaded with them to stop the treatment. "You get it," she said to Jess. "You of all people have to understand that some people are just too broken. They're better off dead. You must feel like that."

Jess blinked. The room spun. She couldn't speak, there were no words. Pamela's stare bore into her. She was looking at her like she could see things no one else could.

Pamela reached up to her collarbone to pull out the imbedded scissors but the second paramedic stopped her. "Don't touch it. You need to leave it in to stop the bleeding. A doctor will take it out at the hospital. If you're in pain I can give you something for it."

"Leave me alone," Pamela fought her. She wanted to bleed out.

"Ma'am, I need you to stop." The paramedic struggled to subdue her. Pamela wanted to die.

Jess looked up when someone ran into the room.

"Jessie. You're okay. Thank God." Jamison stood at the foot of the bed, a deep crease between his dark eyes where his brow knitted together with worry. "Get this handcuff off her," he shouted. He held up his badge to be inspected. "She's an FBI agent."

The same officer who had tried to cuff her leaned in to remove her shackle. "No," she said, pulling her hand away. She didn't have time. She needed to find Lindsay.

Jamison bent down to help her up. His skin was hot against hers. "You're bleeding,' he said.

"I'm fine. I need to find Lindsay. Where is she?" Jess towered over Pamela. "Tell me where she is." Her body vibrated with rage.

"We need more naloxone in here." A third paramedic came into the room. "I have another overdose and he's still unresponsive."

"Where is she?" Jess screamed.

"Jessie." Jamison reached for her hand again. "She's in the other room."

Jess spun on her heel. "Why didn't you tell me? I need to see her. Is she okay?" She had to hold her hands out to keep from falling as she ran from the room. The floorboards creaked as she ran to the bedroom next to Peter Reid's. She knew immediately that was where Lindsay was because police officers stood huddled outside the open door talking in hushed tones.

Jess pushed her way between them and went in, Jamison behind her.

Like Peter's room, everything was either black or white. She ran to the bed. "Lindsay. I'm so sorry I got you involved." Lindsay's eyes were closed, her thick, honey-colored hair cascaded over the pillow. Her top lip was blue but there was no blood on the sheet. That must be a good sign. She had stopped bleeding. There had been so much blood at her house. She had been so worried that she would bleed out but she hadn't. "Lindsay, I'm here. You're safe. It's going to be okay. Open your eyes." Jess stroked her cheek to try to get her to wake up. Her skin was cold to the touch. She turned to scream over her shoulder, "She's freezing. We need to get a blanket. I need a paramedic in here. Come on, Lindsay, wake up." She grabbed her by the shoulder. "Come on, Lindsay. Wake up." Jess turned and screamed again, "We need a paramedic. Help!" She screamed to anyone in earshot, "Please help!" Unease crept along her skin. "Come on, Lindsay. Just open your eyes for me."

"Jessie."

"She needs naloxone!" Jess screamed so hard her throat burned. "Get the paramedics in here now! They should be in here not working on Peter Reid. She just needs naloxone. She's going to be fine. She has to be."

"Jessie." Jamison shook his head. Sadness clung to him. His ever-present cool demeanor had slipped. He reached for her good hand, his fingers wrapped around hers, but she pulled away.

He was trying to comfort her but she didn't need comfort, she needed help for Lindsay. "She needs naloxone. That will help her. She'll be fine."

"Jessie," he said again. "She's gone."

"No!" Jess screamed. If her hand was not already in agony she would have smacked his face for even suggesting that. Jess leaned down and gathered Lindsay in her arms. "Come on. I need you to wake up." She pressed her cheek to hers as she held her. Lindsay was so heavy and rigid in her arms. And her cheek was so cold. Jess pulled back to look at her. There was no color in her lips except the outline of dark blue. There was no rise and fall to her chest. "Please," Jess whispered. She looked up to the sky, silently begging a god she didn't even believe in. "Please," she whispered again. "Lindsay, I need you." Hot pressure built behind her eyes. She bent and whispered into her ear. "I can't do this without you. I don't have anyone else. I need you. Please, please be okay," she begged. She cuddled her hard against her chest and remembered all the times Lindsay had wanted to hug her but she had refused. Why hadn't she just let Lindsay hug her? She would give anything to go back and feel her arms close around her. She closed her eyes because she couldn't see through the pool of unshed tears. "Please," she cried again. "Please."

"Jessie."

She wiped her eyes with the pad of her hand. "She's gone, Jamison. Lindsay's gone," she sobbed.

"I know. I'm so sorry."

"She's gone," she repeated, still not able to fully comprehend what was happening. Her chest convulsed with the onslaught of tears. It didn't make sense. None of this made sense. Lindsay should not be part of any of this. She wouldn't be if Jess had not spoken to her, if she had not relied on her for everything. She should be in her office now, seeing clients or cracking jokes. She couldn't be gone. Jess had never envisioned a life without her in it.

She remembered what Ava's mom had said about the transition to death, that people could still hear even after they had died. "Lindsay," she whispered against her ear. "You are my best friend and my champion. You are the best person I have ever known. You're the funniest and the smartest. Because of you I felt loved and safe. I loved you. I didn't tell you and I should have. I should have said the words. I love you. Thank you for being my friend and loving me and all my broken pieces." There was so much more to say but grief robbed her of the words.

Jess held Lindsay against her and wept while Jamison stood guard over her. Several times people tried to enter the room to move Lindsay's body but Jamison sent them away. She didn't know how long she held her, but eventually there were no tears left in her.

She pulled back. Blood from her hand had smeared over Lindsay's forehead. "I'm sorry. I should have been a better friend. I'm so sorry," she whispered.

"You didn't do this. You were a great friend to her." Jamison rubbed her back.

Jess squeezed her lids together but the tears streamed through the barricade. She shook her head. She didn't want to be told she wasn't guilty. She knew the truth.

CHAPTER THIRTY-SEVEN

Stan barked when the entry bell for Jess's apartment buzzed. It was probably a delivery for next door. They were single-handedly keeping Amazon in business. Jess considered ignoring the buzzer but she didn't want whoever it was to ring again and upset Stan. He had already been through enough upheaval.

She leaned down and gave him a scratch behind the ears. "It's okay, buddy. That's just the doorbell. You're going to have to get used to it because you're stuck with me. It's just you and me, Stan."

His ears perked up at his name. He nudged her hand up with his nose, begging to be pet.

The buzzer went again before Jess reached the intercom. "Hello," she answered.

"Jessie, it's me."

She squeezed her lids together. *Don't be nice to me.* She couldn't handle Jamison reaching out to her now. They both knew where they stood. He had made his feelings very clear. He had once said they were too messed up but that wasn't true. It was her—she was too messed up.

"You don't need to check on me. I'm fine."

Jamison had always been a good man, always trying to do the right thing. He thought pretending that they were okay was the right thing. But it wasn't. She wasn't a wounded bird that needed tending while her wing healed.

At least he had known to leave her alone at Lindsay's funeral. Everyone had. She had sat in the back pew with her face in her hands, willing the service to end. She had only gone out of respect for Lindsay's family. A cold church was not where she wanted to say goodbye to her. Someone had once told her that funerals were for the living. Maybe that was why she had hated the service so much, because she still felt dead inside.

She had worn the one dress she owned, which fortunately was black. She pinned a purple flower to her collar as a sign for Lindsay. If she was there somewhere watching, Jess wanted her to see the purple and know that Jess was trying to say something. She wasn't sure what she was trying to say but Lindsay would get it; she always just got her.

"You didn't stay for the wake," he said through the intercom.

"I had to get home for the dog." It wasn't exactly a lie. Stan did need walking but she had come home because she couldn't stand to be around people. Lindsay was the only person she wanted to speak to and she was dead.

"A few of us are going to grab a few drinks at The Waiting Room. Do you want to come? I'm the designated driver, I can bring you home after."

Jess stared down at the floor, looking for the strength to say no. She wanted to go out with him and pretend that everything was okay, but it wasn't. Lindsay wasn't here so things were never going to be okay and she needed to get used to that. "No. I have plans."

"Oh," was all he could say. They both knew that "plans" was her code for going out to find a man to make a bad life choice with. "Fine. Be safe." Antipathy dripped from his deep voice. He didn't bother trying to hide the disappointment.

She was glad she couldn't see him, to see the disappointment on his face. He should know better than anyone else that she could only ever disappoint. That's what she did. No one should depend on her for anything; she would only hurt them. She was the woman who fucked strangers in bathrooms and got her best friend killed. It was best that he remembered that.

Jess pulled back the curtain and watched Jamison get in his car and drive away. She held her breath until his taillights faded around the corner.

She knelt down beside the dog, her dog. "Stan, I need you to hold down the fort, buddy. You're in charge until I get home." She stopped short of telling him why she had to go or how long she would be gone. Talking to dogs was okay, but full analytical conversations weren't.

Jess went down to the garage and got in her car.

She turned on the music full blast. The bassline pulsed painfully in her ears. She hoped that it would quiet the voices but it didn't. Nothing did. She pounded her fingers on the steering wheel to the beat of the music as she drove. She parked away from the building and kept her head down as she walked in so no one would try to speak to her.

Once she was confident that there was no one around who was going to approach her she looked up and smoothed back the hairs that had fallen out of her ponytail. She knew she looked rough but she could at least make an effort to be somewhat presentable.

She walked down the hall to the very end of the corridor and knocked. She looked around to make sure no one was watching. She wasn't embarrassed but it was no one's business what she did on her own time. She wasn't sure if this was the right decision but she knew she couldn't feel like this anymore. She couldn't be this raw. She had a high threshold for emotional pain but this was more than she could bear.

"Come in," a familiar voice answered.

Jess opened the door. When he realized it was her surprise flashed across his face. She was surprised too to be seeking him out but she would do anything to make the pain stop.

"Hi." He put the papers he was sorting down on his desk. "Come in."

Jess paused for a second as she tried to decide if she should go through with it but the need to numb some of the pain pushed her forward. "Are you busy?"

He glanced up at the clock. "I can make some time. How are you?"

Jess let the door close behind her. "Not great," she admitted. She took a deep breath and forced herself to finish what she had started. "Um-I-ah," she stammered. The need to run was overwhelming. But there was no place to go, no way she could outrun this or numb it away. She had to deal with it head on. "Before Lindsay died she asked me to consider coming back to therapy. I told her I was too busy. But I'm always too busy. I'll always have an excuse. I don't want to make excuses anymore." She took a seat on the couch opposite Dr. Cameron's desk. She looked up toward the heavens as she suddenly realized why she had worn a purple flower. She hadn't been sending Lindsay a message, it was the other way around. Lindsay was reminding her to look for the hope, to cling to the small beautiful moments in life, to find any happiness she could. She wanted that. "I want your help. I want to get better."

A LETTER FROM KIERNEY

Thank you for reading *Cross Your Heart*. I am truly grateful when readers choose to spend their time and money on something I have written, so thank you again. If you enjoyed the book, I would very much appreciate if you left a review. Reviews are the lifeblood of writing: they are how new readers find a book, so even a short review would be tremendously helpful.

If you enjoyed this book and would like to keep up to date with all my releases, just click on this link. Your email address will never be shared and you can unsubscribe any time.

www.bookouture.com/kierney-scott

I love hearing from readers and I always respond to messages. If you have a question or a comment, you can contact me at KierneyScott@gmail.com. You can also find me on Facebook and on Twitter.

I hope to see you again very soon when Jess and her team are back for their next adventure.

 www.facebook.com/kierney.scott

twitter.com/Kierney_S

ACKNOWLEDGEMENTS

Thank you to all the readers, reviewers, and bloggers. I am tremendously grateful for all of your support. Thank you for every review, message, and tweet. They are greatly appreciated.

Thank you to everyone at Bookouture. I am so fortunate to write for such an amazing publisher. Thank you to my editor, Helen Jenner, for being able to see my blind spots. You always know what I need to do to fix a scene. A special thanks to Noelle Holten and Kim Nash, AKA the best publicity department in all of publishing. You ladies are fantastic. I appreciate you both so much. Thank you for putting my books in the hands of bloggers and readers.

Thank you to the other Bookouture authors. You lot are the wittiest, most generous bunch of people. I love seeing your books at the shops and being able to say I know you. Being your friend is like getting to sit at the cool-kids table. And you all are so lovely you don't even ask me to leave.

Thank you to my CrossFit coach, Rachel Mackenzie for helping me to not merge with my couch after days on end of writing and not moving. You are the only person who I will run for, other than that I operate under a strict run-only-when-chased policy.

And finally thank you to my Baby Girl. Everything is better with you.